Once
Upon an Island

By Marion Seabrook

Published by:

Books for Pleasure

22 Norton St. West, Box 916

Cayuga, Ontario N0A 1E0

ISBN: 1-55349-010-X
Printed in Canada

FORWARD

In long ago days, Nanabush carried his grandmother on his back in search of the home of the great Manitou. They had journeyed long and he was very tired. They were crossing over a lake, and in spite of all his efforts to hold her, she slipped off his shoulders and fell face forward into the water. She lay there, semi-kneeling, and her grandson tried valiantly to lift her. However, the task was too great, and he had to leave her in the water. Nanabush had magical powers. He changed his grandmother into a beautiful island. She was called Mindemoya by the People, an Ojibwe word meaning "Old Woman". She is still there, and the waves of Lake Mindemoya lap, as they did then, against her shores.

In a later time, Ojibwe families following the game found the island. They made their summer camp there on the fertile north point. Fish and beaver, mink and muskrat were plentiful. While the men harvested the fur their children played on the shore, turning over the stones at the edge of the water and laughing as they watched the crayfish scurry backwards to new hiding places. The breeze carried their laughter to the women filling their birch bark baskets with berries. It was summer in the hearts of the People. Until, one day, in silent canoes, the Iroquois came.

Many years later, the MacPherson family bought this island which was now called "Crown Land". They did little to change it except to build a small house and tool shed. The animals that lived here scarcely noticed the intrusion of humanity and continued to roam quite independently, even venturing to the verandah after dark.

The MacPhersons sold their island to Jean and Joe Hodgson in 1928. To these new owners the Old Woman gave many gifts--forty years of rich soil in which to nourish the seed they planted. Joe loved gardening. Every spring his one-furrowed plough turned up treasures from an earlier time--arrowheads and tomahawks, little bits of pottery and broken tools. He carefully collected these and told his children stories of the People who had lived here so many years ago. Joe planted every kind of vegetable in his garden. Beside the house he tucked in roses and climbing clematis. By the kitchen window he heeled in a yellow rose. In a large flower bed in the front grasses he coaxed lilies into bloom, their fragrance heavy and sweet. He scattered hollyhocks everywhere, and giant dahlias and sweet peas. He grafted six kinds of apples on one tree, right beside the kitchen door. Everything he planted grew. The Old Woman and Joe were an awesome team.

Meanwhile, Jean cooked and preserved the bounties of their garden. She scrubbed and scraped and painted every board that made their home. She filled the air with music. Joe often teased her, "You can play that violin whenever you want. Only the birds and the bears will hear you!" And she'd laugh.

Then one day, in 1968, Jean lost her precious Joe. His death was sudden and kind, but how she missed him. She sold the island. She built a home on what was once his family farm that overlooked the lake. Every morning she watched their island rise from the mist.

Today their friends own the island and they keep the trust, planting the flowers, polishing the boards, giving back the gifts.

People live as long as they are remembered. But islands are forever.

CHAPTER 1

Maxie read the noisy hum of the crowd milling around the items set out for the auction. Yep, this would be a good one. A lot of junk, but some interesting pieces mixed in that would turn a good buck. He looked over the crowd. They were all here. You got to know the auction family as well as the people who sat around your kitchen table. And you could count on them bein' here the same as you could count on your family showin' up for supper. He smiled. There was Allie and Mae. He loved those two old girls pokin' around the dishes on the table. Never bought anything, but never missed comin' all the same. They'd come a long piece today, all the way from Mindemoya to Evansville in that old Chevy. Allie kept her tuned up pretty good, though, and she looked after Mae like a mother hen. Thinking of Mae, he could almost taste those home-made biscuits she always had on hand whenever you dropped in. Yep, two great old girls. Hoped he was as spry as them when he got that old.

He shifted his gaze. There was that nice kid, Jamie. Been to every auction this summer. Good lad. Away from the Island since his folks died, but came back out of the blue this spring. Should drop in and see that kid. Knew his dad well. You never knew when a friend like that's goin' to drop out of your life.

He spotted Sheila Peters standing by the wagon. Newcomer. Never missed an auction, though. Raised a fuss about somebody takin' something out of a box she'd bought. A pair of china rabbits, that was it. Never heard the end of that story.

And there by the wagon, too, was that guy in the red plaid shirt. Tryin' to pass himself off as one of the locals. Strange one. Always smiling, but a hard guy to get to know. Well, he bought a lot of stuff, and his money was as green as the next guy's.

He searched the crowd. Brian wasn't here yet. He was a good one to have at an auction, helped keep the bids moving on the farm stuff. He could find the darndest use for old tractor parts and odd bits of machinery. Not a lot of good junk for him here today, though.

The usual dealers were here, lookin' for bargains. Cagey bidders. Had to watch for a flick of a finger or the slight jerk of the head to catch their bid. Pretty cool, but the locals had their number. Got to read them the same way he did.

Well, it was almost eleven. Time to get a move on. Warm up his throat before he got into the full swing of the auction lingo. Took a bit out of a guy keepin' up a perpetual chatter, but he'd learned his trade well and once he got started he could play the crowd and fine tune the bids like the showman that he was. He lifted the hand mike. "We're just about ready to get started, folks." He smiled, waiting for their attention. "If any of you don't know how this auction works, come over here and get your number from Sadie. She'll keep track of what you buy and put it on your bill. You don't have to pay until you leave." He paused and grinned at the upturned faces. "Likely that will be about six o'clock."

They groaned in unison. He continued. "Just kiddin' folks. We'll rush along. Whenever you want to leave, just come and get your bill from Sadie and take it to those good lookin' ladies over there by the porch and they'll gladly relieve you of your money."

The "good lookin' ladies" smiled, accustomed to the auctioneer's banter. They knew Maxie well, and this was all part of the pre auction ritual. They rearranged the cash box and two pocket calculators on the small wooden table set up on the porch. A red checkered tablecloth refused to square in spite of careful hands pushing and pulling at the corners.

It was a warm July day. A playful wind stirred up a barnyard of summer smells – wild strawberries, yellow roses and freshly cut grass – then tossed in a touch of soggy soil and rotting manure. The resulting potpourri hung heavily in the warm air. The locals paid no attention. The tourists wrinkled their noses in obvious distaste. Was it really worth enduring the stench just to see a country auction?

A push of men crowded closer to the old hay wagon. Their eyes swept over the clutter of cardboard boxes bursting with carelessly sorted odds and ends collected from the lean-to shed next to the barn. They touched the articles, searching and examining: a deeply scarred wooden plane, blade missing; a rusty sad iron, bereft of handle; a covey of spark plugs, corroded and greasy; a coil of rope; a lidless gas can; some fishing reels and an old green tackle box; a hoe with a shattered handle; some spikes in a box; two sections of chain; three shovels; a brown bottle, half full, labeled "horse liniment". They catalogued all these things in their minds. If they wanted something they would have to remember the box, as there would be too many pushing to the side of the wagon when the sale started to get a second look.

Gary Westicott, in a red plaid shirt, rifled through a box a rusty bolts and broken tool pieces. He had a list in his mind of all the things he needed. He fingered the objects in the box. Well, there was nothing he was collecting in there. He moved to the next box. His hands assumed a careless shuffle through its contents. There was a cigar box in fairly good shape, some leather straps, a good horse halter, and a small object down in the corner. He touched it. Was it possible? A small shape he recognized immediately. A tiny jackknife! He picked it up, hand still in the box, and felt it carefully. It was exactly what he was looking for, and he had never expected to find it here. A little knife in the shape of a lady's high buckle boot, carved in bone like the others, perfect in every detail, even to the tiny buckles for the lacings. The knife blade worked. His hand knew all this although his eyes looked elsewhere. No one else need to know what he had found. Concealing his treasure in one hand, he picked up the halter with the other, assuming great interest in the buckles. It was the knife he wanted desperately. He had to draw attention away from what he had found. He replaced the halter noisily and closed his fingers carefully around the knife. He would not steal it. By chance someone might see him and he could not risk that. He would simply move his hand carelessly to the next box of junk and drop his treasure in there. Luckily it was a box of rusty bolts and broken tools. It would hide the knife and he could buy this box for a song. He heard it drop softly and disappear. His heart raced as he realized that this knife was going to be his. It would be time to take count again of the articles in his collection. He would assume his usual carefree expression and no one would take notice of his desperate eagerness to possess this little knife. No one would suspect...He didn't allow himself to finish the thought. Not now.

The men pushed closer to the wagon like threshers to the dinner table, ready for the meal to start. They knew this load would be sold first. That was the pattern. Maxie would keep the best stuff to the last to hold the crowd. There were very few women around the wagon. They were more interested in the long table lined and laden with dishes and linens, boxes of trinkets, clothing, costume jewelry and kitchen nick knacks. There was one woman though – a newcomer to the Island who frequented the summer auctions, and she was rummaging through the boxes carelessly checking out their contents.

Maxie could sense the auction fever coming on and skillfully read the temperature of the buyers. It was rising steadily. He recognized at least three antique dealers. That was good. And there were some local collectors who would pay a high price if it were something they really wanted. Yes, this would be a good sale – another payment on his house in Florida.

"We're ready to go now, folks. The terms of this sale are cash. You will be charged GST and PST to keep those government boys happy. You are responsible for what you buy...Don't leave it around in case I sell it twice. Now if you chaps will just push this rig over next to the wagon we'll get this show on the road."

On cue four lads pushed the auctioneer's platform closer to the wagon. This outfit was an elaborate homemade contrivance, half trailer, half rickshaw. It had a raised podium in front and a speaker arrangement fastened to it. Maxie used that to keep the attention and control of the crowd. Auction bills papered the side of the platform listing times and places of future auctions. Sadie sat on the stool at the back flipping her sales books as she assigned numbers to the prospective purchasers.

Maxie smiled as he listened to a couple of tourists rooting through some boxes and talking about the treasures they had uncovered. "Look at these horseshoes! They'd look great over my cottage door." "Check this out! One of those horse collars you can use for a frame for a mirror. I'm getting this for sure!" The crowd quieted and listened in, following Maxie's attention. Realizing the sudden hush, the men grinned in embarrassment as Maxie patronized them with a smile. "That's okay fellas, that's pretty good lookin' stuff you've found. Just dig your fingers deep in your wallets and that can be all yours. Now, we're ready to go. This is a big sale and we got to get movin'. We'll start with that load of goodies over there. Just hold that box up good and high, lads, so the folks can see. What have we got there? Hold up some stuff. The business part of a hoe, a bunch of six inch spikes, a piece of chain, some leather straps for a harness...What am I offered? Toss in that fishin' tackle box. What's in it, boys? Show the folks. Everything you need to catch the big ones. I hear the perch are bitin' pretty good down at the Kagawong dock. Pete here caught a two pounder there yesterday, right Pete?"

Pete raised an arm to cover an embarrassed grin. Maxie continued. "Now what am I offered? All this for the price of one. There's lots of hooks in there, and sinkers it looks like, and some pretty high test line, may be in pieces, but you can tie it together."

A few laughs erupted from the crowd as the boys held up a veritable jungle of broken line, sinkers and hooks that would defy all sorting.

A voice from the crowd. "I'll give you a dollar."

"One dollar, one dollar, do I hear two?"

"Two."

"Two, two, do I hear three?"

"Five."

"That's more like it! Five, five, come alive, six, six, do I hear six?" Going for five, last time. Sold. To Jamie, that guy in the yellow shirt. Number 69, Sadie. Good luck with the fishin' lad. There's a chap down in Tehkummah mounts the big ones...Okay boys, now we'll take the next box."

CHAPTER 2

Jean had given Joe the tackle box for his birthday. It had cost $3.49 in 1938. She had saved the change from the cream cheques until she had enough to buy it from Dave's Hardware in Mindemoya. She knew Joe needed the box, for he could never keep his fishing gear in any kind of order.

She smiled as she thought about him. He was always looking through the drawers in the kitchen, especially the junk drawer, home to all the useless things you couldn't throw away – broken pencils, rubber jar rings, half used paraffin wax slabs, strings, an old egg beater, a ball of twine. Sometimes he'd stash some sinkers and leaders in here, and maybe some fishing line. He did keep track of his hooks, though. They were stored high and dry on a shelf. Once he'd got a fishhook in his finger, the barb lodged tightly below the second joint. As Joe said, "It hurt like the devil getting it out." After that, no more hooks in the drawer.

Now he'd have a place for all his gear. She carefully hid the box under the stairway. Joe never looked in here. This was the way they loved each other, saving, buying little gifts, and hiding them until the right time came.

Joe loved the box. It had two sets of shelves. Perfect. "How'd you know I needed this, Jeannie?" He laughed heartily, a laugh that quickly spread infectious good humour.

"Now don't let me catch you putting your fishing stuff in my kitchen!" she said.

Joe began to collect all his gear. Jean helped him in the search. By the time they had gathered bits and pieces from every nook and cranny in the kitchen, and Joe had checked out all his pockets, they had a fine collection. Joe carefully sorted and arranged it all in the little compartments. It was tidy for a week.

If there ever was a fisherman, it was Joe. It didn't matter to him if the fish were biting or not. He knew they were there. The challenge was to see what they were eating. Sometimes popcorn did the trick, especially in shad fly season. You could bait your hook with a nice white popcorn, and let it lie casually on top of the water. If a fish mistook it for a juicy shad fly, you had supper in the net. Sometimes a little chunk of fish flesh did the trick better than a minnow. It was smart to have a little smorgasbord ready and waiting in case the fish weren't interested in a regular diet. Joe chuckled as he prepared his delicatessen. It was 4:30 A.M.

There were a number of guides on the lake. They were all friends and respected each other's expertise. A bit of good-natured rivalry kept the competitive spirit alive. That was the reason Joe was up at this ungodly hour. 'Old Fred', across the lake, had caught some whitefish on a hook and line. Usually the only way you caught whitefish was in the springtime, in spawning season on the end of a spear. Illegal, of course. But to actually find a whitefish hole and catch them with a hook and line was something else.

It didn't take long for the fish gossip to make the rounds. "Yes, 'Old Fred' had found the hole." "Yes, it was very deep, about sixty feet." "No, it wasn't very big. Just big enough for one boat to anchor on top." "It was in the gap, somewhere. Closer to the island than to Wagg's point." That's the way the stories went.

Joe would drag the gap this morning, before 'Old Fred' was up, and he'd be parked on that hole when Fred brought out his tourists. Maybe he'd even have a few fish to show them.

The old five horse Evinrude started on the first pull. What a morning. It was late night quiet. The sun would just be creeping over the trees by the time he reached the gap. The smell of soft breeze over fresh water always invigorated Joe. His senses were always alive and appreciative, a skill honed to awareness by five years of training at the Ontario College of Art. But this was no morning to be distracted by Nature's beauty. It was nature's secrets he was after. He slowed down as he reached the point of the island. He'd shut the motor down and drift. The sun was just beginning to edge over the shadow of the trees. He let out his line.

At first the dying force of the motor kept his line adrift, straight from the stern of the boat. Then it settled with the weight of the sinkers. He snagged the bottom promptly. His hook was likely caught in an old sunken log, or snagged in behind a rock. He played the line, loosening it, then pulling it taut. After several such attempts, it pulled free. He reeled in the line and removed the hook. He added two sinkers. Much less likely to snag. He dipped the oars, propping his feet against the rear seat, the line held securely between the toe ends of his laced rubber boots. It became a pattern – pull the oars, test the depth, pull the oars, test the depth. He kept a straight line between the two points. He repeated the process again and again. He had to be lucky soon, or Fred would catch him hunting his hole.

He leaned on the oars and checked his sights: straight out from the point of the island, the edge of the West Bay point on his right. He steered a little to the west. He let his line fall loosely. It spun out. Suddenly it dropped, straight down. He grabbed the line. He knew he had the hole. He threw the anchor, but it touched at thirty feet. He'd overshot, but he must be close. Paddle a little to the right. He quickly took the sights. He couldn't lose the hole now that he was so close – the birch at the point, the mushroom tree to the south, Farquhar's barn to the east. He paddled gently northward, testing the line. He lifted the anchor and threw it slightly to the right. The rope started spiraling from its coil, all of it, all sixty feet. He was on it. Now he'd mark this spot very carefully. The second mushroom tree to the west on the south side, the peak of the roof of the red barn, the eagle's nest tree, top branch, on the island. By golly, he had it.

He had nailed the hole, but just in time. He could see Fred's boat taking off from shore. He wouldn't stay to fish this morning. He'd rather have a catch in his boat when Fred pulled along side. No, he'd go back and tell the news to Jeannie. Tomorrow he'd have his guests anchored on the spot before Fred was even up.

The fun had just started. And this was just the beginning.

CHAPTER 3

"Let's move along now, boys. What have we got here? Hold it up so everyone can see. An old lantern. A genuine antique. The glass is a bit cracked, but you can still buy the new ones. A little paint and she'll be like new. And in the box, a couple of stove grates and a lifter. Any lids there, boys?"

Allie and Mae had one ear tuned to Maxie, but they were really not interested in the things on the wagon...They were standing by a makeshift table, eyeing up the dishes.

"I think I've seen some of these dishes before. I've got a feeling I've seen that rooster pitcher somewhere – in somebody's house. If I could just remember..."

"There's not likely many of those pitchers around. Pretty old, I'd say. Now that you mention it, I think I've seen it too." Mae picked up the pitcher. It was about ten inches high, brown and yellow, with a curled green tail feather handle. The rooster's comb was spread wide at the top for the opening. Its eye was brown with a red accent. He was a mean looking rooster. If he were alive, it would take a brave soul to approach the hen house. She turned over the pitcher. SLOVACIA was printed there, and a clear stamp with number 14 inside the circle. This was an old one, all right, but it looked like new. Not a chip or a crack. It had a creamy smooth touch to the fingers. She gently replaced it on the table.

"It'll come to me," she said.

They had to move with the crowd as they circled the table. Allie said, "I'm pretty sure I've seen that plate with the lily of the valley. Do you recognize it?"

"I can't be certain. That and the rooster pitcher seem familiar."

"Could be anybody's. This is a consignment auction. Maxie collects stuff from all over the place and makes a big auction when he gets enough. So there's no telling who belongs to what, or what belongs to who."

They both chuckled and started checking out the boxes as they filed with the traffic around the table. "I think we've been around this table six times now. Let's see if we can find a shady place to sit for a while. There's a bench over there that ought to hold us."

They tested the legs before they sat. Off to the right, Maxie was dealing with the stuff on the wagon. "What's he got in his hand?" Allie said.

"Beats me," Mae replied.

"Genuine old fashioned leg traps, folks. Pretty small. Maybe for a rabbit, or a mink. This one's got some pretty cloth wrapped around it."

"I never could stand the thought of trapping," Mae said. "I had a neighbour who set traps and didn't check them until the next week or so. Most of the animals he caught starved to death."

"I've heard a beaver will chew a foot off to get out of a trap."

"Yes, I've heard that, too."

"Why do you suppose there's a cloth on that one?"

"Heaven knows. Maybe a marker. Set the trap in the snow and the bright cloth shows up."

"Never thought of that. Starve to death or freeze to death. Pretty gruesome way to go, I'd say."

"Okay, what am I offered for these traps?" Must be ten or so here. Maybe more. How about a start of ten dollars? Ten, ten, do I hear ten? Five, five, come alive. What's your bid, folks? Any Greenpeacers here? Buy these and put the trappers out of business. Let's move along now. Three, three, do I hear three?"

"One."

"Sold. This young lady in the blue jacket. Number 27. It's hard to say what a young gal will do with these traps. Watch out, fellas."

Sheila had bought the box, but she certainly had no interest in the traps. She had a reason for buying them, though. She had seen the man in the red plaid shirt hide something in a box of junk. When she was sure he was out of sight, she looked in the box. She searched carefully, getting dirt and rust on her fingers as she rooted through the old bolts and nuts. In the corner was a small object. It was a little ornament of some kind. She did not want to be seen studying it. Very casually she retrieved the object and slipped it in with the traps. She wasn't sure what she had, but if he wanted it, it must be good. It would be very gratifying to see him buy the box of junk and not find what he had sneaked in there. He had played a dirty trick on her. Let's see how he liked a little of his own medicine. A small shiver of excitement brought a smile to her lips.

CHAPTER 4

Joe and Jean brought the fish fillets down to the shore dinner place by boat. Joe selected pieces of kindling, slivering long strips with his jackknife, and placing them at careful intervals among the logs to keep a constant heat. Jean floured the fish and emptied two packages of butter into the huge frying pan lying in readiness on the grate. When the fire was right, they shared the job of frying. Joe tested the hot grease with a perch filet and nodded approvingly as it sizzled and curled at the edges. They enjoyed these few minutes of privacy every Sunday, moments stolen from the busy week of complete attention to caring for tourists' every request. The season was short, and they didn't begrudge the long hours they spent, assuring themselves of business the following season. At the same time, they relished these few minutes to chat and enjoy one another's company.

Soon the hum of approaching outboards indicated that this little retreat was about to end. In no time at all, the tourists had landed, the meal was served, and everyone was still sitting around on the makeshift benches. The girls were tidying up. Only a few bottom scrapings of scalloped potatoes were left in the grey roast pan on the picnic table. The fried fish were all gone, and a few flies buzzed over the last spoonfuls of baked beans. Two pieces of banana cream pie relaxed in the sun, spreading themselves comfortably in the pan.

"Now's the time for the fish stories," drawled Chuck, a guest from Ohio who found an excuse to return to Treasure Island at least four times a season. "Joe, did ya clean up that big booger I caught this morning, or is he still in the ice house? He was one big son of a gun, and gave me a pretty hard fight."

"Nope, he's on ice, Chuck. If it had been last week at this time he would have been cooked, but fishin's been good this week, and we didn't need him. Some of these new guests are finding your holes, Chuck."

"I guess all's fair if you can find them. Do you remember the time we were on the whitefish hole with a net full and Fred pulled up beside us? I'll never forget the look on his face."

A new tourist broke in to the conversation. "Is the whitefish hole where that marker is in the gap?"

"Well, I'd like people to think so," said Joe. "When two or three boats get tied up to that marker, there's just enough room left for us to sit right over the hole, about a boat length to the west." The old timers chuckled. This was the trick. Anchor the marker twenty feet from the hole to lure the competition, then come along and park right on the hole beside them.

One story led to another. Then Chuck said, "We'd better hear the mink story, Joe. Some new folks here won't have heard it."

Joe was putting back his last bite of lemon pie. They'd often asked him for this story. He must have told it a hundred times. In response to good humoured coaxing, Joe set his empty plate on the table. With one hand he pushed the old felt hat off his forehead, found a good spot to prop up his foot, and leaning forward on his bent knee, began the story.

"When Jeannie and I bought this place there wasn't a lot of money," he began softly. The place hushed. "We had a big payment – $500 – to make on the island in the fall. Might as well have been 50,000. Anyway, it was before we got into the tourist business, and we were scraping pretty hard to make ends meet. My brother, Geordie, and I had a fox farm on the home place, and when Jeannie and I bought the island, I brought my share of the foxes over here. We had quite a few pens, and every year, if things went well, we had several litters of puppies. Then we'd have to kill off some of the older ones and send the pelts away to Barrie to be tanned and made into furs. You could get pretty good money for a cape – up to $150 in the good times. But you had to find somebody with enough money to buy it."

"How many pelts could you get off one fox, Joe?" shrilled a voice from a back bench.

Tourists asked the galldarndest stupid questions, thought Joe. But without a smile or a blink of an eyelash he answered, "Oh, about six in a good year." A chuckle rippled through the crowd. Jeannie cast a knowing look at the staff, which read, "Don't laugh. Customers are always right."

"Anyway," Joe continued, "My friends, Roy and Jim, raised mink as well as foxes. We talked about the future of fur farming every time we got together. Mink were becoming the big thing. I really wanted to get into them, but Jeannie didn't think we had enough money to buy the first pair. We needed that money for the first payment on the island."

Jean smiled at this, and nodded knowingly. Joe slipped her a grin. "Anyway, I was over in town one day and got talking to Jim. He told me he could get me a pair of mink for $300. He thought I could double my money in no time. I got pretty excited about it, but dash it all, when I mentioned it to Jeannie, she put the kibosh on it. No mink.

"Well, I couldn't help thinking about it. Somebody else was going to buy the mink if I didn't move soon. We had a bit of money set aside, and if I worked like the devil peddling turkeys which we raised, I thought I could still make the payment in the fall. We also had a big garden, and I could take the turkeys and the vegetables to Espanola and sell them door to door.

Without a word to Jeannie, I bough the mink. I brought them over to the island one evening and left them in their cages overnight by the dock. I'd muster up enough courage to tell my sweet wife that this was a good investment – in the morning. I was short of nerve that night."

Jean smiled.

"Next morning I went down to check my mink." He paused. "But son of a gun, that she mink had chewed her way out of the cage. I was frantic, but I had to use my head. Telling Jeannie I had bought the mink was bad enough. Telling her I had lost one was unthinkable.

Not likely that mink would swim the lake. She'd check the food supply close at hand first. I was a pretty good trapper. I'd done a lot of that to make a bit of money when I was a kid, and I had some good traps. I thought I'd bind those traps with cloth so they would hold the mink and not hurt her. So I took some old print flour bags from Jeannie's kitchen drawer, and ripped them into strips. I wrapped the traps carefully, making sure the snap would hold but not kill my prize.

I set those darn traps all over. One I set down here in a hollow log over by the fireplace. I put some meat in the middle of the log, nicely hiding the trap. Some of the others I set around the fox pen where I'd put the male mink. I thought she might go there.

Anyway, there was nothing to do but wait. I checked the traps close to the pens. No sign. I came down here pretty despondent. I peeked into the end of the log. There she was! Just sniffing the meat. I grabbed my hat and stuffed it in one end of the log and ran around to the other end. I unbuttoned my shirt and stuffed it in there. I knew my hat wouldn't hold, so I ran back to the other end, holding my hat with my leg while I took off my pants. I stashed them into the log with my hat. Then I took my shoelaces and tied them around the shirt and the log at one end and the pants and the log at the other. I had her!

Stark naked, shoes flapping, I hoisted the log on my shoulder and I carried my prize to the house. I opened the kitchen door. I shouted, 'Jeannie, I got her.' My wife thought I'd gone over the edge. She said, 'Joe, what's the matter?' Then out poured my whole story. Together, we go that mink safely in the pen."

"And did it work, Joe? Did you make lots of money with your mink?"

"No, we never did. We made the payment all right – with the turkeys. But I gave up skinning mink." He laughed and his laughter was contagious. "I decided to skin tourists instead."

Next shore dinner there'd be someone else who hadn't heard the story.

CHAPTER 5

Sheila made room for the box of traps at her feet. There was no hurry to see what Gary Westicott had hidden there. She could enjoy seeing what it was in the privacy of her car. Now she would bide her time and watch for his response.

As Maxie coaxed the bidders in his singsong soprano, Sheila catalogued in her mind what little she knew about Westicott. It was at one of Maxie's auctions she had first become aware of him. The memory flashed vividly in her mind. She had found, in a box of assorted glass and china, a little set of three rabbits – two small salt and pepper shakers and a mustard jar – nestled on a small blue china platter. The rabbits had shiny, mottled bodies, orange ear liners, and orange eyes with pupils of glistening gold. Little white whiskers added a quizzical expression to the rabbits' faces. These rabbits had conjured up a rare happy childhood moment. Her aunt had owned a set like this. Whenever they visited, as a child, she saw these rabbits nestled on a ruffled doily on the sideboard. Sometimes she had been allowed to play with them. And now, here was a set exactly the same. It might cost her quite a bit, but she was prepared to pay.

As she thought back, she could still hear Maxie's voice. "We'll start with that box right there," he had said. One of the lads had held up the box. The bidding advanced quickly. She bid thirty-eight dollars. She held her breath. Maxie tried for forty, but there was no response, "Last call," he shouted. "Sold."

The boys had handed her the box carefully. She placed it on the ground and lifted a plate and saucer to uncover the rabbits. She searched through the box. They were not there. Her rabbits were gone. Her dismay had registered with Maxie. The words blurted out. "There were china rabbits in that box," she said.

"Did anyone remove a set of rabbits from this box?" he asked the crowd.

No response.

"I'm sorry, ma'am, we must get on with the sale. If someone has removed the set by mistake, please make sure this lady gets it back."

Even to-day, the disappointment enveloped her. It was at the next auction that she learned what had happened. A young man –

18

actually, the one who had bought the tackle box – had approached her shyly, explaining that the man in the red plaid shirt had asked him to help load a heavy cupboard into his truck, and in the move he was sure he had seen the rabbits. Sheila thanked him. She felt like approaching Westicott directly, but she did not want to involve the young man. Instead, she would bide her time. She would get her revenge.

She studied Westicott now. He was a good looking man, about thirty eight she guessed, dark complexioned, still wearing the red plaid shirt. This must be his auction uniform, she thought. He had a pleasant expression. There was really nothing about the man's appearance to arouse any suspicions.

Sheila had casually inquired about him. She learned that he bought antiques and trucked them away. Presumably, he had an antique store 'down East', as the locals put it. He had stayed at various places on the Island. Rumour had it that he visited a lot of elderly ladies, presumably buying up old articles that they didn't know had antique value. The moccasin telegraph traveled pretty fast and if she kept her ears open she would likely learn a lot more. She wasn't in any hurry. She would wait, and watch, and see how he liked being tricked...That would be enough for a start.

At this moment, Maxie was still a few feet away from the box of junk in which Westicott had hidden his treasure – or thought he had. Now one of the boys was holding up a mounted peacock. What a strange creature to see at an auction. Old and dusty, thin of tail feathers, it still maintained a regal pose on a twisted branch. Iridescent teal neck feathers glistened in the sunshine. Its wings were folded snugly to the body, the feathers smooth and colourful. Only the tail feathers were shaggy and sparse. One of the boys blew on its head and a mushroom cloud of dust sent him into a spasm of coughing.

"Better use a vacuum, laddie. You're apt to clog up your lungs. Now folks, a genuine mounted peacock. Clean him up a bit and you've got a perfect trophy for your family room. Look at those shiny eyes. Not a scratch. I tell you, folks, he's a keeper. Let's start off the bidding at forty dollars. Forty, forty. Do I hear forty? Thirty-five, thirty-five, who'll give me thirty-five? What am I offered? C'mon folks, we've got a lot of things to go through yet. Fifteen, do I hear fifteen? Fifteen, fifteen..."

"Ten dollars."

"Okay, I've got ten, ten, ten, give me twelve..."

"Twelve."

"Twelve, twelve, now fourteen, fourteen..."

"Fifteen."

"Fifteen, fifteen, do I hear seventeen? No takers? I've got fifteen folks. Going once, going twice, going three times. Last call. Sold. Number 46. Brian Peterson, Mindemoya.

19

CHAPTER 6

"Joe, that peacock will bite you," his mother said. But the warnings went unheeded. He would lie on his stomach in the grass and wiggle up quietly behind the peacock, reaching out to touch his tail feathers. Sometimes, if Joe stood really still, the inquisitive peacock would come close to him. Then, Joe would reach out and pet his shiny neck. When the peacock screeched, Joe thought he was saying, "Joe, Joe," in his squawking voice.

Joe's family had been on Manitoulin for two years. George, Joe's father, had bought the farm in 1883, but it was eight years before they moved. George loved it here, and returned from his farm in Ayr several times before he thought it was time to move his family. The two years had not been easy, but they were all filled with the spirit of adventure, and the pioneer families bolstered each other's spirits.

George's parcel of land was three hundred acres, and it had cost him fifty cents an acre. The land was covered with maple, spruce, oak and pine. The flat land by the lake gradually rose to a limestone hill from which jutted small limestone cliffs. In the spring, the land above the hill was carpeted with trillium, a beautiful forest floor of solid white and green. In late June, wild strawberries grew in profusion. Joe and Janet were often sent to fill their cups with strawberries.

"You're not supposed to eat any until you have your cup full," Janet said. Joe liked to pick far away from Janet so she couldn't see him. The berries were just too good not to eat them. After all, mother wanted them for the table, so he would eat his share now. Janet was so bossy. He sneaked another berry into his mouth.

Janet, who was nine, was expected to do some chores, but Joe, only five, escaped most of the work. He spent most of his days chasing the rooster, playing with the peacock, and drawing pictures in the dust with a sharp stick. He loved the little nooks and crannies in the hill. The limestone ledges made perfect little spots for him to sit. He loved to watch the clouds and make up stories about them as they sailed across the sky. He loved going down to the lake but mother was so afraid of water that he had to sneak down without her seeing. He wished he could go to that wonderful island out there in the lake, but there was no way to get there. The old elm tree boat they had come in still rested there on the beach, but nobody ever put it in the water.

The world of play and make believe was soon to end for Joe. His brother, Will, never strong, became very ill. Will's coughing was lasting longer and longer. The neighbours brought medicines, but there was no doctor close by. There was a kind of hushed activity that chilled Joe to the bone. He was left on his own, worrying and wondering what was going on behind Will's closed door. Then, one day, the coughing stopped. Joe heard the word 'coffin'. He cried and cried. Jane, his older sister, held him in her arms a long time. His mother was sobbing, and his father held her in his big arms. The next three days were terrifying. Neighbours came to call, and Will was lying in a wooden box. Nobody would let Joe look inside.

After the funeral, the family returned to the cabin. Joe stayed outside. He took a stick and drew pictures in the dust by the door. Then, he wandered out to the chicken pen. He found two brown eggs in the nest and put them in his pocket. Mother might be happy to get the eggs. He would take them to her.

He turned to run to the cabin. At that moment, a strange cat came from behind the henhouse. It made a beeline for the peacock. Before the peacock had a chance to run, the cat attacked. Joe dropped the eggs and ran. "Father. Father!"

By the time George arrived, the cat had bitten the peacock's neck. Joe ran to his pet. It was too late. The terrible sadness of the last three days, and now his friend dead. He sobbed, "Don't put him in the ground. Please, father!"

George picked him up and held him close. "Joe," he said. "First, I will shoot that cat. But more importantly, I will have our friend, Jim, fix up your peacock. He will clean his feathers and mount him on a strong branch. We will keep him in the house. That's a promise."

Joe was comforted by his father's words. He snuggled into his shoulder. Finally understanding a little boy's grief, the family gathered around, and Jane coaxed him from their father's arms. "Come, little Joe, let's go to the lake. I'll tell you a big story about that island out there."

George kept his promise. The beautiful peacock was mounted, and Joe kept him all his life.

CHAPTER 7

The auctioneer's mesmerizing monotone had slipped into cruise control, weaving in and out the traffic line of boxes on the wagon. The crowd was responding well, the prices fairly high. One of the boys picked up the junk box. Sheila watched. Westicott's face revealed disinterest. "What have we got here? Lots of old nuts and bolts. A bit rusty on the edges, but clean them up and they'll last you a lifetime. You know what the commercial says, 'Hold the country together with our nuts and bolts.' Who'll start me off with three bucks? Three, three, do I hear three? Two, two, toodledeedo. Let's have a bid, folks. What else can we add, lads? Put in that..."

"One dollar."

"Sold. Your name again, sir?"

"Westicott."

"Sold to Mr. Westicott, number 26."

Westicott didn't look in the box, just held out his hands to receive it from the boy and placed it casually at his feet. If he thought he had a prize in the box, he did not reveal it.

The bidding continued. Two lanterns brought $150. A cream can went for $95. A dented copper boiler collected $125. Maxie was now auctioning off an antique wooden duck decoy. "It's real old, folks, a genuine hand carved decoy. This belonged to my old friend, Ted. He's been shooting arrows at it for forty years and hasn't hit it yet."

The crowd laughed. The decoy brought $130. Maxie was now ready to move from the wagon. Allie and Mae watched his contrivance come closer to the table where they were standing. Once more, they surveyed the table's bounty. They were close enough to reach out and touch the dishes. The quality china was not in boxes. Each piece was separate, polished and sparkling in the sunlight. Allie was concentrating on the golden rooster pitcher.

Suddenly, a bolt of memory struck her. "Mae, I know whose pitcher it was! It was Jean's!"

"Of course! And the plate. That was Jean's too. She told us about them that day Joe took us to the island."

"Right. Joe's mother had brought them with her when they moved here. They were wedding gifts. When the steamer landed in West Bay, and their things were unloaded, the crate her gifts were in broke, and they had to leave it there, on the shore. It was over a week before they could get back to pick it up. There it was, safe and sound, nothing taken out of it. Some of the West Bay women had kept their eye on it to make sure it was safe."

"I remember that story. Why do you suppose these dishes are at the sale? Surely the family would want to keep them."

"You'd have thought so."

"Well, I'm going to bid."

"So am I."

"I'll bid on one, and you bid on the other."

"Which one?"

They were oblivious to the fact that Maxie was ready to start and was grinning at the two of them.

"I'll bid on the rooster."

"I'll bid on the plate."

By this time, the whole crowd was watching them, so intent on their own conversation that they had lost track of what was happening. Everyone was enjoying this little drama.

"That's all right, ladies. No better place to visit than at an auction. Best social entertainment to be had. Hand up that pitcher, lads. This is an old one, folks. Not a crack or a chip. At least a hundred years old, I'd say. We'll start it off at fifty dollars. Fifty, fifty, do I hear fifty?"

"Fifty."

"Fifty-five, fifty-five..."

"Fifty-five."

This was more than Allie had dreamed of bidding. "Sixty dollars," she said.

"Sixty dollars, right down here," Maxie said, looking at Allie.

"Sixty-five."

"Seventy."

"Seventy-five."

"Eighty."

"Eighty-five."

Allie drew a deep breath. "Ninety dollars," she said.

The crowd clapped. "Ninety, ninety, last call. Going, going, gone –
to Allie, number 66. Hand that down carefully, boys."

Allie took the pitcher carefully. Her hands caressed its smooth shape. It wasn't so much the pitcher. It was because of Jean. All the memories came flooding back. What times they'd had. But there was no time for reminiscing. Up came the lily of the valley plate. "Here's another oldie. Genuine Bavarian china plate. Little flowers all over the bottom. In perfect shape. Let's start this off at forty. Forty, forty, do I hear forty?"

"Forty."

"Forty-five."

"Fifty."

"Fifty-five."

"Sixty."

"Seventy." That was Mae's bid. Mae, who had to scrimp and save to buy the groceries, had bid seventy dollars on a plate.

"Seventy, seventy, going to the little lady in the pink sweater. Last call. Sold."

One of the boys passed Mae the plate. She took it carefully, a flood of memories overcoming her. The sale moved on. Allie and Mae withdrew from the crowd. The enormity of what they'd done settled on them like a shroud. In the heat of the auction, too excited, they had both bid higher than they had intended. Where would they get the money? They lived in the same small town that had recently been serviced with water and sewers. Everyone had to be a part of the plan to make it affordable for all. People like Allie and Mae were feeling the pinch. There was certainly no money for careless spending.

They looked at each other in disbelief. Maxie would take a personal cheque, but Mae's bank account wouldn't handle seventy dollars. Not until her old age pension money came in, and that was the end of the month. Allie was in almost similar circumstances. She had saved all her life, and had put a little away. However, the new town improvements had taken almost all of that. She always paid everything up front. Although she knew Maxie well, it would be too embarrassing to tell him she didn't have the money.

"Allie, I don't have seventy dollars."

"I wish I had money to lend you, Mae, but I'm pretty strapped myself. It took so much for the water."

"I know. I only have forty dollars until my cheque comes in."

"I brought forty dollars with me, but I spent five dollars at that yard sale on the way up for that box of old clothes for my grandkids to dress up in. They'll be here this summer, and they love to dress up and act out skits. I wish I hadn't bought that, now."

Mae was close to tears. She held her arms tightly around her plate. It was some consolation to know that Jean would be glad she

25

had it. As she thought of her, a little of her panic dissipated. If Jean were here, she'd laugh – they'd laugh together – and find a way out of this mess.

"Mae, this sale will last a long time. I'll take the car back home and see if I can borrow some money. Will you look after my rooster? And my box of clothes. I left them over there by the bench. Do you want me to get you a coffee and a cookie?"

"I couldn't eat a thing, Allie. I'm so embarrassed. I got caught up in the excitement and lost my head."

"Never mind, Mae. It will turn out all right. Take care of my things. I'm off. Try to enjoy the rest of the day." Allie left abruptly. Mae sat down on the bench beside Allie's box. She carefully placed the rooster and the plate in among the clothes. She would sit here and watch the people. Her stomach was too jittery to even think of a cookie.

Two hours passed. Allie was not back. What would she do if she didn't come back? It didn't bear thinking on. She tried to concentrate on the auction. Her body was a bundle of nerves. "My lands," she thought, "I have to calm down or I'll have a heart attack." She had to think of something to do to keep her mind busy. She'd look at the plate again. And the pitcher. Then she'd check out the clothes Allie had bought for the grandkids.

She carefully placed the plate on the grass by her side. She picked up the pitcher, recalling Jean's voice as she had told its story. Then she took out the clothes, one at a time, and folded each one up after she had looked at it closely. This one was a party dress, a horrible char-treuse trimmed with black sequins. Whoever wore it likely thought it was beautiful. Nobody would be caught dead wearing it to-day, that's for sure. The next garment was a circle skirt, made of felt. She used to have one of these. Yes, there was the white poodle and his long leash. It took her back to the fifties. What a time that was! All the memories came flooding back. She and Ernie had loved to dance. She thought of the Sandfield dances, so crowded that one night she and Ernie had started out in one square and ended up in another during the à la main left. She carefully folded up the skirt, making sure the little poodle with the sequin eye ended up on top.

She groped around in the box and hauled up a sweater. She had knitted that pattern once. It was in a Beehive book. She remembered how hard it was to knit in the pockets and the buttonholes. The direc-tions had been hard to follow. You knit the front of the pocket then left those stitches on a needle while you knitted up the back. Then you had to remember where the buttonholes went and how to get them in the middle. Whoever had knit this had done a good job. Even the button-holes were perfect. She examined the technique as she undid the but-ton on the pocket. This was nicely done, all right. She reached her hand inside. There were some crumpled bits of paper in there. No, it wasn't a Kleenex. What was it? She unfolded it carefully. Was it a bill? What on earth was it? Money? She couldn't believe her eyes. A one hundred-dollar bill. She looked around her. Was anybody watching? No. She reached in again. Another one. And there were more. There were ten – at least ten. Legal tender – that was on the front. She replaced the money and buttoned up the pocket. She must be dreaming – or delirious. She looked in the pocket again. Yes, it was real! She was sane.

Excitement thrilled through her. They would have lots of money to pay for the dishes. But was it really theirs? Wouldn't it be stealing to not report it? Her mind raced. Maybe she should tell somebody. No. The money was Allie's. She had bought the old clothes. They would decide together what to do.

Maxie was working the next table. One of the boys was holding up a quart sealer chock full of buttons. "What am I offered, Ladies? There's enough buttons here to redo all your husband's shirts. And there's some real purtty ones, too. Will someone start me off at five dollars? No? Do I hear two? Two, two toodledeedo...These aren't your ordinary buttons, folks. There's all kinds in here, shiny ones, little pearl ones, maybe the crown jewels hidden in this little jar. And when you use up all the buttons, you can put your preserves in the bottle."

There was no response.

"Somebody give me a dollar."

"One dollar," said Sheila.

"Sold to that young lady. Maybe you'll find enough buttons to sew on all those fur coats you're gonna make when you set those traps." He grinned as the jar was passed to her. The crowd responded with a chuckle, and smiling eyes turned her way. People didn't seem to mind being made fun of publicly. She played along, and smiled back.

In the bottom of the jar was a ruby button.

Chapter 8

Joe checked his assignment: MAKE TEN SKETCHES OF STILL LIFE SELECTED FROM ANY DISPLAY AT THE ROM. HAND IN MONDAY. How could he keep his mind focused to-day? He could scarcely keep his feet on the ground. He had just received a letter from Jean. She had set the date for summer. Finally she had found the nerve to tell her father that she already had her engagement ring, and she really loved Joe, and they wanted to get married in the summer. She told him she had her speech all planned, but when the time came, all the words came spilling out. Her father was not surprised. "I wondered when this would happen," was all he said.

Joe knew how hard it was for Jean to tell her father. Jean's mother had died when she was seventeen, and that left all the responsibility of the household, as well as the care of the children, to Jean. She had taken it upon herself to hold the family together even though relatives and neighbours had offered to take some of the children into their care. One aunt had been especially helpful with the two-year-old, but Jean had insisted on keeping the baby. It hadn't been an easy job, as her father used to spend months prospecting up north.

Now that baby was seven. Jean would take the little boy to live with her and Joe. No problem there. He liked the little kid. Summer, summer, they'd be married in the summer. His mind was incoherent and his feet were falling suit. He was wandering all over the museum, paying no attention at all to where he was.

Suddenly he was jerked to attention by the commanding voice of a guard. "This is not a dance hall, young man. If you wish to view the displays, please control yourself. This is the costume room."

"Exactly what I was looking for. I was just so excited to have found it. Here's what I was to draw," he said. His quick eye caught the name of the display: Queen Victoria's Gown.

The guard eyed him suspiciously as Joe set up his canvas stool and easel. He made a production of selecting his charcoal and paper. Then he pinned on his identification: Student of the College of Art. He started to sketch furiously.

From the corner of his eye he observed the guard. Then a group of students and their teacher came into the room and diverted the guard's attention. Joe remembered he was to meet his friend, Orval, somewhere. He'd forgotten the spot. Anyway, why not sketch the old Queen's dress. He was pretty good at shading, and maybe he'd pick up some extra marks for catching the lights and shadows in the folds of the skirt.

He wished he could buy a dress like that for Jean. It would look better on her than on Queen Victoria. For a moment his mind saw Jean in the beautiful satin dress, the lace trim and little roses curving softly around the low neckline. How much would a dress like that cost? Did brides buy their own dresses, or was the groom responsible? Who could he ask?

"Joe, what happened to you? I waited by the Grecian urn for twenty minutes! Thought you hadn't come."

It was Orval. "Sorry, old chap, I had a whole lot of stuff on my mind."

"Does a 'whole lot of stuff' have anything to do with that letter I see in your hand? Is it from Jeannie, by any chance?"

"Orve, I've got great news! We're going to be married in the summer. I got her answer right here. She's dold her that, and he says it's all right."

"Slow down Joe. Have you been sniffing that charcoal?"

"I'm perfectly fine. Did you hear me, her Dad says it's all right. He's not such a bad old bird after all!"

"Well congratulations! I never thought she'd marry a starving artist."

"Now, I'm a pretty good catch Orve, well spoken, serious, studious, dedicated to my work..."

"Especially well spoken. Maybe you'd better fix that sketch of yours to reflect some of those characteristics."

Joe looked at his drawing. Orve was right. It wasn't very good. He'd better take a good look at this dress. A little railing separated him from the garment. He leaned closer to study the lace detail – little raised roses held together with fragile thread. A line of red buttons closed the back of the neck and ran all the way down to the waist. One hung a little loosely at the bottom.

Almost without thinking, he leaned forward, picked his jackknife from his pocket, checked out the guard instructing the students, and in one quick movement, sheared the red button from the dress. Just as quickly, he deposited the button in his pocket.

This action did not escape his friend, Orve. "Joe, if anyone caught you, you'd go to jail! For Pete's sake, quit fooling around. Your bride won't be too proud of you if you flunk this course and end up in the pen to boot!"

Joe settled into serious sketching. The button was loose. It didn't look good there, out of line with the others. He'd really done the old Queen a favour to remove it. And he had a little red button to give to Jean. She could wear it on her wedding dress. Something old...

The little red button felt good in his pocket.

CHAPTER 9

Sheila took her purchases to the car and placed them in the front seat. She got in, shut the door, and started going through her box. The traps were certainly of no interest to her. She did wonder, though, about the colourful pieces of cloth wrapped around them. She dug beneath the tangle of rusty traps and found the little article she had taken from the box of bolts and old tools...So this is what Westicott wanted so badly.

She looked at it – a lady's high boot, brown and white, carefully carved out of bone. Little buttons were raised in relief up the front, perfect in every detail. The whole thing was scarcely an inch and a half long. Was it a brooch? No. Both sides were exactly the same. Why would this be of interest to Westicott? She inspected it carefully. There was a little ridge of steel along the side, with a small indented slit. She slipped her thumbnail in the slit and pulled gently. Maybe there was something in behind the bar. Suddenly, a little blade snapped out. This was a jackknife. Must have belonged to a woman. She wondered how old it was. Perhaps it was valuable. Why else would Westicott want it? Anyway, now it was hers, bought and paid for – well, not exactly – she had to get into the lineup at the porch to pay, and maybe she would still buy something else before that. She slipped the little knife into her jeans' pocket, tucking it down under a collection of Wurthers and loose change. She left the box of traps on the seat where they could easily be seen. She didn't bother to lock the car. It seemed that people on the Island seldom did. They had some crazy philosophy that if you locked things up it made people think you had something worth stealing. She'd just take the keys. If anyone wanted to steal the traps, let them. She walked casually back to the auction, joining the steady stream of people who had just stored their purchases as she had. They passed Westicott, whistling a little tune, his box tucked under one arm as he opened the door with the other. She wished she could become invisible for a few minutes and watch him look through his box of nuts and bolts and scrappy old tools.

As soon as the truck door closed, Westicott placed the box carefully beside him. He began to look for his treasure. Where was it? It had to be here. He'd tucked it into the top corner. Not there. He clawed through the nuts and bolts, staining his fingers with rust. He hated the gritty feeling on his hands. It had to be here. One more time. No knife. He overturned the box and the contents rattled onto the seat, old broken bits, a small saw blade, a screwdriver with no handle. His head began to pound. Not here. He picked up each bolt separately. Then he did the same with the nuts, sorting them as he went. He liked things orderly. He could feel the pressure building in his head. "Get a grip on yourself," he said out loud. Maybe it had slipped off on the floor. He searched under the seat, sweeping the floor with his fingers. His movements became frantic. Nothing there. He breathed deeply, forcing himself to keep calm. Someone had tricked him. Someone had taken his knife. His head felt as if a band of steel were slowly tightening around his forehead. He must be calm. He closed his eyes. He began to count…one thousand, two thousand…Slowly he forced his mind to take control. Finally the turbulent emotions were lessening. The vise was loosening around his forehead. His heartbeat slowed perceptibly. Whoever had taken that knife would pay. He would go back to the auction and study every face. He would know. He took a slow deep breath and opened the door. He had forced himself to hum a tune he'd heard at a revival meeting in the prison. It had stuck in his mind. "When the trumpet of the Lord shall come, and time shall be no more." It was taking on a special meaning in his mind. He saw himself, alone, blowing the trumpet. He felt the Power. Someday, people would take notice of him. That time would come. He was now in complete control. He would return to the auction.

He began to study the crowd. Who had been standing around the wagon? There was that kid who had bought the tackle box. Not him. He'd helped him load stuff at several auctions. He'd given him a few bucks for his help. No. Just a local clod with more brawn than brains. Who else was there at the time? The stupid tourists, jabbering away about the horse collar. No one else stood out in his mind. He racked his memory. There was that whey faced farmer who bought the peacock. Probably the town nit wit. He passed him over. There were a few women – that broad who was moaning and groaning about lost rabbits last fall, for one. He chuckled to himself. And those two old dames blabbering together, but they didn't stay at the wagon long. All the other faces seemed a blur, all typical local yokels buying one another's junk. They had no idea of the value of anything. The wind swept dust over his face and he brushed his eyes. Dumb drivers, parking too close to the crowd, spitting up dust with their tires.

The driver who emerged from the cloud of dust was Allie. She spotted Mae, still sitting where she'd left her, on a little side hill where she could watch the crowd. She was guarding their purchases, one arm leaning on the box of clothes. Likely she had the dishes tucked in there for safekeeping.

Mae spied her and rose, stiff-kneed, waving. Maxie saw her hand and said, "Are you in, Mae? Twenty-five, twenty-five…"

"No, I'm not bidding," she said. She pulled her hand down quickly.

"Have to be careful, waving your arms around at an auction," Maxie said, laughing. "Now, where were we? Twenty-five, twenty-five…"

Allie hustled towards Mae. Her face revealed the bad news before she spoke. "I wasn't as lucky as I thought I would be. I was only able to get fifty dollars. I tried to get a loan from Hazel, but she was a bit strapped, too…"

"Never mind, Allie," Mae said. "I've got something to tell you." They leaned their heads together conspiratorially, like two rag dolls sitting side by side on a toy shelf. "I was sorting through your clothes, Allie, trying to pass the time. I picked up the sweater and looked at the pattern. It was the same one I knit that time from the Beehive book. Do you remember? The green one with the pockets."

"Yes," she laughed. "I remember the time you had with the buttonholes. You were so frustrated."

"Yes, that's the one. Anyway, I was checking out the buttonholes, and I opened the pocket. Inside I felt little balls of paper, and I knew someone had washed the sweater with tissues in the pocket. So I reached in and pulled out a wad of paper. Allie, do you know what it was?"

"No, what?"

"A bill."

"A bill? Money?"

"Yes, a one hundred-dollar bill. Legal tender, it said…"

"I can't believe it."

"Yes. And there were ten more."

"Ten more? All hundreds?"

"Yes. Eleven hundred dollars."

"My saints. Eleven hundred dollars. It can't be true."

"Yes, see for yourself."

Sheila, at the edge of the crowd, had kept an eye on the two old ladies. It was so funny that the auctioneer thought they were bidding. Now they were rummaging through some clothes in a box. They were so intense on what they were doing. She had watched them earlier when they had bought some dishes. After that, she hadn't seen them buy anything else. Auctions probably were a social highlight in their lives. She couldn't imagine herself getting old and going to auctions, although she had certainly enjoyed them herself this summer.

Maxie was at the furniture now. The only thing she really liked was an old walnut dresser. It had two long drawers at the bottom, and two deep drawers on either side of a central shelf accessed by a hinged door. Sheila had chatted with a local lady when they were looking at the dresser earlier. Apparently, the center space was a bonnet drawer. What a lovely idea. Coming home from an afternoon tea, storing one's bonnet in a special cupboard. It would certainly be nice to own it. It was in good shape. Even the keys were taped inside the drawers. She wondered how much it would bring.

They were starting the bidding now. Four hundred already. Now five, five-fifty, six. There seemed to be several bidders, as Maxie was concentrating on four or five places in the crowd.

"Seven hundred, do I hear seven-fifty? Seven-fifty, seven-fifty, last call, seven-fifty. Sold. Number 26. Mr. Westicott. You've got yourself a good cupboard there, sir." The crowd applauded. They appreciated the excitement of the bidding, and the best man won. Sheila joined in the applause. Better to act like all the others and not stand out. Westicott smiled graciously at the crowd. He seemed charmed by their friendly applause. Jamie appeared as if by magic, and asked if he needed help loading it. It was a heavy dresser. "Thanks so much, young man." In a matter of minutes two other men appeared to lend a hand.

This piece was a good buy at any price. The dresser would serve Westicott perfectly. There were things needed to be locked.

CHAPTER 10

When the fire started, Joe's mother was alone at the cabin. Joe was playing at his favourite spot on the hill, in among the limestone caves. There were little places to hide in the side of the hill. George had gone to Providence Bay for flour, a ten-mile hike. He would be back by suppertime. The boat with supplies was due in that morning, and they were almost out of flour for bread. Geordie was at the neighbour's farm, helping with the threshing, and Janet and Jane were both working at the store.

How the fire started was beyond Jean. It must have been sparks from the chimney. It had been very dry, and the cedar shakes would be quick to ignite.

She had been washing when she noticed smoke. Her homemade soap was not touching a stubborn stain, and she straightened up to check it out. Her washstand was out on the porch, and it was quite pleasant washing, rinsing, and hanging out the clothes on a makeshift line. She went into the kitchen to fetch another kettle of boiling water to add to the wash, and a cloud of smoke met her at the door. She did not panic. What could be saved was up to her. She thought after, what strange things people save. She grabbed an armful of dishes, the rooster pitcher, the lily of the valley plate, the little clock that played 'Annie Laurie', the cookie jar with the money and the letters, and put them outside on the ground. She ran back in. The bedroom was full of smoke. She couldn't handle the bed, but she got all her force behind the dresser. Pushing and coughing, eyes stinging with smoke, she somehow got it to the door.

The neighbours had seen the smoke, and came running. They found Jean, such a little person, slumped on the ground, sobbing and coughing. Joe was beside her. The men were able to save a few more things from the kitchen, but the cabin was lost.

Already the men were forming in their minds plans to help George build a new house. They would help him quarry the limestone from this very hill. He had dreamed about doing that anyway, and had often talked about building a big house where there would be more room for the family, so cramped in the cabin. Well, they'd help him with his

35

dream. It would be a chance to repay some of the favours he had done for them.

Geordie comforted his mother. "Father will be home soon," he said. "Everything will be all right. No one has been hurt. We can build a new house."

Joe looked at his brother with big, brown, trusting eyes. Geordie would build a new house, and father would be home soon. Mother could stop crying now.

Chapter 11

Maxie was a good auctioneer. He knew how to keep the people interested to the very end. He had saved a beautiful maple table on white glass rollers to the very last, and people, if they were not interested in it for themselves, were curious to see who would buy it and how much it would bring. Finally, it sold – $325 – probably a bargain at that. Maxie started to put away his gear. Sadie was handing out the last bills.

The lineup to pay was a long one, and it was not moving fast. The ladies at the cash could handle only one at a time. They seemed a little flustered with so many people waiting. Everyone was tired, but people were standing patiently, lost in their own thoughts. The lively conversations of the afternoon had quieted. Many were rethinking their purchases. Did they really want what they had bought, or had they just been caught up in the auction fever?

Jamie was first in line. He had just made one purchase, the tackle box. For him, it had been a great day trading stories with the hometown folks. When he was growing up here, he hadn't appreciated the people. His mom and dad had a lot of friends, but as a teenager, he hadn't been really interested in them. He thought about that now. Back then, everybody seemed to know everybody else's business. There was no privacy for a teenager. You walked down the street feeling that one of your mother's friends was making note of your long hair and your jeans with the holes in the seat. As if any of this mattered.

Then the accident had happened. It crashed into his memory now as it had six years ago. Would he never get over the horror of that moment? All the neighbours, even people he didn't know, had come to help, but he had lashed out in bitterness and anger...He wanted to be left alone. He realized now how rude he had been. But no one seemed to remember that now. They had welcomed him back without question. He soaked up the stories they told him – stories about his mom and dad. He couldn't get enough of them. All the time he had been away, he had purposely erased all the memories from his mind. Now he was filling up the spaces, savouring the pages as he filed them in his mind.

He thought about the tackle box. It was almost the same as the old one he had as a kid. His dad was always after him to keep it tidy. He smiled as his memory called up the familiar voice: "How can you catch a fish if you can't find a hook?" On a sudden whim he had bought the box, with the twisted and knotted line. He would untangle it now, one piece at a time. He smiled in the darkness as he handed the $5.65 to the cashier.

Brian Peterson was next in line. He was glad he had the peacock. It was a bit of a mess, but he could fix it up. A few extra feathers could be pushed into that scraggly tail. It would be a beauty. It was strange, he thought, what came over a man at an auction. He had no notion of buying anything – had just come for the fun of it. He liked visiting, catching up with the local news. Besides that, he liked watching Maxie. And often there was a part for a machine or a piece of scrap he could use. He had arrived a bit late, and the bidding had already started. He was standing at the back of the crowd when Maxie was jabbering away about the peacock. He heard his own voice shouting out six, eleven, thirteen, and fifteen...The peacock was his almost before his mind made the connection. He smiled to himself. If Carol were here, she would think he was crazy. Why would anyone in his right mind buy a dusty old stuffed peacock? Surely there was enough junk in the house already.

He had forced himself to forget her. He never wanted to relive the disappointment he had felt when he first brought her here. He thought about that now. The memory washed over him uninvited. He was bringing her home. They were going to be married, and he had told her all about the old homestead, vacant now since the death of his parents. The same old coming home feeling had welled up inside him. He turned down the lane and parked the car beside the porch. "Home," he said, and turned to her. At first she was quiet. "Is this it?" she said. "Is this rundown shamble of a house the home you promised me?"

He could handle all that now. Yes, this was home. And he loved every part of it – the house, the barn, the yard, the chicken house, the rail fence. And he would put this peacock right in the living room. It could sit on the table and focus its eyes on the laneway. If Carol ever came back, let her squawk. He smiled wryly at the thought.

Behind him in the line, someone offered Mae a stool to sit on as she waited. She accepted it thankfully. Her one shoe was feeling very tight, and she was anxious to take her weight off her feet. She sat there contentedly, her arms encircling the plate. In one hand she held a tightly scrunched one hundred-dollar bill. Mae smiled to herself. She would treasure this plate forever. She would put it on the sideboard beside the little framed picture of Jean and Joe. A perfect spot. She would write the story of the plate and tape it to the back. That way, when she was finished with it, someone else would know the story.

It suddenly struck her how important it was to write down the stories. Just think, all of those things at the auction had belonged to somebody. Somebody's hands had carefully cared for all those dishes on the table. Where had they come from? Someone had knit that sweater. Someone had folded up that money and stuffed it in the pocket. Think of all the stories that were lost. Why, she had lovely things in her own house. What would happen to them? She had things of her mother's. There were wonderful stories about them. Was she too old to write them? Of course not. She could remember things from long ago as if it were yesterday. It was the present day stuff she had trouble with. My lands, she'd almost forgotten to take that cake to the church bazaar last week. That would have been so embarrassing. From now on she would jot down on the calendar all the important things to remember.

Now she started to plan. She had a little book that Allie had given her last Christmas. At the time she thought it was funny to get a book with blank pages. Now she knew what she would do with it. She'd get that book out as soon as she got home and...

"You can move your stool ahead, Mae," Allie's voice broke into the silence.

"Oh, my mind was somewhere else. I think I'm getting stupid, Allie." She got up from her stool and moved it ahead.

"That's all right, Mae. It's getting dark and hard to see. My mind was wandering too."

Allie was a little worried about Mae. She seemed a little frailer lately. And her mind wasn't as sharp as it used to be. She'd almost forgotten that cake for the bazaar last week. That was certainly not like Mae. She was always the one who reminded everyone else. Well, she would keep a sharp eye out for her. She watched her now, so happy with her plate. What a miracle they had found the money! The Lord sure did work in mysterious ways.

Behind them in the line was Westicott. The darkness conveniently hid the seething fury in his eyes. Who had the nerve to take his knife. It was his knife. Who dared touch it? Which one of these stupid hayseeds had betrayed him. His knuckles tightened within his jacket pocket, squeezing his auction bill into a sweaty wad. Control was slipping. He started to count, slowly, methodically. One thousand, two thousand, three thousand...He had learned this from a counselor in Kingston. Gradually his fist relaxed. At least, jail had taught him something useful. He wished that fat broad at the cash would move her ass. He needed to get into his car and drive.

Sheila leaned on the porch railing. Westicott was in line three people behind her. She strained to hear any conversation, but no one was talking. Probably everyone was thinking about getting home. It had been a long day. She wondered what Westicott was thinking. He might think twice about cheating at an auction from now on.

She let her mind wander. Sometimes she could hardly believe she was here. After the quarrels with Jim, the accusations, the angry confrontations, the hurt and emotional abuse, she finally got hold of herself to get a lawyer and end the relationship which was draining her of all self confidence. The divorce finally was settled, and she decided to put as many miles between herself and Jim as possible. The morning it came through, she started to pack. Then, she simply got in her car and headed north. She felt she could drive forever. Three hundred kilometers later, she saw a fruit stand and stopped. While the man was making her change, her eyes fixed on a sign behind the vegetable display. "Why not visit Manitoulin? Help yourself to a brochure." SheP did that. She had never heard of the place. What a perfect idea. Get completely lost on an island. There was the sign. Turn left. With a sudden sense of purpose, she threw her purchases in the car, and followed the sign. She hadn't regretted this decision for one minute. She had hidden herself away with all the tourists on the Island. She had picked up a day-tripper at a store and started with day one. She had seen more sights than most of the locals. Checking out real estate and auctions were her favourite pastimes. She hadn't missed one of Maxie's auctions since she came. He brushed past her now on the way to the cashiers.

There were the two ladies, still here. The light on the front porch highlighted their features. They were leaning over the table now, paying for their things. Westicott was watching them. Then his voice broke the silence. It was a friendly voice, quiet and polite.

"Do you ladies need any help carrying your things to your car?"

"Thank you so much, but we already have most of our things packed," Allie responded.

"Here, ma'am, let me help you down those stairs." He took Mae's arm, guiding her gently down the steps. "It's pretty dark. Let me walk you to your car."

"You are so kind," said Mae. "It is a little hard to see at night." The threesome walked along the path together.

"You are the young man who bought the cupboard," Allie said.

"Yes, I love old things. My grandmother had one like that. It reminds me of her. Guess I'm sentimental about things like that."

"Is your grandmother still living?" asked Mae.

"No, I'm sorry to say. She passed away last summer. I do miss her so. She spoiled me awfully."

What a fine young man thought Mae. She wished she had been a grandmother, but they had never had any children. Now that she was old, there was no one to dote on her. It must be comforting to have a grandson. She imagined how safe she would feel if this young man were looking after her.

40

"I don't believe I have seen you before," offered Allie. "Are you new to the Island?"

"I'm originally from Toronto, but I've been to the Island several times. My mother has a small antique store. I pick up odds and ends for her."

"Well, there have certainly been lots of auctions this summer. The paper's full of them."

"Yes, I've managed to get to a few. Now, please tell me who you ladies are."

"Oh, I'm sorry. My name is Allie White, and this is my friend, Mae Bennet. We live in Mindemoya."

"Gary Westicott," he said. "I've been in Mindemoya. Pretty little town."

"Well, next time you're down there, drop in for a cup of tea," Mae said...Strangers were always welcome at her table.

"I can't get over how friendly Manitouliners are. In Toronto no one would invite a perfect stranger to tea," he said.

She patted his arm. "Well, we're not like that here. You just come along. Stop in at any of the stores and they'll point you over to my house. Everyone knows me in Mindemoya."

Westicott opened the car door and gently helped her in. "Thank you. I'll take you up on that offer. I'll stop in on Wednesday. I'm going down that way and I'll be happy to try a cup of that tea."

"I'll bake a batch of biscuits," she said as he closed the door.

CHAPTER 12

Mae opened her eyes and almost immediately started humming a tune under her breath. That nice young man was coming for tea today. Right after breakfast she would tidy up a bit, and then toss up a pan of biscuits. Well, maybe she'd make the biscuits first, just to make sure they were done when he came.

She bustled about the kitchen, getting out her utensils. The stainless steel bowl was best for a big batch. My lands, it was right in the very back of the cupboard. She practically had to crawl in to get it, and those knees seemed harder and harder to bend lately. Well, she should be thankful that was the only thing wrong with her at this age. Best not to complain. She put everything else she needed on the counter. Then she flipped on the little TV. Might as well get the last of Canada AM. She prided herself in being caught up on the news.

She knew the recipe by heart. Six cups of flour, one and a half cups of shortening, twelve scant teaspoons of baking powder, and a touch of sugar.

"Good morning. This is Wei Chen with the morning news. This morning in Ottawa..."

One cup of shortening, add the milk and the raisins, toss to mix.

"The Prime Minister is attending a trade conference in Mexico. It is hoped that..."

Flour the board, knead the dough gently, roll it out. Cut with a small glass. Cook in a hot oven.

"This morning in Iraq, the women and children are expressing a need for..."

The phone interrupted Wei Chen.

"Hello. Oh, it's you Allie."

"Are you getting ready for your visitor?"

"Yes, I've just put a pan of biscuits in the oven."

"Don't work too hard Mae. He may have forgotten."

"Well, he did say he'd come. Why don't you drop in about one?"

42

"I have an eye appointment in Little Current, or I would. I'll drop in when I get back."

"Thanks for calling, Allie. Bye."

Now she mustn't forget the biscuits in the oven. Fifteen minutes should do them...And there was hawberry jelly in the fridge and the butter was soft on the counter. She'd be ready. While they were cooking, she would have time to dust the sideboard and put up her plate. Carefully, she removed all the articles and placed them on the chair – the tatted handkerchief that she always put under the moustache cup, the violin vase, the candles, and the picture of Jean and Joe. Lightly, she shook the crocheted doilies and began the business of dusting. She rubbed the old wood until it glistened, then replaced each item, after swishing the dust cloth over each before placing it back. There was a plate stand somewhere. In the top drawer. Carefully, she placed the lily of the valley plate on the stand and centered it behind the picture. Perfect. There Jean, you've got your plate.

The biscuits. She hurried to the kitchen. Thank heavens, they were just right – lightly brown, the raisins plumping up against the crust. She'd try one of these right now, with butter and honey. That was the good thing about living alone – you could do what you wanted when you wanted. She savoured it. Just the right amount of salt, and sweet enough. Now, she'd just lie down a moment before he arrived.

A light tap on the door awakened her. She had no idea how long she'd slept. She sat up quickly, patting her hair in place. He must be early. Surely she hadn't slept long. Another tap.

"I'm coming." She opened the door.

"Sorry. Were you resting?"

"Oh, I should have been up. I just dropped off for a few minutes. Come in."

The TV was blasting. A rerun of Unsolved Mysteries. She loved that show, even though it was a bit scary. Fortunately, this was a safe little town. But now she had company. She turned it off.

"What a lovely little home you have here."

"I like it. Not very fancy, but good enough for me. Come into the living room and find a comfortable seat. I'll put on the kettle."

He walked in. It was a quaintly charming room. Every surface was laden with nick knacks. He looked at the sideboard. "I see you have a place for that pretty plate you bought at the Evansville auction."

"Yes. I paid too much for it. But I suddenly remembered who had owned it and I couldn't resist. That lady, there, in the picture. It was hers."

"Was she from around here?"

"Oh, yes. We were the best of friends. She died a few years ago." Mae brought in a tray of biscuits, jelly and tea, and placed them on the coffee table. "Now, sit down and try one of my biscuits. Have some hawberry jelly."

"What are these hawberries, anyway? I see signs all over the place."

"When the pioneers came here they spent some pretty tough winters. The only thing that grew plentifully were hawberries. I guess they practically survived on them. The Indians put them in their pemmican."

"What's that?"

"It was a mixture of dried venison, fat and berries. Doesn't sound too tasty, but there were lots of vitamins and protein in it. Are you going to be staying on the Island?"

"I'd love to. I really like it here. The pace is so quiet. It's a break to get away from city life."

"Why don't you stay?"

"I wish it were that easy. My mother is not well enough to handle the store herself. I've been after her to give it up, but she insists. I'd like her to move in with me, but she wants to be independent."

"You should bring her up here."

"Maybe I will. What do people do in this little town?"

"Oh, a lot of people have their own businesses. We have quite a few stores in town. We've got hardware, groceries, clothing, gifts, plumbing, gas stations, whatever. Once you're here, you never have to cross that bridge again." She laughed.

"Sounds wonderful to me. Couple of people at the auction told me there was nothing to do here in the winter. Said they were really bored stiff."

"Folks around here have got a saying for people like that."

"What is it?"

"There's a road off and it ain't crowded."

Westicott laughed. "Pretty good way to put it. As for me, I could live here forever." He reached for another biscuit. "I'm afraid I'm making a pig of myself, but I've never tasted better biscuits."

"Help yourself. I've been making biscuits all my life. My mother said you have to have light fingers to make biscuits. I practised that."

"I guess it's an art." The two of them chatted comfortably for over an hour. Gary would endear himself to this old woman. You never knew when time spent like this might be useful later on. Finally, he said, "I would like to stay all afternoon, but I really have to go. I'm certainly enjoying your company."

"I'm so glad you came. Come in again, whenever you're in Mindemoya. The kettle's always on."

He stood up. "Let me carry the tray to the kitchen." He picked it up carefully, pausing at the sideboard. He looked at the moustache cup. "That's a lovely old cup. And that doily underneath. That looks like fine hand work."

"It's really not a doily. Just a handkerchief with a tatted edging. I thought it looked nice under the cup."

"It certainly does. Such intricate work. It must take a lot of patience."

"Oh, it's just a matter of making little knots with a shuttle – in and out and under and pull. That's all there is to it."

"You make it sound so easy." He leaned the tray on the sideboard and touched the tatting with his free hand. "It's beautiful," he said. His eyes fixed on the tatting as he picked up the tray. A tatted handkerchief!

Mae led the way to the kitchen. "Now, I want you to come back," she said.

"I will. That's a promise. I'd like to spend a little time in this town. Could I use your name if I need room and board?"

"Of course." Her mind raced. "Better still, I have a spare room I could let you have – if you could put up with my cooking."

"Well, I just might take you up on that offer." He smiled. "Goodbye, Mrs. Bennett. May I call you Mae?"

"Oh yes, everyone calls me Mae."

He took her hand gently, careful not to hurt that frail hand that made such good biscuits. "Thank you so much. You've made my day." He walked down the path to his truck, turning to wave before he drove away.

Mae could hardly wait for Allie to come so she could tell her all about the wonderful young man. Wouldn't it be marvelous if he did come to stay? She'd be the envy of the whole town.

Chapter 13

Sheila was beginning to feel more relaxed. Coming here had been a good thing. She smiled to herself as she thought of that spur of the minute decision. The sign had said: Manitoulin Island. It was only a name, not a place in her mind. She had been daydreaming and in the left lane anyway. Why not turn left? This would be as good a place as any, and the idea of an island sounded adventurous.

She made the turn, bumped over an uneven railway crossing and found herself walled in by gigantic rocks. Graffiti read: WELCOME TO AFRICA. Well, it did seem a continent away from Toronto. Half expecting to see lions and elephants, she slowed her car, obeying the caution signs. No lions. Just a bridge under construction. A slow line of cars preceded her. What a stench! The wind was blowing her way from a paper mill, belching forth smoke and vomiting dark foam into what might have been a beautiful river. She held her breath as long as possible, then gulped in more of the putrid smell. Finally, she was across the bridge.

When she dared breathe again, she began to take note of the signs. The highway wound through bush and mountains and it was obvious that this was cottage country, although none of the places advertised could be seen from the road. After about a half hour's drive, she stopped at the first traffic light she had seen for thirty miles. She had come to a bridge of some sort.

As she waited for the long line of traffic, she let her mind wander. She thought about this bridge. Maybe this was her sign. A place to cross from one life to another. Lost in her thoughts, a loud honk from the car behind snapped her into reality. Obviously, not everyone daydreamed at this bridge. She accelerated slowly, conscious of the narrow, bumpy road ahead. Once over, an information booth quickly presented itself on her right and she turned in. She located a map and picked up a handful of brochures. She would turn into the first motel she came to.

She hadn't regretted any of it. She was an explorer, and the natives were friendly. She had stayed in various places, a bed and breakfast here, a motel there, and had even rented a cabin for a week by a pretty little lake. She read the local papers from cover to cover. She was determined to get the 'feel' of the place before she got personally involved with any of the people. She was beginning to recognize some of them at the auctions, and she had a feeling that they were interested in her. But apart from a casual 'hello', no one forced attention on her. Sometimes she felt them watching her, and if she looked up, they smiled. They seemed to be checking her out, seeing if the cloth she was made of would fit into the fabric of their lives. There was no hurry. They were giving each other time.

She usually had supper at a restaurant, and since summer evenings were long, she went for a drive afterwards before she went to her lodging for the night. She had no destination in mind, just turned the car down a road she hadn't traveled before. To-night she'd had supper at Jessica's in Mindemoya. She drove to the corner, turned left at Ben's, proceeded along the highway and turned right at the first side road.

There was absolutely no traffic on this road, just sky above and trees and rail fences on either side. She turned a corner and came upon a scene reminiscent of one of her grandmother's tapestries. She wondered where all those works of art had gone to. Her own mother never had time for needlework, but Grandma had always been busy with some kind of fancy work. Sheila could visualize that busy needle, darting up and down while she played with the coloured wool. A wave of memory washed over her. On a whim, she stopped the car, got out and walked over to the rail fence close to the side of the road. She leaned her arms on the top rail and took in the scene around her. Actually, she'd never paid this much attention to the landscape before. It was absolutely beautiful. What colours would one have to choose to paint this picture? Blue for the sky, green for the trees, and brown for the fence. No, that wasn't right. She studied the colours. The sky was pink and purple and a hundred shades of blue, with puffs of white clouds. The trees were not green. They were brown and rust and hunter green and olive. Right now a pair of blue jays were darting up one tall pine tree, seeming to follow a well-worn path, probably searching out supper. The fence was not brown. It was many shades of gray, lined with black shadows in the creases. Softening the zigzag line, weeds and grasses melded into the bottom rails. There was green here, and little orange flowers, and lacy white weeds.

She looked at all this, as a critic would study a painting. It could be called...A Tapestry of Trees. Right. Good name. Well, maybe a bit trite. She smiled at her romanticizing. As she looked around that little pair of blue dots caught her eye again, flicking in and out, filling in the blue. Could she ever feel as at home in this landscape as these blue jays did? She held this thought as she got back into the car. Maybe, just maybe.

47

It was still quite light. She would continue on. She turned left at the main highway and in no time found herself at Providence Bay. She hadn't realized that this road led here. She had been to this beach several times, walked the boardwalk, had an ice cream, relaxed on one of the seats provided, enjoying the wide expanse of water and sand. This was a place she really did enjoy. She parked her car. Then she took off her shoes and walked towards the water.

She found a quiet spot and sat down, watching the swelling waves roll in, swish up and then retreat from shore. The movement of the water and the accompanying sound mesmerized her. She lost all track of time, soaking in the sounds and smells, her eyes half closed, almost asleep. When she jolted awake, everyone on the beach had gone. The sun was almost behind the lighthouse. The sand was still warm, but when she dug in her toes, she felt a cool dampness. Responding to an inner urge, she walked toward the water. She stood at the edge, her toes in the water and her heels in the sand. The cold splash of the encroaching waves spread over her feet, then withdrew, pulling the sand in their wake. She closed her eyes, concentrating on the flow of water and the wash of sand on her skin. The wish and wash of sand filled her ears. Her feet sunk deeper with each wave.

Anyone watching would see her as part of the landscape. But was she? Could she ever belong here? She seemed to sense the presence of something almost supernatural, something larger than life. A kind of spirit that lived in this miracle of space was tugging at her, holding her in a way she had never experienced before. This Island was a spiritual place – she'd read that somewhere. The home of the great Manitou. Was this the home she longed for? A shiver electrified her body. A great throb of sadness. She began to shake uncontrollably. The tears ran down her face, falling from her cheeks to the water. She pulled her feet from the sand and sat down beyond the rush of water.

The wash of water, the movement of sand, the gathering coolness of wind over water enveloped her. All the anguish of the past that she had controlled so long was suddenly spilling out, a cup overturned, its contents lost, mixing with the water and the sand. She didn't even try to right the cup, just let it all empty out, and when it was all gone, the throbbing eased, and a calmness gradually stilled her body. It was a sensation that defined definition. Her usual clinical mind could not touch what had happened to her. It was enough to know that for once in her lifetime she felt at home with herself, and with this place. It was getting dark, and certainly time to go back to the motel. But she would never forget these moments. She had come to an important realization. It was time to come to terms with the rest of her life.

She had a hard time getting the sand off her feet. Maybe this was part of the message. She smiled to herself. The outpouring of emotions had left her calm, more than at anytime since she had crossed that bridge. She made her decision. She would stay.

She cleared her head. Staying meant finding a job, buying a house, putting down roots. She was a good nurse, and there were two hospitals on the Island. She would try the one at Mindemoya first. It was a smaller place, and she was already familiar with the little town. There were places to buy – lots of them. She would tell that real estate agent that she was serious now about buying a house. Her mind was so full of plans, she could hardly remember driving to the motel. She felt an excitement she hadn't experienced for a long time.

In no time she was ready for bed, willing morning to come. Just as she felt herself drifting into unconsciousness, something would jolt her back to wide awake awareness. She lay there, eyes wide open in the darkness. Her bed faced a window, and all she could see was sky. It looked like a black blanket with pin pricks of light poking through. She studied the night. There was no apparent pattern to the stars – bright, pale, big, small, twinkling, still, scattered. The architect of the universe had not thought it important to make a pattern – just scattered the stars and let them land wherever. An untidy sky, she thought. And there is much beauty in untidiness. And that thought took her back to what she used to call home in Toronto.

What a masterpiece of untidiness that used to be. She and her friend, Janie, had found relief from the tensions at work in attempting every craft under the sun. Jim, who never spent much time at home, would come in late at night and say, 'The make-it freaks have attacked again.' At first he didn't make a fuss about it, just ignored both them and the mess. She never questioned where he went after work – he never bothered with what she was doing. Then things started to change. He became very angry when she left some wool in his chair, and patterns scattered on the coffee table. She couldn't believe how something so small could loom so large in his mind. She had intended to deal with the clutter, but suddenly things at work changed abruptly. There were layoffs. She was transferred to emergency, and Janie lost her job. The pressures at work were intense – long hours, and fewer staff. She had no time for crafts, and no time to pay attention to little collections of cloth here and there, and glue and ribbons and patterns lying about. Jim was furious at her housekeeping. "If you're not going to use this stuff, get rid of it!" he'd shouted.

There was more to it than that, but this was the beginning of the end. She had retaliated with her own accusations. Maybe he could come home earlier and help with the house. He pushed her into a chair, holding her shoulders, staring into her face. "I'll help, all right!" he yelled. They had argued many times before, but this was the first time she had detected how capable he was of violence. She had tried to forget the feel of his hands on her shoulders – strong, hurting. Even now, remembering, she could feel the pain. The next night she had come home, bone-tired, and the living room was bare. The coffee table was empty, her books were gone, the shelves were cleared. She went into her sewing room. Her boxes of fabric, her quilt blocks and wool, her wonderful odds and ends – her sewing machine! She was thunderstruck. Jim was there, waiting for her. "You wanted me to help," he said. "But my sewing machine! I waited so long to buy it. I bought it with my money!" "I returned it. Got five hundred bucks for it. You never used it. Just cluttering up the place." "But you did it without telling me!" He raised his hand and walked towards her. "Any more complaints?" he said.

After that, one thing led to another. He was home more often now. She didn't ask why, afraid to start another tantrum, but she was sure he'd lost his job. He painted the kitchen a bilious yellow. Her favourite brown teapot lay broken in the garbage. Some of her things went missing. If she dropped anything on a table and left it there, it disappeared. "I'm simply teaching you a lesson," he announced. "It's the only way you'll learn to put your things away."

From that time on, she made no decisions around the house. She was living with a meticulous, dangerous landlord, possessed with teaching her a lesson. Any attempt to explain her frustration kindled his fire. She was leading two lives – at work, a coolly efficient emergency nurse, at home a whimpering, idiot housewife. Jim enjoyed his power over her. He was obsessed with teaching her. He analyzed every statement she made, showing how wrong she was. She began to lose confidence, even in her ability to prepare a simple meal. She forgot to put an egg in a cake mix, and found herself hiding the soggy results in the bottom of the garbage can. Everything she touched spilled or fell out of her hands. She couldn't even make a simple decision. Well, thanks to Janie, she did make one decision, and a good one. She saw a good lawyer and filed for a divorce. Thanks to him, she had half the money from the sale of the house to help make a new start. No more of that. She was free. Legally, emotionally. She would make all the decisions now. At one time, Jim had destroyed her self confidence. Now she was getting it back.

This was the first time she had gone over these things in her mind since she'd crossed that bridge. She could handle it. She smiled up at the stars. She drew a line to one of them, and fell asleep.

CHAPTER 14

Lorene was sitting very quietly on a stool, watching her father paint. Suddenly, Joe was aware of a pair of big brown eyes staring at him. What a beauty this almost-five second daughter was. Sitting on a stool, quiet as a mouse. How long had she been there? He hadn't even noticed her coming. Once he got into the mood to paint it was as if he had entered another dimension.

He grinned at her. "How long have you been there, Renie?"

"A long time."

"You've been very quiet."

"Mommy says I have to be quiet when you're painting."

"You're a good girl. Do you like my picture?"

"No."

"Oh. Why not?"

"Why are you making those trees blue?"

"What colour should they be?"

"White. Or brown."

"They will be when I've finished."

"I think it's funny to see a purple cow."

By gosh, this kid of his had some head on her shoulders. She was really taking note of what he was doing. He'd better explain. "This big shadow shape here is our island. I'm going to put the sun here, and some clouds in the sky. The trees are going to be those big birch ones in front of Uncle Tom's. And the cows are his. They are wading in the water."

"I know. I saw the cows in the lake. 'Member? I thought they would drown."

"No, no. They were just getting a drink when we saw them."

"But the trees weren't blue."

"That's right. Want to know why I painted them blue?"

"Yes."

"It's because I want to paint the inside of the tree first. You see, I drew the shape in this colour." He pointed with his brush to burnt umber on his palette. "Because the very inside of the tree is a kind of brown. You can see a little here, under the blue. There are a whole lot of colours in a tree, you know."

"My big tree is white."

"All right, little lady, I'll just put my stuff up here so Gyp doesn't knock it over, and we'll go and take a look." He put the palette in a safe place, away from the dangerous wag of the big Newfoundland's tail. Of course, the dog had no notion of staying if Joe and the kid were going outside.

They walked down to the big birch tree by the lake. It was the favourite playing tree. There was a great place to sit between the branch joints, and a long, sturdy limb to swing on. Renie was not quite big enough to climb to the tree seat.

"When am I going to be big enough to climb up there all by myself?"

"Pretty soon. How did you get up there yesterday? I saw you when I was down at the dock."

"Marion lifted me."

"Well, she's five years older than you. So, I guess it will be five years." He teased...

"Stop fooling, Dad. I can almost reach now. See?"

"Of course. I was just kidding." Joe got out his jackknife. "Now, I'll just make a little slit here in the bark and show you the colours underneath." He wasn't going to be talked out of the painting lesson.

"But Dad, the tree will die."

"Not if I make just a tiny slit."

"But you said so, Dad. Don't pull any bark off the trees. 'Member? When I wanted to make a canoe you said 'no'."

This kid had the galldarndest memory. "Yes, I remember. So we won't pull any bark off the tree. We'll just peek, if we can find a little spot where somebody else had pulled some off." He put his knife in his pocket. The only place he could find to prove his point was down near the bottom. "Come here. Look down in here. Get down on your knees so you can get a good look."

He was squatted on his haunches, pointing out the spot. She got down on all fours. "What colours do you see?" he said. "There's a whole bunch."

"I see brown."

"What else?"

"And black."

"And?"

"And...grey."

He pointed with his finger to a particular spot. "And what colour is this?" The little monkey was purposely avoiding this one.

"I guess it's...blue. Kind of." It was a joke. She saw the blue all the time. She had fooled her Dad. She laughed and pushed him as he crouched precariously by the tree. He tumbled back.

"You little monkey," he said. They both laughed as he caught her and tumbled her to the ground.

Jean was watching from the kitchen window. The two of them were laughing their hearts out by the big birch. She went to the door and called out. "It's time for dinner, you two."

They waved and laughed. She was tugging on his hand as he half pulled her up the little hill to the house.

"Whatever are you two giggling about?" her Mom asked.

"This little kid-kid is trying to fool her old dad. She didn't like my tree in the picture, and I was trying to show her why I was painting the tree blue. Now Renie, stop laughing and tell your Mum what colours you saw inside the tree."

"What colours did you see, Renie?"

"I saw brown, and black, and grey..."

"And?" he prompted.

"PINK."

"They all joined in the joke and walked into the wonderful smells of the kitchen.

CHAPTER 15

It was a rainy afternoon. Mae was going through an old box of music that had been cluttering up a corner of her living room for months. She had brought it down the last time she went up to the storage room upstairs. Now it was time to decide what to keep and what to throw away. Maybe the church could use some of it. Here was an old piece she used to play years ago. Well, she would keep that one and try it again some day. And here was a book of duets she and her sister used to sing. My, how the years went by. Mamie was gone six years now. Perhaps one of her kids would like this book. They were all away from home now, but sometimes one of them returned in the summer.

The opening of the door diverted her attention. "Mae, are you home? It's me." Allie was letting herself in, putting a plate of muffins on the table.

"Come on in, Allie," Mae said. "I'm sorting out an old box of music."

"I picked up your mail on the way in."

"Thanks. It's early today." She reached for the bundle of paper. "Here's a letter from Sarah. Funny, I was thinking about her. I wondered if she would like some of the music her mother and I used to sing. Here's one I don't recognize. Handwritten. Who can this be from?"

"You go ahead and read your mail. I'll just make myself at home and read your Expositor."

Mae handed her the paper and opened the letter with the unfamiliar handwriting. She glanced down at the signature. "Allie, do you know who this of from? It's signed Gary Westicott. You remember that nice young man we met at the auction."

"Yes, I do. That was quite a time ago. What does he say?"

"Here, I'll read it. 'Dear Mae, I hope I can call you Mae. You may not remember me, but a few months ago you shared your hospitality with me one afternoon. Do you remember? Well, since then a lot has happened. My mother has not been well, and after a stay in hospital, she finally consented to live with me. Now she's improving, and anxious to live on her own again. I'd like to see if she could handle living alone at my place for a while. It's closer to the hospital, and her friend lives right next door. If it's too hard, I'll be able to convince her that she needs me. She is in a hurry to get back to her store and wants me to pick her up some more things from the auctions. Maxie sent me some fliers, and there are several good ones coming up. Now to get to my point. You were gracious enough to offer me a room when I visited you that afternoon. I certainly do not want to impose, but I would be eternally grateful if the offer is still available. Your friend, Gary Westicott.' Allie, isn't it wonderful! He wants to stay here."

"Where would you put him?"

"I'd have to clean out the upstairs bedroom. It needs a good house-cleaning, anyway. I've been storing things up there, and there's a lot of junk to put away. But I'd love to help Gary out. He seems like such a nice young man."

"Well, I'll help you with the room. Mae, I can just hear the tongue waggers." She laughed. "Guess who's living at Mae's," she mimicked. "Do you think he's a little young for her?"

"Allie, I wouldn't care. They'd just be jealous, that's all. Let's get a look at that bedroom right now. Then we'll know what we have to do."

Together they walked up the narrow stairs to the first landing. They paused to take a breather. "You know, I don't remember when the last time was I came up here," Mae said. "I used to come up more often, but lately my knees have been hurting, and I haven't been tackling the stairs. Funny, my knee doesn't seem to be bothering me today. I can make these eight steps with no trouble."

The attic bedroom was quite large, with plenty of room for a three-piece bedroom set, even though the walls, snuggled in by the roof structure, were short in places. One large window looked out on the street. The mahogany spool bed was almost hidden by the boxes and bags that were piled on its surface. "I never dreamed I had so much stuff up here."

Allie walked over to the dresser – a large bonnet cupboard with carved walnuts and leaves for handles. "I always loved this old cupboard, Mae."

"Yes. It holds a lot. I suppose all the drawers are stuffed full, if I remember rightly." She pulled open a drawer. A bundle of strings and fabric swelled up as she opened it.

"Whatever is that?" asked Allie.

"This is my old marionette. My mother made that for me when I was a child. I had started to untangle it, but got too discouraged with it, so I stuffed it in here." She took it out carefully. All the strings were in knots. "I wonder if it still works. Nothing seems broken. Look, the same little crooked smile. Mother used to make her dance. I'll take her downstairs and see if I can fix her up. It'll take some patience to untangle her."

"Maybe you could put on new strings."

"I'd never know where they went. It's pretty complicated. I'll try to get the knots out first." She bundled up the marionette into a bag from the bed. "Now, let's see what has to be done up here. Where to start?" Her eyes swept the room. The dresser was covered with little figurines and boxes – presents she had stored here until she found a better place for them. There were quilts piled on the blanket box, old books leaning together on a shelf, clothes scattered here and there. The school children knew they could always get costumes from Mae for school plays. Mae would dig them out, and never really get them put back again. Her eyes rested on the bed. "Tomorrow, I'd better start with the stuff on this bed. At least find a spot to sit," she laughed.

"Then you won't need me tomorrow. You will have to decide what to keep and what you don't need."

"Whatever you like. I'd be glad of your company. It's too late to start now." She glanced at her watch. "My lands, we've almost missed our show." The two ladies hustled downstairs, not pausing at the landing. Mae flicked on the TV. They settled themselves comfortably, then Allie remembered the muffins. She rushed out to the kitchen and brought in the plate.

"We're too late," Mae said. "It's just ending. Listen."

TWO YEARS AGO TODAY THE BODY OF A YOUNG WOMAN WAS FOUND IN A LAUNDROMAT ON A BUSY STREET IN TIMMINS, ONTARIO. SHE HAD BEEN STRANGLED WITH A FINE COPPER WIRE. HER HANDS WERE FOLDED ON HER CHEST, AND IN THEM SHE HELD A SMALL GLASS ANGEL. PRINTED NEATLY, IN A BOLD HAND, WERE THE WORDS: 'AN ANGEL WITH FEATHERY WINGS'. THE ANGEL HAD SMALL WHITE FEATHERS STUCK IN ITS WINGS.

TWO MONTHS LATER, AN ELDERLY LADY WAS FOUND MURDERED IN SAULT STE MARIE. SHE TOO, HAD BEEN STRANGLED WITH A FINE COPPER WIRE. HER HANDS WERE FOLDED ON HER CHEST, HOLDING A CERAMIC WHITE AND BLACK COW. PRINTED IN THE SAME BOLD, NEAT PRINT WERE THE WORDS: 'A COW CHEWING BARLEY AND MALT'.

THREE MONTHS AGO, A SIMILAR CASE WAS DISCOVERED IN HAMILTON. THE MANNER OF DEATH WAS THE SAME. ONLY THIS TIME, THE FOLDED HANDS HELD A THIMBLE WITH THE NAME 'GRACE'. PRINTED BENEATH WERE THE WORDS: 'A THIMBLE FOR MAE AND FOR GRACE'. NO MOTIVE HAS BEEN FOUND. NO ONE HAS BEEN APPREHENDED. WHAT IS THE CONNECTION BETWEEN AN ANGEL, A COW, AND A THIMBLE? IS THERE SOMETHING SIGNIFICANT ABOUT THE FEATHERS AND BARLEY AND MALT AND A THIMBLE WITH THE NAME GRACE? IF YOU HAVE ANY INFORMATION THAT COULD LEAD TO THE SOLVING OF THIS CRIME, HELP

BRING A CRIMINAL TO JUSTICE. CALL THE NUMBER FLASHING ON YOUR SCREEN. ALL INFORMATION WILL BE TREATED AS CONFIDENTIAL, AND YOU WILL NEVER BE ASKED TO TESTIFY IN COURT. TUNE IN AGAIN NEXT WEEK FOR UNSOLVED MYSTERIES.

The familiar theme music ended the program. "I wish we hadn't missed the first part," said Mae. "I like it when they act out the story. Whatever would possess anybody to kill all those people? The world is getting worse and worse." She flicked off the TV. A soap was on now, and she hated soaps. The things that were on soaps these days were not fit for human eyes. "Next week, we'll remember the time – not get carried away with my attic!"

"Mae, did you remember to bring down your marionette?"

"No, it went clear out of my mind."

"I'll get it for you. Maybe you can get it working. My grand kids are coming sometime. Sandra and Bill have rented a cottage on the lake. Little Amy would love to see that puppet."

"Well, I'll do my best. I'll be a bit busy getting that room ready, but I can sure try to get it working. I love little Amy. You're right. She'll love it."

Allie went upstairs to get the marionette. Yes, this room would take some doing, all right. She'd have to help Mae with it next week. She looked around the room, already planning what to do. The furniture would need a good dusting, the window would need to be scrubbed, and the floor should really be waxed. She could handle that. Mae could tend to the little boxes of stuff, and the clothes and the blankets.

She came downstairs and gave the bag to Mae. "I have choir practice tonight, so I had better get going."

"See if Helen would like any of this music. I've got a whole box full, and it's just collecting dust around here."

"I'll ask. I'll see you tomorrow. I suppose, as soon as I go, you'll be writing a letter to that young man," she teased.

"Now, Allie, stop that. You'll like him as much as I do." Mae gave her a hug, and opened the door to a cool breeze that was settling in after the rain.

Chapter 16

The upstairs room was sparkling. Mae and Allie had worked wonders. The bonnet cupboard shone, the mahogany spools gleamed warmly. A hand quilted patchwork covered the bed and stretched up over the plump pillows, squeezing itself into the smooth brown headboard. A fresh breeze tumbled the newly ironed curtains and cooled the attic room, carrying with it fragrances of late summer, a combination of geranium, marigold and chrysanthemum.

Mae gave the room one last look. Her boarder was to arrive anytime now. Satisfied that everything was in order, Mae negotiated the stairs one more time, careful to hold on to the rail as she descended. The bold fragrance of cinnamon met her, fingering its way up to the attic having already claimed every little nook and cranny downstairs. She hurried to the kitchen to check the oven. She opened the door, the moist heat of apples misting her glasses. She waited until they cleared. Just a few more minutes and the pie would be ready. The phone rang.

"Hello?"

"Hello, Mae. This is Gary. I'm at the Shell station in Little Current."

"Then you should be here in a half an hour. I'll have lunch ready."

"Great. Sure you don't mind my coming for lunch?"

"Of course not. I'm looking forward to seeing you."

"I'll be there in a few minutes. Bye for now."

Mae hung up the phone. She lifted the receiver, listened for the tone, and immediately rang Allie.

"Hello, Allie. He's coming for lunch."

"He is?"

"Yes. He's at Little Current now. Come on over and have lunch with us. It will help him feel more welcome."

"I'll be right over."

"See you soon!"

In less than five minutes, Allie arrived. She was breathless, carrying a plate covered with a blue checked tea towel. "Smells good in here!"

"I just took a pie out of the oven. Thanks for the cookies. You didn't need to bring them."

"You can save them for snacks. You have enough here for a threshing!"

They busied themselves with the table fixings, giggling like schoolgirls. The table looked perfect. Mae had used her pink dishes with the little roses, all arranged neatly on a crocheted tablecloth.

It seemed no time until a truck pulled into the driveway. Mae opened the door before the knock came. "Come in," she said, almost falling against the man, his hand poised at the knocker.

"Hello there," he said.

"Come in, come in," Mae said. "We've been waiting for you."

The smells from the kitchen embraced him. "Thank you," he said, and stepped inside.

"You remember my friend, Allie."

"Of course. How do you do?" They shook hands. Allie took his coat and hung it on the hall stand. He turned to Mae. "Mae, I'm so grateful to you for taking me in like this."

"I'm just happy to have you. Make yourself at home. You and Allie go in the living room while I get the food on the table."

They accepted her invitation. Westicott's eyes swept the room, slowly focusing on the sideboard. The moustache cup still rested on the tatted handkerchief.

He smiled at Allie. "It's very nice of you both to make me feel so welcome. Are all the people of this town so friendly?"

"We like to make visitors feel welcome."

"I've never lived in a small town. What do people do around here?"

"Oh, there's lots to do. There are all sorts of sports – golf in the summer, hockey and curling in the winter. Then there's all sorts of volunteer groups to get involved with."

"Like what?"

"Oh, adding a new room to the arena, keeping the parks in shape, raising funds for the hospital and local churches. There's scads of things to do."

"Sounds pretty interesting. I would like to get involved with something like that."

Mae called from the kitchen. "Can you sing? The choir needs men's voices."

He laughed. "I can carry a tune, but I never sang in a choir."

"You should take him tonight, Allie."

Allie chuckled. "You can see how easy it is to get involved, Mr. Westicott."

"Please, call me Gary."

"Well, not tonight," he said. "But I might consider at least going to church. First, I'd like to get settled."

"As soon as we've had lunch, I'll show you your room. I think everything is ready now."

They responded eagerly to her invitation. "You can sit here, Allie. And please take this chair, Gary."

The meal was steaming on the table. They settled themselves comfortably. "I always say grace," Mae said, "Bless this food to our use, and us to thy service."

While the ladies closed their eyes in thankfulness, Westicott lined up his knife and fork exactly with the crocheted motif on the cloth. He shifted his plate a little to the left, precisely in the center. Then he fixed his glass completely within the circle of a flower in the crocheted design.

Chapter 17

As soon as Sheila saw the house, she knew it had to be hers. It was an older house, not fancy on the outside, but the builder had taken every advantage of the magnificent view. Built on a side hill facing the water, the front windows offered a panoramic vision of sky blue lake and emerald island. The agent had told her a little bit about this island. Apparently, Nanabush, the trickster god, was carrying his grandmother on his back. She fell off and landed in this lake. Nanabush, who had magical powers, changed her into an island. From certain vantage points, it looked like a woman on her hands and knees, arms outstretched above her head. The island was called Mindemoya in the old days, meaning 'old woman'. He said he wasn't altogether sure about the story, but she could find out about it from any number of people.

Looking through the windows from room to room presented different pictures. From the bedroom, a close-up of the island. From the dining room, a long shot of the same scene. From the living room, a panoramic view. In every room the outside scene presented itself as a backdrop. It was truly beautiful.

She was experiencing the same kind of feeling she had at the beach. She could still feel the wind in her mind; sense the wash of sand between her toes. What was happening to her? Was this island a spider's web and she'd crawled in? Well, if she was caught, she hadn't seen the spider yet. She smiled. Or maybe you didn't until you were more firmly trapped. She would know pretty soon. She had invested all her money on this house, living in the hope that the part-time job she had got at the hospital would turn into something permanent.

The deal was to close this afternoon. She would sign the final papers at three o'clock. She turned her car left on the Ketchankookem Trail, driving slowly to drink in the beauty of her surroundings. As her car bumped over the little bridge, two mallards flew up, taking refuge in the cattails in the bay. She stopped the car. A flock of wild geese were assembled further out, probably checking out plans for fall. On the left, the river ran through a golf course. Fallen trees and loose branches provided the perfect homes for mink. She had watched them the other day. Sheila had never been in a canoe, but a sudden desire to see around the bend in the river excited her. Well, she was going to spend a lifetime here. There was lots of time to learn how to paddle a canoe.

Having resolved that, she turned on the ignition. Only twenty more minutes before she signed on the dotted line. Might as well be on time. As she slowed to turn left towards her house, her eyes caught sight of a young man sitting on a lawn chair in front of a cottage right by the turn. She recognized him from the auctions. This was the young man who told her about her salt and pepper shaker rabbits. On an impulse, she braked, and called out. "Hi! I'm going to be your neighbour."

He looked up, then dropped what he had in his hand. "Hello." He walked toward her. "I heard the house was sold. Yes, I remember you, from the auctions."

"Yes. My name's Sheila. And yours is Jamie. The auctioneer called you by name when you bought the old tackle box."

"Right. I'm working on that right now. I had a lot of work to do around the cottage and didn't get around to the fishing gear until now. Quite a challenge. I made a bargain with myself not to cut the line."

"That may be quite a task." She smiled. "I'm going to need some work done around my house. I'm calling it mine and I haven't signed the papers yet! Maybe I could hire you?"

"Thanks for the offer. But I won't be here much longer. I have a job to go back to. I've spent so much money on this cottage I need a paycheck."

"Do you know anyone around who is a carpenter? I suppose I can check the phone book."

"Actually, I do know somebody. He's not a carpenter by trade. He's really a marine biologist. He opted out of city life and came back to the family farm. I've seen some of his carpentry though. Makes great cupboards. I don't know how busy he is. People are beginning to find out what he can do."

"What's his name?"

"Brian Peterson. He lives on the east side of town. A farm with a long lane. He's really fixed up that old homestead. Likely if you dropped in he'd show you some of his work."

"Thanks so much, Jamie. Oh, I see I'm holding up traffic. I think I'm fitting in with island life already."

"You bet. That's a good sign. See you around, Sheila. I'll drop by sometime." A car with a license plate too dusty to read cut between them. She waved at Jamie, and turned left towards home.

The real estate agent was already there. He walked over to her car as she parked. "You've got yourself a beautiful place," he said. "I know you won't regret this decision."

"I can't believe it's mine," she said. "Come on in."

He unlocked the door, and gave her the key. She smiled, and pocketed it. He put his briefcase on the table. "Here are all the papers. I'll need your signature here, and here, and...here. You'd better read it first."

"All right." She scanned the draft. "Yes, this seems fine to me. May I use your pen?"

He nodded, smiling at her eagerness. "It's all yours, now. Officially, my job is over, but if there is anything you need, give me a call."

"Thanks. You've been great." They shook hands, and she followed him to the door. Alone in her own house at last, she surveyed her castle. Complete joy filled her and spilled out through her fingers and toes as she danced from room to room, moving her arms to the rhythm of her excitement. "I'm acting like a child," she thought, and she flopped down on the chesterfield.

The house was partly furnished. There were boxes in every room filled with books and dishes and who knows what else. It would be fun going through them. Right now, though, she had to do some shopping and get some food in her cupboards. There were dishes in the kitchen, and some pots and pans. She checked for a teapot. No, there wasn't one. She'd buy one at the corner store. She hadn't shopped for groceries for a long time, and she was looking forward to it. She'd just splurge, and fill the cart. If there was a cart. She grabbed her purse and hurried out the door.

The old general store on the corner seemed as good a place to go as any. It was handy, and would likely have a teapot as well as groceries. She wasn't disappointed. Everything you would ever need was there. And there were carts to boot. She picked one with fairly smooth wheels and pushed it to the back of the store. There was clothing, fabric, wool, toys, cards, dishes – that's where she'd find the teapot. Plates, salts and peppers, bowls – there they were – a flowered one, one that looked like a house, and a plain brown one. That's the one she'd buy. A nice, comfortable, brown teapot. She placed it carefully in her cart. Now, where were the tablecloths? Probably with the blankets and sheets she'd seen earlier. She pushed her cart through an alley, almost bumping into two older ladies who were studying a pattern book. They looked vaguely familiar. Where had she seen them before? She racked her brain. Suddenly she remembered. The auction. Of course, they had bought the dishes at the auction – the plate and rooster pitcher. She smiled to herself. All of Mindemoya must have been at the auction.

They looked up at her over the top of their book. "Hello," they said in unison.

"Hello," Sheila said. "I'm sorry, I almost bumped into you. I was searching for the tablecloths."

"They are over there," said Mae. "On the second shelf by the pillow cases. Here, I'll show you." She bustled to the place. "They are quite lovely, aren't they?"

"Yes, I like this one." She checked the size. "This should be fine."

"Are you a visitor to our town?" offered Allie.

"Actually, I'm a resident. I've just bought a house down by the lake."

The ladies looked knowingly at each other. "Welcome to Mindemoya."

"Thank you very much. I'll be working at the hospital." She couldn't believe she was volunteering so much personal information.

"We heard there was a new nurse coming on staff. That's lovely."

"I'm sure I will enjoy it. It seems to be a well-equipped hospital."

"We hope so. We are so afraid with all the government cutbacks we may lose it. So we all work hard to support all the hospital fund-raisers."

Sheila had never worked for a fund-raiser in her life. "You are pretty dedicated people."

"Well, we know when we have a good thing." Mae smiled at her. "You must drop in for a visit when you get settled in."

"Thanks so much. I'd like that. Now I must get my shopping done. I've got empty cupboards!"

Mae saw her chance. "I've just baked a batch of biscuits. I always make too many. You just stop in on your way home, and I'll have a few ready for you to take for your supper."

"Oh, that is too much. I don't want to impose."

"Don't give it a thought. What are neighbours for, anyway? Just look out that window. Do you see that house with the blue roof? That's mine – just a stone's throw away. I'll be looking for you."

Before Sheila could refuse, the two ladies left her holding the tablecloth. This town was something else. It might take some getting used to.

Chapter 18

The blade of oars dropped water pearls, trailing into long neck-laces on the bare shoulders of the lake before being sucked into the funnel of swirl spun by the oars. Each dip of the blades ushered forth more strings. Jean watched them form and disappear.

"Look at the pearls your oar makes, Joe."

"Beautiful," he said.

The floor of the lake must be covered with jewels," she said.

"I'd rather if it were covered with fish," he replied, and grinned at her. She looked lovely in her white dress, her blue sweater hanging loosely on her shoulders. How did he get so lucky.

"Joe, you are the limit," she laughed. Then her expression turned serious. "Do you really think they'll sell, Joe?"

"I hope so. William usually has his facts straight, and he's been their caretaker for years. He's really a good old bird – been a friend of our family for years." "Old" was a term of endearment to Joe. "If he says the island's for sale, I'm sure it is."

"Oh, I hope they'll sell. But can we afford it?"

"We'll cross that bridge when we come to it. Geordie won't want us to move, but he'll help if we need him, I'm sure. And he knows the island would be a good place to raise foxes."

"I don't mind looking after your mother. And Geordie, too. He's great with little Pat. But it would be so nice to have a home of our own."

"Poor Jeannie. First you look after your own family, and now you're looking after mine."

He paused. "If I could own that island, I'd feel like a king." He chuckled. "Then you'd only have to look after me."

"There'd better be room on that throne for a queen," she said smiling. The excitement in his heart could be seen in the rhythm of his strokes.

Finally, they landed on shore. There were three small boats pulled up here. Each had a name: The Siwash, John Little Bear, and the Lo-tus. There wasn't a stir on the front lawn. They followed the little path up the gentle slope to the house. They stepped onto the veranda, and rapped on the door. No sound. Joe rapped again. Suddenly, a male voice called, "Just a minute, I'm coming."

The door opened, and a man in a grey housecoat, still groggy with sleep, was standing there, perusing them. Joe blurted it all out. "We heard you wanted to sell the island. Jeannie and I want to buy it."

Another head appeared at the door. "Come in, come in. Mac and I were still in bed." She pushed past her husband, and ushered them in. They introduced themselves, and entered the living room. There was a stairway leading up to the right, shiny with varnish. The room was furnished with comfortable chairs, a big chesterfield, and several small tables spilling with papers. Jean dared to look around. The walls were covered with strange objects. There were large clubs covered with fancy ends, a pair of boomerangs, carved gourds, an old gun, and a model of a ship in full sail. Mrs. MacPherson caught her studying the walls. "Those strange things belong to Mac. He collects them when he travels. And we've spent a long time in Australia. The clubs are from there. The boat is a model of the Bluenose. The gourds are from India." She smiled. "Now there is no more room on the walls, and we have to sell. Come into the kitchen. I'll make some coffee." She led them through a small dining room into the kitchen. A lovely glass enclosed cupboard caught Jean's eye. It was filled with beautiful china on the top two shelves. The bottom ones were lined with books.

"This is our kitchen. The pump has good cistern water. We carry our drinking water from the lake."

"There's a good cellar," Mac added. He lifted a large trap door to reveal a set of steps. "The cistern is down here. The whole basement is cool. You can keep butter and milk for a week. Vegetables store very well." He turned to Eva. "I'll show them the upstairs while you make the coffee."

"No, I'll make the bed before you show them the upstairs. Mac, why don't you go and get dressed while I make the coffee?" She turned to her guests. "Please make yourself comfortable. Sit down here at the table."

She busied herself at the cupboard. There was a moment of awkward silence. Joe caught the excitement in Jean's eyes. It wasn't hard to see she loved the place. How he hoped they could swing the deal. No mention yet of money. Soon Mac appeared in a green plaid shirt. He rolled up his sleeves as he sat down at the table.

"So you kids really want to buy my island?"

"We'd love to," in unison.

"I've made up my mind to sell. The price is twenty five hundred dollars. I'll write down the terms of purchase on this paper." He took a sheet out of his shirt pocket. They watched him write. Then, Mac read out what he had written:

Mindemoya June 29, 1928

I agree to sell my island property 62 acres in Lake Mindemoya County to Mr. Joseph Hodgson of Mindemoya for the sum of $2500.00. First payment of $1000.00 to be made on Dec. 15, 1928 – a mortgage to be given for the balance – and payment on same made of $500.00 per annum and payment to be made Dec. 15 of each following year.

The sale includes everything on the island. House, Furniture, Rugs, Carpets, Boats, Boathouse, Carpenters tools, garden tools, verandah chairs, etc., etc.

Signed and agreed to

Eva MacPherson   R. MacPherson

Jean Hodgson   Joe Hodgson

The whole thing had been decided in one meeting. They signed their names. It was hard to believe what had happened. This beautiful island Jean saw every morning from their bedroom window – this magical, beautiful island was going to belong to them.

CHAPTER 19

Mae had planned it all. Wednesday, at eight o'clock, they were going to surprise that nice young lady, Sheila, with a house warming party. A few days ago, when she had come to accept Mae's biscuits, they had had a lovely chat. That dear girl was all alone in the world – at least she must be, because she never mentioned anything about family. It was only right that the community should welcome her.

Mae had told Allie, who had told the choir, and each member of the choir had told a friend. Then Mae went to the corner store, settling herself in the pattern book section. Whenever a woman wandered back within earshot, providing she knew her, she told her about the party, Wednesday, at eight P.M.

"Bring a pot luck, and if you want, a little something for the house."

Mae had already alerted her church group, and the hospital auxiliary board. She hadn't kept any count of how many were coming. The more the merrier. She would make a huge chocolate cake – the moist one, with the mayonnaise – and spread it with that good old-fashioned brown sugar icing. If some people forgot to bring lunch, it would go a long way.

At first, she was going to ask only the ladies. But then she thought it would be better to ask the husbands, too. There might be things Sheila needed to have fixed in the house, things that would be easy for a man.

Then an idea visited her, walked around in her mind, and stayed for lunch. Gary should come, too. Lately, he was always up in his room working in the evenings. It would be good for him to get out and meet the people, too. In a way, it could be a party for him. Wouldn't it be lovely if they could become close friends, both strangers in a new town.

She would keep that little scheme in the back of her head – she wouldn't even tell Allie, who had accused her of playing cupid on other occasions. My, life was so full these days. There were so many things to do. She had never yet found time to write in that little blank book Allie had given her. It seemed like such a good idea at the time. And she did his washing and ironing, too. She did not have to clean his room, though. He insisted on doing that himself. He said he knew the stairs were hard for her.

She heard his truck drive into the garage. She had supper all ready to put in the oven. They would have time for a little chat while it was cooking.

"Was it a good auction, Gary?" She asked as he opened the door.

"Yes, I got quite a few things. Mother will love them."

"Were there many people there?"

"No, not a lot. That's why I was lucky, I guess. And I got something for you."

"For me?"

"Yes. I'll go get it." He went out to the truck and returned with a small box of linens. They looked new, almost as if they had just come from a store. There was a long lace table runner and two matching doilies. They had ruffled lace around the edges.

"They're beautiful. But where will I put them?"

"You just close your eyes, and I'll perform a little magic in the living room."

She listened as he moved things about, heard the tinkle of china and objects being placed. Pretty soon he called to her. She opened her eyes and walked into the living room. Immediately she saw the transformation. He had placed the long runner in the center of the sideboard, and one doily on each side. The moustache cup was squarely in the middle of the doily, the picture and the plate centered in the other. The other objects were arranged neatly in between.

"Why, that's beautiful. You shouldn't spend your money on me," she said. "You're spoiling me, you know."

"Why wouldn't I spoil you? You spoil me with all that good cooking every day. I'll never forget your kindness. I should really be paying you more."

"No, all I need right now is a little money for the groceries. I never told you, Gary, but at one of the auctions, Allie and I had a lot of luck. We weren't going to tell anybody, but I can tell you. I can trust you to keep it quiet. Allie bought an old box of clothes, and in the pocket of a sweater, I found $1,100.00. I couldn't believe my eyes. Each bill was all rolled up into a ball. I just accidentally undid one and it was a hundred dollar bill. That money was like a gift from heaven."

"Lucky you. Just like winning the lottery."

"Yes. And Allie, she's such a good friend, insisted we divide the money between us. She said she would never have found it herself for she was going to let the kids play with the clothes. So we paid for our dishes, and divided the money."

So, the old girl didn't have money. He had been wrong about that. Aloud he said, "Such luck couldn't have happened to anybody nicer."

"Now, when that money is finished, I'll have to ask you for a little for your room."

"You are a dear," he said. Westicott plunked himself down on the chesterfield. She handed him the paper. "I'll check supper," she said.

"Mae," he called. He suddenly had an inspiration. "If you're short of money, I have an idea. You know that big dresser in my room? The one with the oak leaves? I heard a guy at the auction say he was looking for one of those. I bet he'd pay five hundred dollars for it."

"You think so? That's a lot of money for an old dresser. If I sold it, what would you do to store your things? I imagine, with all the things you've been buying for your mother, it must be pretty full."

"That's true. But last summer I bought an old dresser. That was the night I met you two ladies. I still have it stored. I could use that."

"I suppose that's a thought. We can talk about it later. Are you ready for supper?"

"I'll just wash up a little. I feel pretty grimy after the auction. Want me to put these old doilies someplace? They're here beside me on the chesterfield. I'm afraid I just threw them down when I was planning your surprise."

"You can put them in the dirty clothes basket in the bathroom. I'll wash them before I put them away."

"Okay. I'll be there a minute. Supper smells great."

He took the doilies and crumpled them in the basket. The tatted handkerchief he carefully folded and put in his pocket. She'd never know it was missing.

They had a wonderful supper – chicken potpie, salad and raspberry tarts. Gary complimented her lavishly. He had to keep the old girl happy. She must never suspect.

"Gary, we're having a surprise party for a girl who has just moved into town. She bought a house down by the lake. It's a housewarming. It's going to be next Wednesday. I'm hoping you will come."

"It amazes me how much you do for people. I guess I can come. I'll take you. You'll be my date."

"Oh, you silly man. But I'll take you up on that offer." She said. Mae beamed her happiness.

Westicott was feeling philanthropic. He could afford to. He had the tatted handkerchief, number six, captured in his shirt pocket.

Chapter 20

Westicott was very attentive to Sheila at the housewarming. He had recognized her immediately. Salt and pepper rabbits, number six. Now he was volunteering to take over the coffee pouring. He was graciousness personified, taking the coffee tray to each person, adding just a touch of sugar and dash of cream, as requested. This was his opportunity to impress the locals, and he would pull it off with poise and charm.

Sheila, a guest in her own house, was to sit down and be served, honouring her visitors by receiving, with all the grace she could muster, the attention bestowed on her. It was Westicott's turn.

"Will you have cream in your coffee?" he asked.

"No thank you. I drink mine black."

Sheila had recognized him as soon as he entered the door. Not wearing his plaid shirt tonight. Could this well-dressed, courteous, openly friendly person be the same one she had watched at the auction?

He interrupted her thoughts, speaking quietly. "You and I are both newcomers to this town, Miss Peters. I am sometimes taken aback by the lack of privacy I knew in the city. Do you share the same feelings?"

"Perhaps, a little. Everyone seems very friendly and interested in my well being."

"I have found the same thing. The people in this town have been very helpful. When I inquire about anything, I don't only get an answer, I get help. That's a new experience for me. I appreciate that."

"I must say I didn't know what to do when all these people showed up at my door. I didn't know how to act." She said. Throughout all this conversation, she didn't let on she recognized him.

"You did magnificently. Living up here is like living in a time warp. My Mae is right out of Dickens." He knew his classics, and it didn't hurt to let people know.

Sheila smiled. Westicott moved on with his coffee tray. At this moment, Mae rattled a spoon on a glass and made an announcement. "It's time now for Sheila to open her gifts. We have them all collected here in a basket. Everyone gather 'round."

Sheila opened the first one. It was a golf glove and a package a Lady Titleist golf balls. And there was a note: "Lady's night at Brookwood Brae is Tuesday night, at six. See you there. Fran, Pat and Terri."

"I have never golfed. But I can learn. Thank you so much."

The next package was a broom with long straw bristles. And a note: "See you in the curling rink in December. Allice and Doug, Sue and Rob, Charlene and Pete."

"You are bound to make a sportswoman out of me. What do you do with this broom?"

They all laughed. "We'll show you."

"It's for sweeping out the corners of the arena," quipped a smart-aleck in the corner.

"And the cobwebs made by Manitoulin tarantulas," added one of the funny men.

"You guys, quit kidding," said Sue. "You let me show you how to use it."

The next gift was a package of six mousetraps. And a note: "An auction 'in' joke. Jamie."

Sheila was a little embarrassed. "I did buy some traps at an auc-tion." She could see by Jamie's face that he hadn't thought she would be reading the messages in public. "I didn't really want the traps. There was something else in the box I wanted."

Westicott's mind raced. "There was something else in the box I wanted." The words printed themselves out in his mind. What else was in the box? He hadn't even suspected her.

"There's a few unattached males around here ready to be trapped," joked one of the husbands.

"Doug, don't embarrass her."

She hurried to the next box. It was a package covered with signa-tures from the corner store. Then a little inscription in careful print: "To Sheila. Hope you like the tea. And enjoy these placemats that match your tablecloth."

"How lovely. Thank you very much. A perfect choice."

The next gift, beautifully wrapped, contained a red hymn book, and an invitation to join the choir. "Choir is every Wednesday at seven."

"Thank you. I'm afraid I don't sing very well."

The next parcel contained ten packages of flower and vegetable seeds, and a plastic bag of roots and bulbs. These were from Mae and Allie. "Now, plant these right away." Said Mae. "If you need some help, we'll come down and give you all the advice you need." She laughed, feeling very comfortable among all these people she had known forever.

72

Then she got very daring. "Probably my special boarder might be good with a shovel. By the way, if you all haven't met him yet, that man guarding the coffee pot, is Gary Westicott."

"Thank you, Mae, I have made myself acquainted with almost everyone, I think. But let me take this opportunity to tell you all how happy I am to be a part of this party, and to be a part of your community, even if it is for a very short time. I do appreciate being included. I can't tell you when I have felt more at home than in Mindemoya." Everyone applauded this little outburst of emotion. Westicott had seized the opportunity, and was pleased with the response.

Sheila had one more parcel to open. She pulled off the paper, and held up a large bottle of jelly. She read the label: HAWBERRY JELLY. A little tag read, "From the historical club. Welcome. If you have time, we'd like to share a little Island lore with you. We meet once a month, the second Thursday."

"Thank you so much." Now it was Sheila's turn to make a speech. The guests quieted, waiting for her response. "I can't tell you how surprised and grateful I am – for all the gifts, and the delicious food, but most of all for your wonderful display of friendship. If I seemed bewildered at first, it was just that I have never experienced this kind of hospitality before. I'm a city girl, and I can't say I ever really had neighbours. Thank you all, very, very much."

The speech, simple and sincere, touched the house warmers. She would fit in to the community. She might never be a haweater, but at this moment, she was close.

The party was closing down. Guests were beginning to say their good-byes. Mae and Allie offered to stay and clean up. Jamie started picking up the plastic cups and serviettes. Once more, seeing an opportunity, Gary began folding the chairs.

"I noticed that some of these came from the basement. Can I take them down for you?"

"Thanks," said Sheila.

"I'll help," said Jamie.

The two men each picked up two chairs and walked down the stairs to the basement. There were boxes here, all over the floor. The contents of one were at the bottom of the stairs. Likely she'd been sitting on the bottom step, sorting the contents, when they had all arrived. The men stepped around them, carefully.

Westicott's eyes videoed the boxes for instant replay later. Now, where was the box of traps? He carried his chairs to the farthest corner of the room, panning the area with searching eyes.

"What a lot of boxes," he said. "Did she buy all this stuff at auctions?"

"No, I don't think so. A lot of it was left here by the previous owners. She told me she's been sorting them, but gets bogged down with reading the books as she sorts."

"Do you know her?"

"I'm her closest neighbour. I've helped her a bit since she moved in. I didn't know you lived in town until tonight."

"Yes, I'm boarding at Mae's. Everybody knows her, it seems. I'm working on getting my mother's antique store stocked with stuff I buy at auctions. She's not been well lately, and can't really do the buying anymore."

Jamie turned to walk upstairs. Suddenly he stopped at the bottom step, waiting for Westicott. "I'll get the light," he said.

The women had restored the kitchen to some kind of order, and the three of them were chattering merrily, like old friends. "Here you are, Gary," said Mae. "It's time for you to take an old lady like me home. And likely this lady has to work in the morning."

There was a flurry of farewell, and finally Sheila was alone. What an evening. And wasn't it strange how some of these people she had observed at the auctions were suddenly coming together? She reflected on this. It was almost as if the summer auctions were a prelude to a new chapter in her life. She would live the pages, one at a time.

Chapter 21

Sheila took her coffee to the deck. There was a crisp briskness in the early morning air. The warmth of the mug felt good on her fingers. She sat there, hands clasped around the cup. The warmth of the freshly brewed coffee and warmth of last night's party melded into one. Sheila held contentment in her hands. She consciously willed the moment to last.

The lake was still, and the rising mist was rolling up the curtain on the opening act of morning. The trees on the island revealed themselves, skirts first, a chorus dressed for the autumn overture. A flock of mallards drew a straight line through the middle of the lake. A white huddle of seagulls drowsed on the floating swimmers' raft by the government dock. There was not a sound. It was that breathless moment when all the lake orchestra members poised, waiting for an invisible baton to signal the first note.

Sheila wanted to know more about that island. Someone had told her it belonged to Tom Sellick, but when she mentioned that to Mae, she just laughed. "No, dear, don't believe that nonsense." As she looked at it now, she let her imagination wander. It must have looked just like this forever, always there, visible in the mist for all the generations who had lived here. How far back? She wished she knew more history. Perhaps she should join that historical club and learn something about this place that had chosen her. That was the way she liked to think about it. She was here for a purpose. Someday, she would understand.

The corner of Jamie's cottage was visible from her deck. He was up early. She watched the rhythmic movement of his arms, splitting firewood, breaking the morning silence. He stopped and piled a few sticks by the corner of the cottage. In that moment he looked up, and caught her watching him. He called. "You're up early."

"I've got the coffee on. Come on up."

"Okay. I was going to settle for instant. Yours sounds better."

Sheila went in to check the pot. Lots of coffee. She got a mug down from the cupboard and dusted it out. He was there before she got it filled.

75

"Hi. When are you leaving for the big city, Jamie?"

"I have to be at work on Monday. I'm getting the woodshed full. That's my last big job."

"I'll miss my good neighbour."

"Yeah. Me too. Quite a party you had last night."

"I still can't believe it. Something I never experienced before."

"That's what's so good about this place. I didn't always know that. I thought everybody was just plain nosey." He added two spoonfuls of sugar to his coffee. "Thought I couldn't move without somebody watching me, knowing everything I was doing, and then mentioning it to my folks. It took me forever to realize they were interested in me, not just curious. Quite a revelation."

"Did you always live here, Jamie?"

"I wasn't born here. My folks moved here from Toronto when I was five. Dad was a graphic artist. His business was very competitive. His nerves got pretty frazzled, and Mom talked him into taking a week's holidays. They – we – came up here and fell in love with the place."

"Did they decide just like that? On the spur of the moment?"

"I think so. I was too young to remember the details. It seemed exciting, moving to a new place. But dad was lucky. He found lots of work, painting signs, and designing things for people." Through all this, Jamie was still stirring his coffee. He stopped. "I was seventeen when the accident happened."

"Oh, I'm sorry. I didn't know."

"It's all right. Dad had designed a logo for a business in Sudbury. They were taking it over to the big boss for approval. I didn't want to go with them. It was a head-on collision. Killed instantly – both of them."

"How tragic, Jamie."

"I'm over it now – almost. I was pretty bitter and mixed up at the time. I hated all the town people coming around, offering me this and that. I took off for Toronto. The lawyer who looked after their estate parceled out enough money to get by on."

"What made you decide to come back?"

"I don't know when it first started, but I suddenly got the urge to come back. I had forced myself to forget all my life before the accident. It was as if I had packed all my life in a box and left it here. I had to come back to find it."

"I can relate to that."

"When I first got back home, I was just as mixed up as ever. Then by chance I went to that auction and on a whim bought that old tackle box. My dad had one like it. Suddenly it seemed to me that those tangled lines were the strings that held me together – all messed up, but still there. I decided to untangle one string at a time."

"How'd you know when to start?"

"I looked around the cottage. Every little thing there had been chosen by my parents. I remembered when we got most of the things, and what they meant to them at the time. I took an object and I picked a piece of line. That line became my memory. As I untangled the line I walked around in that memory, trying to recall every little detail. I thought about what was said, what the voices sounded like, what the feelings were as best I could. I made a point never to cut a line."

"You are very wise for someone so young."

"Hey, I'm twenty-two now. And I'm getting a grip on things, finally. Now that's enough about me."

"Good for you. I should have bought myself a tackle box."

"You bought a box of traps." Jamie laughed. "Sorry, I shouldn't have kidded you about that last night. I didn't know you were going to read my note out loud."

"That was all right. Guess I was a bit embarrassed. I really didn't want the traps. There was something else in that box."

"May I ask what?"

"Yes. It was a little knife. I'll show you." She went into another room and brought out the knife.

"Quite a little gadget. Doesn't really look like a knife. Why'd you want it?"

"I didn't. I shouldn't tell you this. You'll think less of me. Anyway, you know Gary Westicott who was here last night?"

"Right. Remember, he was the guy I thought had your rabbits?"

"Yes. Well, I was watching him one day at the auction. And I was still upset about my rabbits. I saw him rummaging through a box on the wagon, and I saw him taking something out of the box and put it in another box of junk – mostly rusty bolts and nuts. So, when he was out of sight, I felt around in the box, found the little knife and slipped it into the box with the traps."

Jamie laughed. "Good for you. Did he find out?"

"No. He bought the junk box and took it to his truck. If he was upset that the knife was missing, he didn't show it."

"There's something about that guy I don't like. I don't know what it is. Seems friendly enough. Paid me enough to help him load his junk. But I just don't trust him."

"They tell me Islanders don't trust strangers."

"Then count me in as an Islander."

"He was certainly pleasant enough last night."

"Well, I still wouldn't tell him about the knife."

"No, I won't. It's a nice little ornament. I thought I'd put a chain on it and wear it as a necklace. No one would know it was a knife."

"By the way, did you ever get in touch with Brian about your carpentry work?"

"No, I've been too busy. I'm working four days now, instead of three. Hopefully, I'll be full time after Christmas. The only thing I really need this fall is a repair job on the patio window. One is a little loose on the bottom. Do you think I should get storm windows for winter?"

"I would. It gets pretty cold in the winter. And you're up on a hill here. The north wind would blow right through there. Look, I'll take you out to meet the guy. He's kind of a loner, a bit hard to get to know at first. Pretty quiet – and he has some strange ideas about the land. Once he gets started on that, though, you can't get a word in edgeways."

"What kind of ideas?"

"He's into that American writer, Thoreau. You know, the guy who planted the beans."

"I remember reading in high school something he wrote. I was too young to get tuned in to what he was talking about."

"Just don't get Brian started. Anyway, he is a good guy. My parents knew him well. He was a bit like my dad, only younger. He had a good education, and a good job. But as they say around here, 'You can take the boy from the Island, but you can't take the Island out of the boy.' All the time he was away, he wanted to come back."

"Why didn't he just come back?"

"His folks spent every penny on his education. They were so proud of him. I guess they thought he owed it to them to have a big paying job and some letters after his name. They're both dead now. Left him the farm. So he came back."

"So now he's just a farmer and a carpenter on the side?"

"Yes. He did go back to the city for a few years. He met a girl there. He doesn't talk much about her. I think he brought her here, but she didn't like it. He never got married. Goes about the farm, talking to the cows and chickens. But don't let that fool you. He has deliberately chosen the way he lives. Like Thoreau."

"I shouldn't put these jobs off any longer. I'd like to meet him. When can we go?"

"It would have to be this afternoon. I've got to see a guy about draining my pipes so they don't freeze over winter. He's coming this morning."

"Should we phone first?"

"No, we'll just drop in. I have to say good-bye anyway, before I go. So, I'll introduce you."

"Thanks, Jamie, I appreciate that."

"Good coffee, Sheila. Keep tabs on my cottage over the winter from this window, will you? Nobody touched the place all those years I was away, but there are more strangers coming to the Island."

"Sure, I'll check it every day."

"Gotta go now. Have to get the wood split. See you at two this afternoon."

"I'll be ready."

Jamie left and Sheila started to plan the rest of the morning. She would treat herself to a few more minutes on the deck, just relaxing. She thought about Jamie. Such a sensitive kid. Untangling the lines, walking around in his memories. Listening for the voices. Quite a nice way to put it. What an effect his parents had on him. Or was it the Island? You can't take the Island out of the boy. That's what he said. Likely both, she thought.

She thought back to her own growing up years. They were always on the move, packing, unpacking, making do with whatever they could afford, usually in very small accommodations. She had hated changing schools, trying to fit in with the kids, always on the outside of the little groups already formed when she arrived. It wasn't really a very happy time. Her parents both worked and never seemed to be home. Most of the problems she had at school she kept to herself. Would her life have been any different had she grown up here? Maybe. The slower pace, the close knit community, the space to call your own. Imagine what it might have been like growing up on that island. How would a kid get to school? Imagine having to cross a lake every day.

Boats were starting to move on the lake. Two were leaving the dock, spurting forward, leveling out, leaving a trail of anxious water tossed around in all directions. There, at the tip of the island, was a smaller boat. She could see the shine on the oars as they lifted and fell in the water. She would have to talk to somebody about a boat. Sometimes the wind got pretty strong. For now, she'd just think about it. No need to hurry. She watched the rowers, two of them, in perfect synchronized movement, bending forward and pulling back, propelling their craft just as surely as those racing about with their high powered motors. There was lots of room on this lake for both. That was the beauty of it.

Chapter 22

Marion and her dad were rowing across the lake. Her strokes were short but fast. "Boy, you can really row," he said. "I can hardly keep up."

"I know. I bet I can turn you in circles." Half standing, she pushed her oar deep into the water and dipped and pulled, dipped and pulled until the boat swung crazily off course. He leaned on his oar, laughing. She grinned and dragged her paddle, letting him swing the bow towards the dock again.

"If you can work half this hard at school, you'll top the class."

"I don't like school. I liked it better when you and mom helped me with the lessons in the mail."

"We want you to be with the other kids. You'll like them when you get to know them better."

"I only like Allan."

"That's because you know him. Ever since you were a little kid you two have played together. Remember in the winter when mum looked out the window and said to you 'I see a little dot on the ice. If it comes closer, and I'm sure it's Allan, you can go and meet him.' You were only four the first time. But now you're ten. You need more friends. There must be nice kids in your class."

"No, there's not."

She was not prepared to like anybody at school. She had taken correspondence courses for four years, even in the summer time, and she was in grade six. But the school teacher in town had said you didn't learn anything from those courses, so he would put her in grade five. Everything was very different at school. You couldn't ask questions unless you put up your hand. And just when something got interesting, you had to put that book away and get another one. The teacher was always saying it's time for this and it's time for that. She didn't like that teacher.

"I hate school."

He glanced at her sideways. He knew the look, defiant, but close to tears. "Well," he started, "I wasn't going to tell you, but your mum and I have a surprise for you."

"What?"

"We weren't going to tell you until..."

"What is it?"

"We've ordered a motor for you. A little Elto. Old Chuck is bringing it up in June, when he comes to fish."

"What does it look like? How fast does it go? Will I be able to take it apart myself?"

"Hey, we'll just have to wait and see. We'll put it on that little green flat you like to row. Then, if anything goes wrong, you can take the oars."

"I can't wait." She smiled brightly. Her smile warmed her dad's heart, for he was more happy in the giving than she in the anticipation. Money was hard to come by, but he could trade Chuck's stay at the cottage for the motor.

The rest of the way went quickly. The oars dipped and pulled together, leaving identical swirling pools in their wake. She could fit his stride when she wanted to. About forty feet from shore, he glanced toward the dock. He saw the school bus slow briefly, then pull away. She turned in time to catch a glimpse of the orange. "The teacher's going to be mad if I'm late. Mike could have waited a minute."

"Don't worry. Mike can't keep everybody late. We'd have had lots of time if the motor hadn't conked out. Dirt in the gas, I guess. We'll just tie up the boat and I'll walk you to school."

They docked carefully, snugging the boat in on a short rope. The boards were slippery with dew and seagull poop.

"This dock's a mess," she said.

"At least we have a dock," he said. "And I'm going to try to get our member of parliament to get us a new dock. Uncle Tom is a senator, you know. Maybe he can help."

"Allan doesn't like him being away all the time."

"Well, that's his job, you know. And he'll be back in the summer."

They started off down the gravel road. It was two miles from the dock to the school. She would be late, but as long as her dad went with her right to the classroom door, everything would be fine. And he would. Crusty old Mr. Brown would forget all about her being late as he joked with her dad at the door.

Knowing this erased all worries from her mind. She skipped along beside him, taking his hand to pull him towards something she'd spied at the edge of the road—a lumpy toad, or a dragonfly easing out of his shell. Each time her dad would stop and study what she had found and there would be stories of other toads and other dragonflies. Finally, they reached the bridge that crossed the river.

"We might as well stop and look awhile," he said. "You're late already."

"Sure," she said. The kids would be doing that stupid times table circle on the board which Mr. Brown thought was so much fun. Well, it would be all finished when she got there. They hunched side by side over the bridge railing. Suddenly a shiver of water distorted their mirrored faces.

"Look, dad," she whispered. "Two beaver."

"Shh...be still. Here comes some babies."

The adult beaver splashed their tails, showering their offspring with river water. Then the young ones splashed in response. They frolicked at the river bank, nuzzling each other, slipping into the water and jet propelling noisily.

Marion and her dad watched breathlessly. She moved her head a little and the moment's shadow warned the beaver that they were not alone. In an instant they slid under the bridge and were gone. "They are smart critters," her dad said. Then he told her all about the beaver. He explained about their special teeth and pointed out a poplar standing like a pencil on a sharpened point, ready to fall into the water with one more night's work. He told her about beaver houses, and said he would take her to the beaver dam up the river. Maybe that poplar would be there by then. They'd remember to check that out.

The beaver lesson lasted for a mile and a half. She was anxious now to get to school to find out more about beaver in the library. Maybe she could find out something that her dad didn't already know.

Suddenly, they were at the school. They grew quiet. They climbed the concrete steps, not even acknowledging the purple iris her dad had planted in the flower bed. She hesitated.

"I'll go with you to the door," he said, and took her hand.

The creaky stairs filled the hall with unwelcome squeaks. There was no one at the fountain. The library door was open, and the musty smell of old books filled the air. They stood outside the classroom. Teachers' voices slid out under closed doors and echoed in the varnished silence. Joe squeezed her hand and winked. He rapped on the door. Mr. Brown's footsteps approached. He opened the door, glanced briefly at Marion, and smiled broadly at her father. As they spoke, she slipped silently through the doorway and took her seat at the far side of the room.

In a few moments the teacher returned, acknowledged the girl's presence with a look, but no comment. He turned to the board and erased the times table circle. "The arithmetic period is now over," he said, looking at the girl as if to remind her of how late she was. "It is now time for English. We shall begin with conversation. Let us share some observations you may have made on the way to school today. We will begin with you, Marion."

Should she tell about the new motor she was going to get, or should she tell about the beaver? The beaver would be best. Maybe the class could do a project on the beaver. They were such smart critters. She smiled and stood up. The words tumbled out. "My dad and I walked to school this morning because our motor broke down and I missed the bus. But there were lots of things to see on the way to school. There was a spotty toad and a dragonfly being hatched. And best of all, at the bridge we seen two beaver..."

"Marion, what did you say?"

"The motor broke down and I missed the bus, but there was a spotty toad and a dragonfly being hatched and we seen..."

"Marion, what was that?"

"There was a dragonfly being hatched and we seen..."

"Marion!"

All eyes were on her. She slid into her seat. Allan, who sat behind her, poked her shoulder and whispered, "Say SAW, stupid."

Mr. Brown's commanding voice rang out. "Now, Marion? Stand up and tell us what you saw on the way to school."

She seemed fastened on her seat, like a bug on a pin.

"Marion. We are waiting."

Slowly she stood up. "We saw two beaver."

"Now that's better. What were they doing?" he asked eagerly.

"Nothing," she replied. The magic of the morning was shattered. Later, she might tell Allan, but Mr. Brown would never know about that awesome moment on the bridge.

She decided she would not tell her father what had happened at school. It was enough to know that if she did tell him, he would be right over there and tell Mr. Brown a thing or two about his kid. She smiled secretly at the thought.

CHAPTER 23

    Mae busied herself with the breakfast dishes. She was still basking in the glow of last night's party. The blossoms on the dishes seemed pinker this morning as she rinsed them; the forks and spoons shone brighter under the careful polish of her blue checkered tea towel. The whole world had taken on a rosy hue. Mae had learned from her mother that it was a blessing to bring happiness to others. She was experiencing the blessing. As she cleaned off the counter and rubbed the sink to a high patina, she realized she hadn't even listened to the morning news. Now, Wei Chen was signing off. Well, the world would have to get along without her.

    This would be a good morning to untangle that old marionette. She could relax now that the party was over. Allie would likely be in to talk over the good time they'd had at the party. She took the old puppet out of the basket and made herself comfortable in the rocking chair. She took a good look at it. The feel of it, the scent of it, set off waves of memories. She could almost see her mother working on it, stuffing the face, pinching the cheeks and sewing the cotton batting inside to produce that permanent smile. The eyelashes were embroidered in black wool. Two of the stitches were loose. Perhaps she should replace them all with new wool. That funny little smile. It was just as quizzical as ever. The body was still in good shape. The jacket was a bit faded, but not torn. It was the strings that needed the attention. What a tangle. The little sticks that held them in a major mess. Well, she'd work away as best she could.

    She started with the string that was loosest. Maybe if she could get one free, the others might move more easily. Mae's fingers were still nimble. She twisted and pulled gently on the strings. In a short while she had released one knot. She was pleased with her accomplishment. Tangle number one. As she worked on the next one she thought she should be writing something about this puppet. Something other people could read after she was gone. She could tell how her mother used to work it at the concerts. She could make it dance and spin around and bow. How the people had laughed! She could use that little blank book Allie had given her. No better time than the present. She put down the puppet, and went in search of the book.

She opened it to the first blank page. First, she'd make a list of all the things she would write about. Then she'd make herself fill up the whole book. Now, let's see. She looked around the room. There was the Gone With The Wind lamp, the foot warmer, the cocoa set with the grape design, the butter bowl, the violin vase, the tatted handkerchief (she must remember to launder that and put it away), the covered candy dish, the old victrola. She'd never forget the day they'd got that. A traveling salesman had come to the door. He said he had only one of these machines left and didn't want to cart it back. At first her father said they couldn't afford one, but before they knew it the salesman had hurried to the democrat to get it.

The machine itself sat on a chest with five narrow drawers. The man lifted the lid of the victrola. He explained that there was a little magic needle in the movable arm that ran around the spaces between the ridges in the record. A man by the name of Edison had invented it—there was his name under the lid.

"Now, if everyone will sit down, I will explain how to play the most beautiful music in the world," he said. "Even you, little girl, will be able to play it. Of course, you will have to pull up a chair to stand on. Now we will take a cylinder out of the drawer. Ah, here is a lovely one, 'The Harp That Once Through Tara's Hills'. You just remove the record from the drawer, place it gently on, like this, and turn it until you hear a little click. There. Then you wind up the crank on the side of the machine, like this." He took the handle in his hand and wound it until it resisted. "Now, just move the wee silver lever in the front of the record – like this – place the round end of the arm in the beginning groove of the record, and listen."

Music filled the room. You could see in a minute that mother loved it. "How much is it?" asked father. "Only ten dollars," said the salesman. Dad looked at mother and I guess it wasn't hard to see how much she wanted it, even though she didn't say anything. "Look," said the salesman, "I'll leave it here for the winter. You can give me three dollars now, and the rest in the spring. That is, if you decide to keep it. If not, I'll give you back the money and take the victrola."

Of course, he knew we could never let it go after listening to it all winter. Seventy records came with the machine. There were lots of hymns that mother enjoyed. And there were Irish tunes that dad loved. I liked the dance tunes best, but I couldn't listen to them on Sundays. No sir! Mae smiled to herself. Could she write that story down just as she'd thought it? Maybe. She'd make a start. No sooner than her pen touched the paper, a knock on the door snapped her out of her reverie.

"Come in," she called.

Four men walked into the kitchen. "We've come to get the old dresser from Gary's room," one of them said. When she didn't reply immediately, he explained. "Gary saw us at the restaurant and asked us if we had time to move the dresser before we went to work this morning. He said you knew all about it. Said to tell you he got a good deal."

Are you Martha Givens' boy?" she asked.

"Yes. I should have introduced myself. I'm Pete Givens."

"I thought you looked familiar. Dead spit of your father. I haven't seen you since you were a little codger."

"I've been working in Sudbury for eight years but I always wanted to come back to the Island if I could find myself a good job."

"Yes. All the kids are anxious to leave, but once they get away for awhile they all want to come back."

"Guess you're right. But right now we'd better get that dresser or we'll be late for our shift at Inco. We're on at noon today."

"It's upstairs. It's the one with the walnut leaves. Careful now, the stairs are narrow."

Mae stood at the bottom, while the men went upstairs. They picked up the old dresser as if it were a matchbox and steered it carefully down the stairs, neatly manoeuvring the corner so as not to touch the wall. In no time they had walked the dresser out the kitchen door. "See you later," Pete said.

"Yes. Come anytime. The teapot is always on."

Well, imagine, Gary had got a good deal on the dresser. She hadn't thought about selling it, but she must have told Gary to go ahead. He would never sell it on his own unless she had given him permission. Might as well admit her memory wasn't as good as it used to be. She reached for the phone. She'd call Allie and tell her. As she was dialing, a truck pulled into the driveway. There he was now. She hung up the phone.

"Mae," he said excitedly, "Look what I've got for you." He reached into his pocket and pulled out a fistful of bills and threw them in the air. They scattered and fell all over the kitchen.

"Gary, what ever are you doing?" She laughed in her excitement.

"Here, I'll pick them up. This is what I got for your dresser." He picked them up and showered them on the table in front of her. There were twenties, tens and fives. She put them in piles.

"My stars! There's $495!"

"And it's all yours. Now, what will you buy? Some new dresses?"

"I'll have to think about it," she said.

"I have my old dresser that I got at the auction in the truck. I'll see if I can get some kids off the street to help me get it upstairs."

She heard him call out. "Would you two fellows give me a hand for a minute? It's a couple of bucks for each of you for five minutes time."

Two teenagers, likely on their way to school, jumped at the chance. Before she knew it, his old dresser was upstairs, Gary admonishing them all the way to be careful of the wall. Then they were gone. So much was happening she could hardly get her breath. She sat down in the rocking chair and picked up the marionette. Her fingers were too shaky to untangle any more knots. She could feel the bills bulging in her apron pocket.

Gary came down the stairs. "I won't be here for lunch, Mae. I'm going to... what's that you've got there?"

An old marionette. My mother made it for me when I was a little girl.

Gary's eyes fixed on that crooked grin. He felt himself beginning to tremble. Control. Control. One thousand, two thousand... In a calm and casual voice, he said, "It's one of those puppets. I've seen them on TV."

"Right. I'm untangling the strings. It's been a long time since I've looked at it. I had it stashed away. Next time I pack it up it will be untangled."

He felt a terrible urge to grab it from her hands. Wring the old girl's neck, and grab the puppet. One thousand, two thousand...

"Gary, are you all right? You shouldn't be lifting those heavy things. You didn't have enough help. Your dresser seemed much heavier than mine."

"I'm fine. It's just that I have a bit of a heart murmur and it kicks up once in a while. Nothing to worry about." He walked over and patted her on the shoulder. "Now, you rest up and think how you're going to spend all that money."

He hurried out the door before she could reply. He must stay calm. Everything had worked so well. Got the deed done before the old girl had a chance to come to her senses. Made himself 500 bucks on her dresser and got his upstairs at the same time. And all the locks worked. Nobody could get into his treasures and he would have them all right beside him. But more than anything – and this was completely unplanned – the marionette was right here, under his roof. Right now it was grinning madly in his mind.

CHAPTER 24

Jamie and Sheila drove down the long lane to Brian's. They saw him by the barn, tinkering with a tractor. He had an oil can in his hand and didn't look up at his visitors. Jamie parked the car and he and Sheila walked over to the tractor.

"Brian, I'd like you to meet a friend of mine, Sheila Peters. She's bought a house on the lake, and it turns out we're next door neighbours."

"How do you do?" he said, rather formally, his eyes still glued to his oil can.

"Hi," Sheila said. Then, attempting conversation, she added, "I'm pretty excited about being a Mindemoya resident. Jamie tells me you're a real haweater." When there was no response to this overture, she said, "I need a little carpentry work done, and I hear from Jamie that you're one of the best carpenters around."

Brian didn't respond immediately. Typical outsider, he thought, expecting him to jump at the prospect of making a buck. "I've got a lot of things to do around here before the snow comes," he announced to both of them.

They looked around the yard. It was picture perfect – a freshly painted barn, an open shed full of wood, a small square garden decorated with staked tomatoes as perfectly spaced as candles on a birthday cake. What needed to be done?

"Place sure looks as if it needs a lot of attention," Jamie said.

Brian didn't respond, finding another spot for the spout of his oil can.

"You have a beautiful place here," Sheila offered.

"Just like any other farm. Needs a lot of attention." Brian said matter-of-factly.

Jamie, sensing Brian didn't want to be interrupted for the moment, took the liberty of showing Sheila around. "Look over here, Sheila. Bet you never saw anything like this before." He directed her over to an old pump that stood by the corner of the house. "See what happens when you push that handle up and down."

"Come on, Jamie, I've seen lots of them in books."

"Go on, give it a try."

Sheila looked over to Brian as if for permission. Apparently he wasn't aware of their conversation, and was still absorbed in his tractor. She took the handle and pushed it up and down. Suddenly water splashed on the ground. "Can you drink it right out of the ground like that?" she asked.

"Sure," he said. He reached for the dipper hanging by the spout. "Fill her up."

She pumped again, just once this time, and water filled the tin with enough force to splatter her jeans. Jamie laughed, and handed her the dipper. She didn't relish the thought of drinking out of an unsanitary tin, but didn't want to offend, either. She touched it to her lips and tasted the cold water. "It's really cold," she said. She handed the dipper to Jamie who hung it back on the hook. Then he turned and walked back to the tractor.

"You've got the old gal looking pretty good," he said. "New paint job?"

"Yeah. Just reground the valves, too. She purrs like a kitty."

"I'm leaving tomorrow. I wanted to stop in and say good-bye."

"I'll keep an eye on your place. Got your wood split?"

"Yeah. Piled, too. Can't say I've got my place fixed up anything like yours, but I've made a start."

"It'll come. I'll plough you up a garden in the spring, if you want."

Sheila had approached and was listening to the conversation. "Maybe when you do that, I could hire you to plough some ground for me. I'd love a garden."

"What place did you buy?" Brian asked, seeming to be aware of her for the first time.

"The brown house on the hill by the government dock. I don't know who owned it before."

"I know the one." No offer to plough a garden, no offer to do any carpentry work. Nice guy. The chirping crickets seemed louder as they filled the awkward silence.

"Well, Jamie, we'd better go. Mr. Peterson seems pretty busy."

"Yeah. Good-bye, Brian." Jamie reached out his hand and Brian shook it firmly. "I appreciate all the help you've been. I'll keep in touch."

"See you in the spring," Brian said. What a cold encounter, Sheila thought. Whatever made Jamie so fond of this oil can addict? He was almost rude. She'd find another carpenter. Mae would have an idea who to get. She knew everybody.

Just as Jamie opened the car door, Brian called. "What kind of work did you need done, Miss Peters?"

"Oh, it was nothing. I'll get someone else."

"Was it the windows that need fixing?"

"Yes." She was surprised at his response. "But never mind. It's not much."

"I'll be down on Thursday."

"But I'm working Thursday. I won't be home."

"Just leave the key under the frog."

How did he know there was a frog? And who did he think she was, leaving a key for a perfect stranger.

"I'll check it out, do some measuring, and order what you need."

Sheila couldn't find words for a reply. Jamie broke in. "See you, Brian. Don't take any wooden nickles." He started up the car and drove down the lane.

"I can't say your choice of carpenter is overly friendly," she said.

"Oh, that's just his way. A bit gruff on the outside sometimes."

"Surely he didn't think I'd take him seriously about leaving the key."

"Most people around here don't bother to lock their houses except in the summer time when there are a lot of strangers on the Island. It's common to let workmen in whether you're there or not. Everybody knows everybody here. It's not like the city."

"I guess there's a lot of things I have to get used to. Your friend, Brian, didn't seem anxious to work for me."

"That's just his way. He'll be down Thursday, like he said."

"He may not get in! Anyway, thanks for taking me. Will I see you before you leave?"

"Sure. I'll drop by for a coffee before I go. Gotta go now and get my packing done."

Sheila walked toward her house. The magic of the morning had dissipated. It just took one unfriendly encounter to change her mood. She certainly did not intend to have this man fix her windows. Let him oil his tractor all he wanted. He didn't have to stop for her. She smiled at the frog on her doorstep. She hadn't paid much attention to him before. He had been there when she bought the house. He'd better not touch you, frog.

Her little kitchen seemed warm and inviting. It comforted her and settled her mind. She decided to go right now and see Mae. Settle this carpenter thing once and for all. She would take her some doughnuts she'd bought at the bakery and they'd have a nice little chat about carpenters. In a few minutes she was at her door.

Mae was delighted to see her. "I'm so glad you came," she said. "Come into the living room. My, we had such a lovely time at your party."

"It was such a surprise. I don't think I behaved very well."

"Of course you did. Everybody loved you. Would you spread this cloth, and I'll get some tea. Or would you like coffee?"

"Tea will be just fine. Thanks, Mae." Sheila placed the cloth on the table, admiring the hand embroidery on the corners as she did so. "Mae, I need a little carpentry done. Can you suggest someone?"

"There's Brian Peterson. He's a very good carpenter."

"I just met him. Jamie took me to his place. He seemed too busy to want work. I felt as if I were intruding."

"Oh, that's just his way. He lives all by himself on that big farm. His whole life is wound up in polishing it up to the nines. Loves every little bit of it. Too bad he never found a good wife for himself."

"He did say he'd come on Thursday, but I'm working. He had the nerve to tell me to leave the key under the frog and he'd just go in and check the windows. And how did he know about the frog?"

"Probably he's been there lots of times. He was a friend of the lady who used to live there."

"Well, I'm afraid he's not going to get to know the lady who lives there now," she said. She was surprised at her own vehemence. That man had got her riled up.

Mae brought in the teapot. "Brian's lived here all his life, except for a few years when he went to school in Toronto. He worked there for a while after university, but his heart was always here."

"Jamie told me the same thing. I thought haweaters were supposed to be friendlier than that."

Mae smiled. "We may take a little getting used to. Here, try a little honey on that biscuit."

"Thanks."

"Do you have a lot of work to be done?"

"Not a lot. The front window needs some attention. I suppose there are other jobs to be done, but I'm not in a hurry for them."

"I'll try to think of somebody for you."

Sheila looked around the cosy room. "I love your living room, Mae. Do you mind my asking just what is that piece of furniture?"

"It's a victrola. Open one of those drawers and you'll see what kind of records it plays."

91

Sheila pulled open a drawer. "You mean these tubes?"

"Yes. You can read the names on the edges."

Sheila examined a record and read the label: THE LETTER EDGED IN BLACK; BEAUTIFUL DREAMER. "I've never heard of these songs."

"I'm not surprised. But I remember them well."

"Does it still work? I'd love to hear it."

"Yes, dear, it does. And I'd love to play them for you. But you know Gary, who rents my room? Such a nice young man. He was doing some pretty heavy lifting, and he has a bad heart. Right now he's resting, and I wouldn't want to disturb him. But one day we'll spend a whole day playing those old tunes."

In a softer voice Sheila asked, "What does Gary do?"

"He works very hard. His mother is not very well, and she has an antique store which she refuses to give up. He buys all the things he can for her, and refinishes the furniture and fixes everything up before he delivers it to her."

"Oh. Well, Mae, I'd better go now. I haven't got my phone in yet, so I'll drop in tomorrow to see if you have thought of somebody."

"All right. I'll check around, Come in for tea, and we'll play some music."

"Thanks, Mae. You're a friend. I brought you some things from the bakery. Maybe I'll learn to cook like you someday."

"What a treat. Gary and I will enjoy them. See you tomorrow."

Upstairs, Westicott had strained to hear the conversation. Would he love to get into that house. Maybe she would leave the key under the frog after all. It would be a simple thing to get it, copy it and return it, and no one would be the wiser. Things might just work out if he played his cards right. He would make sure he was around for tea tomorrow to help things along.

Chapter 25

Mae hustled about the kitchen, preparing a tea tray. She had invited Allie who had just returned from a holiday with her kids, and Sheila was coming too. Now she heard Gary's truck pulling into the driveway. These were the occasions Mae loved. She had made Swedish cakes, delectable little cookies rolled in crushed nuts and filled with jelly. It was just as if this was her own family dropping in for tea.

"You're home early, Gary."

"Yes. I got the first finish on an old table I'm sending to mother. It will take a few hours to dry."

"You haven't talked about her lately. How is she?"

"Very well. Better than expected. She wants to stay at my place until after Christmas, and then set off on her own. Can you put up with me for that long?"

"Of course. You're just like family. Sheila and Allie will be here soon. That's why I'm getting a special lunch. You're just in time."

"You'd almost think I had it planned," he said. "Coffee smells great."

"Would you carry this into the living room? I'll get the cloth. By the way, Gary, you know that tatted handkerchief I had on the side board? Do you remember where you put it?"

"I put it in the dirty clothes."

"I've looked and can't find it anywhere. Sometimes things are right before my eyes and I can't see them. Maybe it fell down behind the washer."

"I'll look for you later."

"It's not that valuable. But tatting is a dying art. I had it in mind to give it to Allie. She always wanted it, and I might as well let her have it now."

"As soon as I get a minute, I'll look for it. I'll get a hanger and use it as a hook to reach down behind the washer. I'll fish it up."

"Thanks so much. I'm getting to count on you for everything. You don't know how much it means to have someone like you look after things for me."

Before Gary could respond, there was a little tap at the door. Allie walked in, arms outstretched and pulled Mae close in a big hug.

"It's so good to see you. You've only been away a couple of weeks and it seems like months," Mae said.

"I've missed you, too," Allie replied. "I'm glad to be back. I love my grandkids but I'm past the stage of looking after little ones. They're a handful." Allie walked into the living room. Gary stood up as she entered. Such a lovely gesture. Most of the men around were not skilled in polite gestures of deference to women.

"It's good to see you, Allie."

"Thanks, Gary. I'm glad to be back." She settled herself in the rocking chair. She looked around. "Mae, you've got a new dresser set."

"Yes. Gary got it for me. Isn't it lovely."

"It is indeed." She looked at the tray. "Who else are you expecting?"

"Sheila's dropping in. It's her day off. She doesn't have a phone yet, so when she needs something, she calls in. I'm glad you got home early, Gary. It will give you a chance to get to know her."

"Watch out for Mae, Gary, she's a matchmaker."

"Don't think I haven't noticed," Gary said. "She's been hinting quite a bit, lately. Not that I don't think Sheila's a good catch. It's just that I'm too tied up with mother's problems to pay attention to my own right now."

A light knock on the door indicated Sheila's arrival. She had walked the two miles and looked fresh and invigorated. Her skin glowed with heightened colour from the exercise. She was wearing jeans, and a denim open necked shirt framed a matching turtleneck knit. Her only adornment was a gold chain pulled taut by some kind of heavy ornament, hidden beneath her shirt.

"Come on in."

"Oh, you have company."

"Just Allie and Gary. We have the tea ready, and some Swedish cakes waiting to be eaten," she said. They walked into the living room. Gary stood, and graciously helped each of them to a chair. Almost unconsciously, Sheila put her hand to her necklace, feeling it safely tucked inside her shirt. "It's good to see you both," she said. "I've had a wonderful walk. It's such a beautiful day."

"It is lovely," responded Allie. "But be ready for winter. One day you'll wake up and the ground will be covered with snow."

"I'm almost ready. But I would like to get my window fixed before it snows. Did you find someone, Mae?"

94

"I tried some carpenters I know, but they are in the middle of jobs. They both said they'd do it, but not right away."

Allie broke in. "You're looking for a carpenter? I'm surprised, Mae, you hadn't thought of Brian."

Sheila laughed. "You too? Everybody is impressed with this Brian except me. I did see him, Allie, but he was so abrupt. He did condescend to help me, but I didn't like his conditions. He wanted me to leave the key where he could find it, and go in my house whenever it suited him. I'm too much of a city girl for that!"

"From what I hear, he's very trustworthy," broke in Gary. "He's honest as daylight. He'd never touch a thing that wasn't his. I'd take him up on his offer, if I were you. First thing you know it will be hunting season, and you won't be able to get anybody."

"What do they hunt?" Sheila asked.

"Deer. Thousands of people come on the Island to hunt. It's Manitoulin's big time sport. It's the last good rush of business for the locals before winter."

"Why would anyone want to kill those beautiful creatures?"

"A lot of men think it's the macho thing to do," said Gary. "As for me, I'm not a hunter. I hate guns."

"I wish everyone thought like you do," Mae said. She smiled at him appreciatively. Such a gentle man. They talked of other things for a while, all seemingly comfortable in one another's company. Finally Sheila said it was time for her to head back. Gary said he would fix her windows if he could, but he was no good with a hammer and saw.

"Why don't you reconsider and get Brian. I'll call him for you," Mae said. "He'll have it fixed in no time. Then you won't have anything to worry about."

Sheila was thoughtful for a moment. "You're sure it's okay? You'd never let strangers in your house where I come from."

"Take my word for it," said Mae. "Just leave the key..."

"He seems to know where I should leave the key." Sheila cut her off. Gary didn't need to know as well. "All right. Tell him Thursday is okay. Ask him to get back to me about the bill. Tell him I don't have a phone."

"Can I drive you home, Sheila?"

"No thanks, Gary. I may not get many more days to walk." He seemed so gracious, but still she didn't trust him completely. She wondered what his reaction would be if he saw the little jackknife she had around her neck. She had kept it carefully hidden beneath her shirt.

Mae took her guest to the door, then returned to the living room where Gary and Allie were gathering up the dishes. On the way to the

95

kitchen, Allie glanced at the sideboard. "Mae, I hope you put that little tatted handkerchief away that used to sit on that sideboard. Remember, you promised you'd leave that to me in your will." It was a joke between them who would die first, and who would get what.

"Yes, I do remember. And you can have it now. I just have to launder it and stretch it up," she said.

"I was only kidding, Mae," Allie said.

"No, I mean it. You always loved it. But I could teach you to tat, you know."

"Not me. Haven't got the patience for it."

"I'm going to leave you two ladies. I've got some refinishing to do. The first coat should be dry by now." Westicott closed the door softly on the two ladies. His mind was spinning. He would get that key early in the morning, after Sheila went to work. It was wonderful how sounds carried up through the grate. A lovely place for the key—under the frog. He would make a copy and return the original under the frog. All that could be done before the farmer clod went down to fix the window. Then he'd have a key in his pocket, and could search at his leisure for that jackknife. The very thought excited him. Right now he would go down to the shed where he stored his auction things. He would carefully pack up all the things he needed to bring home and lock in his dresser. There was so much to think about. The tatted handkerchief, the knife, the marionette. His excitement grew. Things were moving fast. He could feel the beat of his own heart in his ears.

Chapter 26

Westicott parked his truck in front of the old shed. He took the key from his pocket, fingering its metal smoothness as he walked toward the door. The heavy padlock accepted the key smoothly, and opened with a snap. Everything looked the same as he had left it. He had stored all his things here in the boxes that he had bought them in at the auctions – everything except the special things he had brought here from before. They were all together in a special locked box, hidden completely by the junk boxes piled neatly along the wall. He would get that secret box today.

At first he had been content to leave everything here. He had made friends with the farmer who owned the shed, and knew he could trust him to keep a sharp eye on the building. But since he had finally got the old dresser with the locks in his room, he had a compelling desire to move these things and put everything in order. He longed to have everything physically close. He was at the stage where he needed to check everything, handle it, count it, play his beautiful solitaire game that left him exhilarated and exhausted.

He smiled to himself. All the Islanders were talking about hunting season. Some had camps at the west end, some had shacks in Tehkummah, some had friends to hunt with at Manitowaning. The hardware stores were full of guns and camouflage suits, compasses and ammunition. It was rather ironic that his hunting season was beginning at the same time. He had only a few more things to find before he could start. About the only thing he shared with the farmer clods was the excitement of the ritual of the prehunt. They were collecting their gear, bragging about their former kills, telling off-colour jokes reserved for the hunt camp. Well, he had some bragging to do himself. His first kills had been pretty satisfying. And how easy they had been. Plan carefully, keep your cool, bide your time, and presto, there goes another one. The only problem was that he couldn't tell anybody how easy it had all been. He went over in his mind how it had all started.

He had been arrested on another drug charge. The cops had come right into his room, slapped the handcuffs on him while he was still in another reality, and unceremoniously ushered him into a cell. He had good reason to hate the cops since he'd endured so much from them when he was behind bars. It was in jail that he nurtured his hatred and contempt for the law. Getting even had possessed him. If they thought the little crime of peddling drugs was bad, just wait. He'd show them. They thought they were so clever with their questions and their power over him. He would make them look as stupid as they were. He would plan the perfect crime. What a satisfaction it would be to read about it in the papers. UNSOLVED CRIMES. POLICE BAFFLED BY CLEVER MURDERER WHO KILLS AND LEAVES NO TRACES. Yes, he'd fool them all. The other slobs in prison continually boasted about what they would do when they got out. Not Westicott. He kept everything to himself. He needed time to plan. Time he had plenty of. And when he got out, he had plenty of money stashed away from his last big deal. Just thinking about it gave him a sense of purpose and inner power.

Having made up his mind, he turned himself into a model prisoner. He kicked his drug habit cold turkey. There were some bad moments, but he did it. He volunteered for counselling, went to chapel, earned the privilege of going to the library, and was even approved to sign up for correspondence courses. He picked English. He had been an eager student as a teenager, but was kicked out of school for doing drugs. That was a lot of years ago. From then on, formal education had been downhill all the way. But he remained a compulsive reader. He read everything in sight – the ads on subways, the cereal boxes, the graffiti on the walls, the signs on the streets. He read all the books he could get his hands on. It didn't matter what kind. He had devoured the classics as readily as the lurid novels he could pick up for a dime at the second-hand store. That was the reason he picked the English course. He might learn something useful to him. Besides that, there was something about the organization of the words on the page that pleased him. Every word was placed there, in an exact spot, orderly and neat. Neatness was becoming his obsession.

Prison was almost as good as living on the outside, except for the company and the food. He was several classes above the other inmates. They were all slobs. They had vocabularies of about fifty words. Westicott, on the other hand, liked the precision of words, and continually added to the dictionary inside his own head. He seldom used these words as it was not smart to draw attention to himself, but secretly he scoffed at the language of the cretins in his row, babbling loudly in their sweat-stenched prison garb. That was one of the reasons he hated meal time. The food was terrible, but the stench and the gibberish of the men on either side of him was worse.

Westicott became meticulous about his own person. The collar of his shirt was always exactly even on his neck, the little seam that joined the ribbing lined up precisely with his left shoulder. His shirttail was folded neatly to tuck inside his pants without revealing a crinkle on the outside. At night, he flattened his trousers beneath his mattress, pressing them for morning. When he put them on, always the left one first, he carefully folded each cuff top a precise inch, patting it around his leg to make sure it was even all around. All these little rituals kept him sane. These were the things he could control.

His mind went back now to how it all began. Actually, it was the English course he had to thank for his perfect plan. Wouldn't that old dame, that 0914, have a bird if she ever knew. She had written him all those encouraging little notes: "You are doing fine." "Your prose is orderly and precise." "I am pleased with your careful choice of words." "Your organization is superb." Of course it was.

The plan started to take shape one day when he was working in the library on an assignment. It was a question to do with the scansion of poetry. It came very easy to him. The rhythm of the lines was so patterned, so regular. He had a little chart that named the rhythms, and it was just a matter of discerning the sound of the syllables. The iambic pentameter of Shakespeare was like a heartbeat, regular and resonant. He felt safe inside its rhythm. Then there were the ocean rolls of the spondees, long, ponderous and slow. For contrast, the lesson provided a child's poem and he was asked to identify the rhythm. He read the poem over and over, until the beat patterned itself in his mind – daa de de daa de de daa de de daa. He checked his chart. Those were the dactyls, bouncy, light-hearted, fast, suitable for a child's poem. This was a new revelation for Westicott. He hadn't realized there was an identifiable beat to poetry.

Westicott got so caught up in the rhythm of the little poem that he found he had memorized the whole twenty-six lines. When he got back to his cell after study hours, the words were still bouncing in his head, as regular as the bars on his window. He was in complete control of the lines that controlled the rhythm. They were his:

A is for angels with feathery wings,

B is for beeswax you rub on a string.

C is for cows chewing barley and malt,

D is for ducks filled with pepper and salt.

E is for eagle's nest, high in the trees,

F is for blue fish that swim in the seas.

G is for ghosts that go bump in the night,

H is for handkerchiefs tatted in white.

I is for ink in an indigo blue,

J is for jackknife in the shape of a shoe.

K is for kiwi, a bird that can't fly,

L is for lorgnette you hold to your eye.

M is for marionette, floppy and old,

99

N is for nugget, a rough lump of gold.

O is for owl, with orange blinking eye,

P is a pilot who flies in the sky.

Q is for quill, what you use when you write,

R is for rabbits with whiskers of white.

S is for spoons with the name of a place,

T is for thimbles for Mae and for Grace.

U is for urn that is used to hold tea,

V is violin strings, E, A, D and G.

W is for winkle, that tingles your palate,

X is a xylophone you play with a mallet.

Y is a yule log you burn Christmas night,

Z is a zebra with stripes black and white.

He smiled to himself. It had taken some time for the whole thing to evolve in his mind. When he forced himself to concentrate on it, nothing seemed to come to him. If he spent too long and became too intense, he became edgy and frustrated. He had to learn to relax, and let the ideas walk around in his mind. Then things began to flow. Maybe he could use this poem somehow. The answer would come.

And it did. He was working on another lesson. It had to do with the symbolic use of numbers. The lesson instructed him to read a number of stories and poems and make a note of the numbers used. Then he was to read all of the book of Genesis, and record all the numbers used there. As he did the exercise, the numbers 3, 7, 12, and 40 appeared again and again. The numbers jumped up at him. He would use these numbers, somehow.

The plan suddenly formulated in his mind. He could use the poem and the numbers. It was crystal clear. He would collect the items mentioned in the poem. When he had collected seven of any of them, he would make his kill. The victim would be the third woman he saw after he collected the seventh one. He would write part of the line from the poem and leave it on the dead body. He would wait forty days before he moved into his next place to get ready for his next kill. He would commit twelve murders. His plan was brilliant.

Then he had to decide where to start. No hurry. Let it come. He went over the poem in his mind. It came like a flash of lightening. "S is for spoons with the name of a place." That was it! It would be easy to collect twelve spoons with the name of a place. He would put these spoons in a bag and draw one out. That would determine the place.

It was perfect. The murders would take place in different locations. There would be no motive for the murder. There was no connection between the articles he would leave on the bodies. The only similarity would be that everybody had an object. If by any chance someone knew the poem, they might make the connection, but that would just make it more interesting. There was no way to connect the poem with him.

He then began to think about how he would collect the items. It would be too simple to go into a store and buy them. Besides that, it would be too easy to trace the purchases. It had taken him several weeks to decide what to do. Some of the things in the poem were old, even antique. He could try pawn shops, but someone might remember him. That wouldn't work. Buy them at auctions. That was it. Perfect idea. Travel around the country, and buy the stuff at small town auctions. Perfect idea. Now he had the basic plan. He had only to polish up the details. He went over the game plan again and again. And it was a game. You pitted your brains against the world, but you didn't shake a die. There was no chance involved, just a precise, clear-cut game plan. When you pass GO, collect $200. Only he didn't need the money. It was power he was after, not money. That was what he wanted. Power to get even for the humiliation he had endured at the hands of the law.

And that was the plan he had followed to the letter when he got out of prison. He had been successful three times. The excitement of that first time came back to him now. He had collected six feathery angels. He reached into his bag with the spoons and drew one. TIMMINS. That was the place. He packed up what he needed and went there. How easy it had all been. He had rented a room on the main street. A streak of luck presented him with one more angel. He watched from his window. The third woman to pass by was his victim. She was quite young. He had no trouble following her. She went straight to the laundromat, just down the street. He had seen her before, so there was no need to hurry. He would get everything ready. He watched the traffic at the laundromat. She was a frequent customer. He waited for the right opportunity. He watched her go in the door, and knew she was alone. No one else had gone in before. He had to hurry. He knew the layout well. He grabbed his bag of laundry and hurried out the door. When he entered the laundromat he didn't see her. That was very good. She would be in the far aisle, loading the machine. She didn't even look up as he approached. She was bending over her basket, sorting out socks. He acted quickly, encircling her neck with the wire he had just for that purpose. Caught off guard and off balance, the woman didn't have a chance. In his mind now, he relived the sight of her fingers loosening, a sock slipping to the floor. He laid her down, ever so gently, placed the feathery angel on her chest, and just beneath, the line from the poem. He turned and walked out, not meeting anyone on the way. He whistled as he walked home, just an ordinary guy taking home his laundry.

The local papers had covered it well. YOUNG WOMAN STRANGLED IN LAUNDROMAT. The front page carried her picture. Quite pretty, he thought. In the haste of the moment, he really hadn't noticed. No clues to the murder. No apparent suspects. No motive known as yet. Westicott had made himself a part of the excited conversation that had taken place in the restaurant. How horrible. What a pretty girl. Imagine, she had two little ones at home. Crime was everywhere these days, even in a little place like Timmins. Surely there should be some clues. The police had better turn up something or we will all be murdered in our beds. Sometimes you wondered how smart the police were. That was his line.

He mailed himself a letter and read it in front of his landlady. His mother was not well, and needed him. He showed just the right amount of concern to arouse her curiosity. Then he told her all about his ailing mother. "Just get there as fast as you can," she said. He thanked her earnestly. He was so thankful to not have to pay the next month's rent. He shook her hand. "There's no better people than the folks in northern Ontario," he said. She could see the tears he had manufactured for his mother. Next morning, he left.

The other two murders had been just as easy. Now he was close to number four. He rather hoped it wouldn't be Mae. She was such a good cook. If it were, he would have to be pretty smart about it. A challenge he would have to face when the time came. It would certainly be easy to kill her, but in a town like Mindemoya, where everybody knew everybody, it would take some planning. Of course, he was a superb actor. He could play the sad tenant, speak of her with tears in his eyes, attend the funeral, buy the flowers. He would stay long enough to be helpful. Leave his room immaculate. Give a big donation to the hospital. Say his good-byes, and take off for mother's.

Everybody warmed to mother. He laughed out loud when he thought about it. Mother was the crowning touch. "Mother" was a small, one-room apartment on Church Street in Toronto. It was a place to go between jobs. His rent came off his bank account as regular as clockwork. He never saw the landlord.

Westicott's busy mind recollected all these moments of past glory as he packed his treasures into three boxes and locked them securely in his truck. He would leave them in the truck until he dealt with the key at Sheila's. One thing at a time. Don't rush. Get the key. Copy it. Return the key. Collect the marionette. Number five. Or leave it where it was, ready to collect at any time. Better idea. Distract Mae from the tatted handkerchief. Number six. Everything was falling into place. He was like God. He had the whole world in his hands. The words of the poem rang like a hymn in his ears.

CHAPTER 27

Sheila built a little teepee of kindling in the fireplace and tucked crumpled balls of paper inside. Then she carefully placed three small logs against each other, making another teepee over the first. Behind all this, she placed two big logs. She touched a match to the paper and little licks of flame crackled the cedar shavings. Jamie had taught her how to do this. She felt a great sense of accomplishment. She could build a fire. Sheila Peters, city slicker, could build a fire.

The flames reached up, licking and blackening the cedar, projecting small missiles of sparks on the hearth. She brushed them back, then placed a screen in front of the open fire. Beside her were two boxes she had brought up from the basement. One of these she had packed in Toronto; the other had been left here by the previous owner.

She reached into the Toronto box. The packing tape was still secure. She was just about to get up to get the scissors to cut it when she remembered the little knife around her neck. Might as well make use of it. She carefully pulled open the blade, and slit the tape. Who else had used this knife, she wondered. She folded the blade and tucked the knife beneath the top button of her shirt. Then she reached for the first little parcel inside. She knew, of course, what it was. She unwrapped it very carefully. Finally, she held a small glass tiger in her hands. It was perfectly crafted. The artist who designed him had somehow got the paint inside the glass, leaving the surface smooth to the touch. She studied him, the light from the fire reflecting life into the tiny creature. She polished him with a cloth until he shone. To make sure he was safe, she placed him on the mantle before she reached for the next one. Soon she had twelve little animals, perfectly matched, lined up on the stone mantle. They looked fine there, but would there be a better place? Maybe the small coffee table with the glass top would be better. If she placed it by the west window the sun would reflect in the glass as the fire had, making them look alive. She moved the table, shining the glass top until it shone, and then arranged the glass animals – the tiger, the elephant and her baby, the giraffe, the lion, the zebra, the gazelle, the wildebeest, the cheetah, the monkey, and the hyena. Her own glass menagerie.

Strange how one got attached to things. She had taken them everywhere they moved. Jim said she spent more time polishing them than looking after him. At first it was a joke, and they had laughed about it. When things started going wrong, it wasn't so funny. "How can you spend so much time with those animals when the sink is full of dishes and the floor hasn't been swept for a week?"

Probably at this distance in time and space she could answer that question now. All her working life she had forced an outward calm as she dealt with accident victims and the general turbulence of the 'emerge'. At first, coming home had helped unravel the nervous tensions of the night shift. Then the constant bickering with Jim had held the nerve wires taut. She found a kind of peace polishing each little animal, feeling the softness of the glass. The animals were her worry stones. Rubbing them seemed to wipe away the tensions of the day, restoring a semblance of calmness to her soul. Short lived, though. Jim's parting shot had been delivered crisp and cuttingly as she held the zebra in her hand. "Take your glass menagerie to hell for all I care. This is one gentleman caller who won't be back." And he slammed the door. Of course, he did come back. And he had never mentioned the glass menagerie again. She had carefully wrapped each piece and stored them all away. He had never said "Where did it go?" and she never offered any explanation. He had never put anything on the empty shelf. Nor had she. The empty space spoke volumes. Now, for the first time in three years, the animals were free. And so, she thought, was she.

Sheila reached into the other box. It held books and sheet music. What would she do with all this stuff? Maybe some of it was valuable. It was certainly old. She began to sort through the books. A blue hard copy of ANNE OF GREEN GABLES. A name inside. Marion, 1940. As she leafed through the pages she remembered parts of the story. Gilbert and Anne. She had read that book when she was about twelve. How romantic it seemed to her. And here was another one: KILMENY OF THE ORCHARD. The girl who couldn't talk. She had read that one, too. Where had all her old books gone? Likely sold at yard sales when they were getting ready to move. "Get rid of the junk," her mother had said. "We're traveling light." And Sheila had done just that. Only the animals came with her. They had been a gift from her grandmother. Her mother had never minded the animals. It was the last present grandmother had bought before the major stroke that took her life within a few short weeks. Sheila had taken the animals once to the hospital, showing them to her, one at a time. And even though everyone thought Grandma was beyond human comprehension, Sheila was sure there was recognition in her eyes. And once, when she held up the little zebra, she was sure she caught a glimmer of a smile. Shortly after that, her grandmother had died.

Sheila felt a kind of tranquility as she thought about these things. For so long she had welled up the memories of the past. Now the flood gates were opening up, spilling over her. And it was good. She could handle it now. She felt the tears wetting her cheeks. It was her right to cry if she wanted to. She made no attempt to wipe away her tears. I'll cry if I want to, she thought.

She reached into the box again, and pulled out an old sheet of music. On the tattered cover was a figure in silhouette, leading a battalion of men, swords brandished high. The title read: JOAN OF ARC, THEY ARE CALLING YOU. Words by Alfred Bryon and Willie Weston. Music by Jack Wells. Copyright 1917. Never heard of it. YOU'RE A GRAND OLD FLAG. No date. A lovely scene on the cover. A grand piano on a huge rock by a river. The next one, DEEP IN THE HEART OF TEXAS, a picture of Guy Lombardo on the front. Copyright 1941. What would she do with all this music? Have a yard sale? Never. She'd find a place for them. It was a link to the past – somebody's past – and she felt it was important to keep it. Someday she would ask Mae about it. For sure, she would know these songs. Mae had all those records she was going to hear some day. She could give Mae the sheet music.

In the bottom of the box were some children's books. She had never heard these titles, either. She pulled one out, settled herself comfortably, and started to turn the pages. It was an old alphabet book. The pictures were wonderful.

A is for angels with feathery wings,

B is for beeswax you rub on a string,

C is for cows chewing barley and malt,

D is for ducks filled with pepper and salt.

E is for eagle's nest high in the trees,

F is for blue fish that swim in the seas.

G is for ghosts that go bump in the night,

H is for handkerchiefs...

The fire was so warm, Sheila could hardly keep her eyes open. She snuggled back into the big chair, and went to sleep.

CHAPTER 28

Brian put the pail of milk on the kitchen counter, found the strainer, scalded it with boiling water, and placed it on the large opening of the four gallon crock. He poured warm milk into it slowly, to keep the foam from overflowing its sides. The moist aroma of fresh milk filled the kitchen.

Brian had no need for all the milk his cow produced. She was a Jersey he had bought from a dairy farm outside Toronto. She was slighter than his beef cows and had more character. At least, he found himself talking to her as if she were a farmhand instead of a cow. Daisy seemed to respond to this familiarity by yielding a pail morning and night.

Government regulations prevented Brian from selling milk, but not from giving it away. He knew two families whose yards were overflowing with children who drank it up, no trouble at all. For all Brian's outward gruffness, those who knew him well understood the pleasure he got from seeing the little kids running to meet his truck which arrived as regular as clockwork, right after the school bus delivered the kids home at 3:45 on the dot. Once in awhile he stopped to pass the time of day with one of the parents. Other times he just watched the kids deliver the two bottles to the door, and drove off. He didn't need any more thanks than a child's smile. That was the one regret he had about the whole thing with Carol. Maybe, if things had been different, they might be married now and have children of their own. He forced this thought from his mind.

This morning he had things to do. He had promised to look at the window damage of Sheila Peter's house. He looked forward to it. He always enjoyed the Trail around the lake and hadn't been down there for some time – not at all since Jamie left. He put the milk in the cellar, and grabbed his measuring tape and pencil. In no time the old pickup was heading for the lake.

When he got to the bridge he pulled over to have a look up the river. At one time he had been a trapper, but he didn't do that anymore. Since he'd come back to the farm he'd spent a lot of time reading, thinking things through, being more deliberate about living his life. The slower pace had made him more observant, more respectful of animals. Now he wondered how he could have trapped them at all. He had never been consciously cruel, just unknowing. Now he saw each animal making its way in the world just as he was. Not giving any trouble, just making his way. Right now a beaver was manoeuvring a huge branch down the river. He leaned on the railing, watching this little creature managing something forty times its size, and with apparent ease at that.

The river was quiet this morning in spite of the wind on the lake. He looked down into the water directly below him. River reeds and water cress provided slight obstructions for the gentle current. The flow of water parted, curved and closed as if to give the plant-life right of way on the water highway. Brian heard a vehicle approaching and looked up to see a green truck coming from the direction he was headed. He recognized it as the one that belonged to the man who boarded at Mae's. He had seen him several times, first at auctions, and later at some community activities. He seemed to be well liked by the townspeople, but Brian didn't take easily to strangers. Not that he was anti-social or unfriendly. Some people called it the Island attitude – if you were going to live here, you'd better earn your keep. Maybe he had, for all Brian knew.

The truck passed him, but the driver didn't wave, or acknowledge him in any way – probably he hadn't seen him, partly hidden by his own parked truck. Much and all as it was pretty nice just watching the river, he realized he did have a job to do, and once again made his way around the Trail. As he passed Jamie's cottage, he thought he'd better stop on the way back just to make sure everything was all right there. A few years ago you never had to worry about locking things up, but the world was a little different now, even here on the Island.

He turned left up the hill, and pulled into Sheila's driveway. He had been here many times, especially when he was younger and his folks were alive. Jean, the lady who had owned the house, often invited scads of people to her house to play music, or rook, often both the same night. His dad played the violin, and his mother chorded on the piano. Kids were always invited too. Jean always had time for them, showing them things she had collected, setting them up with games of their own. Brian knew that he was always welcome here. Jean had listened to him and treated him as an adult. She was an old lady when Brian returned from the city but she was always young at heart. He had visited her quite often, and had done some carpentry work for her. In her late eighties she was still going strong, and told him to come on in whether she was here or not, and do what fixing there was to do. The key was under the frog.

Brian tapped the frog now with his toe, pushing him enough to see the key under his belly. He stooped to pick it up. It slipped effortlessly into the lock. He turned the knob and walked in.

A wave of memory caught him by surprise. He could almost see Jean, standing by the stove with bread in her hand. She was tapping the top with her fingers, testing to see if it were done through. He walked past the memory into the front porch. He knew at a glance what the problem was. The wind, or the rain – or a combination of both – had loosened a corner of the frame. It was obvious that water had seeped through, leaving brown drip trails in the plywood. He would have to take the window out to do the job properly. Then he really should try to match the colour and stain the wood.

His eyes lifted to take in the view in front of him. It was breath-takingly beautiful. The island was sitting there stoutly, like a castle surrounded by a moat. There was always something mysterious about this island. Probably because it was out of reach of the passing viewer. Once Brian had gone to the Queen Charlotte Islands and had been taken to see the legendary golden pine. It had the same mysterious-ness about it. It was only a huge pine tree with yellow needles, but it shone in the sunlight like a gold pin on the lapel of the forest. What made it mysterious was its inaccessibility. You couldn't walk there to actually touch it and be sure it was real. And out there in the lake, was an island, a piece of land surrounded by water, but you couldn't walk there. There was all that trouble about getting a boat, and you just didn't bother. And so it remained mysterious.

Probably he knew more about it than most. Jean had told him lots of stories about her life over there. He hardly remembered Joe, but she spoke of him often. At one time, Joe and his dad had been great buddies. Often, around the supper table, his parents filled the com-fortable spaces with tales Joe had told them in his inimitably funny way. He smiled, listening in his mind to his father's voice:

"You know, everything Joe took to the island he had to take by boat. But how do you fit a cow in a boat, or a horse? Joe had a flair for invention. He fastened two boats together and made a floor over them. He called it the Mayflower. On the floor, he built a stall. He simply tied the cow to the stall, and propelled the craft with an outboard motor. One day Joe was taking a cow and a crate of thirty dozen eggs. Every-thing was going fine. He was almost on shore when the cow saw its reflection in the calm water. She yanked the rope, slipped on the boards, and pushed the thirty dozen eggs overboard." Brian's dad mimicked Joe's voice: "The dashed eggs were all over the lake. But I had to get that cow ashore before she broke a leg. Gall darn cow, cantankerous as a rattlesnake and just as deadly."

There were lots of other stories. He hadn't thought about them in years, but being in this house had brought them back. That egg story reminded him of another. Brian and his dad had been fishing. Brian pulled in a whitefish. He didn't know what kind it was, and he asked his dad.

"It's a whitefish, Brian. You know our friend, Joe, from the island? It's a long time ago now, but he found a whitefish hole where you could catch them by the boatload. I'm not sure whether he found the hole, or whether it was one of the other old guides – there was lots of bragging going on. Anyway, Joe got the idea if there was one hole, there should be more. So he and a tourist buddy anchored on the hole. The fish were really biting. Every time they caught a fish, they carefully fastened a long fishing line to its lip, and tied a balloon to the other end of the line. They thought all they had to do was follow the balloon to another hole. In no time at all, balloons were careening all over the lake. Seems the fish were only interested in getting loose, not retreating to a new hole. Eventually, the fish, exhausted, came to the top. Joe and his buddy hauled them in and removed the lines and took them home for supper. As Joe said, "That was one episode that was a gosh darn failure. But we had a good feed, all the same.""

Brian smiled to himself. Then a little sadness came over him. Jean had built her house here, after Joe died, on a hill overlooking their lifetime. She intuitively knew what his old buddy, the philosopher, had taken so long to find out: Nobody owns the landscape. The island had passed through several buyers' hands, but it was always Jean's.

Brian usually refused the luxury of reminiscence. Whatever had come over him today? The minute he had opened that door, he was caught off guard. Now, to get down to business. He measured up for the materials he would need. Then he scribbled a note to Sheila Peters. "There's quite a bit of work to be done on the window. I've taken note of what I'll need. I'll pick it up next week. I'll drop down as soon as I can and fix everything up."

After he left, he realized he hadn't taken note of Sheila's presence in the house. He had no idea what it looked like now, and he had been in there almost an hour. Had she changed things around much? Caught up in the ghosts of the past, he couldn't remember a thing.

Chapter 29

It was music night at the island. Everyone looked forward to this night, but none more than Jean. To her, a group of friends gathered around playing music was the height of happiness. She had baked bread in the morning and made sure there were lots of cakes and cookies to serve at the end of the evening. All the tourists would come up from their cottages to hear the music and she wanted to have lots for all. Everyone raved about her cooking.

The orchestra was arriving. Joe would be making several trips getting them all here. He couldn't play a note himself but he was proud of his kids who played in the orchestra, and he was always glad to see Jean so happy. She just glowed when she played that fiddle! It would be a good evening, and he knew his guests would love it. They always did.

There was the usual tuning up. Alburtta would take charge. She was Jean's cousin, and everyone in the orchestra respected her because she had her ATCM in music. Most of the others played by ear. But that didn't make their music any less sweet. Alburtta would listen to each one. "Let me hear you're A, Jean. That's good. Sound your D, Burton. Is your E too high, Cliff? Marion, give Cliff an E on the accordion. I guess you girls on the autoharps are okay. Play your C chord, Viva. Make sure the guitars are in the front row so you can be heard. Now, is everybody ready? Lorene, hand me my purse. I need my list. Thanks. We'll be starting with Raggedy Ann in the key of G."

The music began. Toe-tapping tunes carried on the still air to the cottages, and the guests, anxious to be a part of this occasion, rushed up to the lodge. Everyone joined in the singing of the old favourites – Let Me Call You Sweetheart, Daisy, Daisy, School Days, I'll Take You Home Again, Kathleen. When the fiddlers played The Kagawong Swamp and Road To The Isles, a few brave guests pushed back their chairs to make room for the dancers. Alburtta whispered to Jean, "Surely they aren't going to dance. I don't approve of dancing."

"They are enjoying the music so much, Alburtta. Why don't I tell them to form two lines for The Virginia Reel? That's more like a game than a dance."

"I guess that is different than a real dance. And it's not as if we're in a dance hall."

Jean made the announcement. "We're going to play for a Virginia Reel. Get yourself a partner and form two long lines down the centre of the room. Ross will call and walk you through the dos si dos, and à la main lefts. The first couple starts off with a forward and back."

In no time two long lines were formed and the music began. The orchestra played the Chicken Reel and Marching Through Georgia until their fingers wouldn't move anymore. The tourists loved it. Most of them got lost halfway through in spite of help from the sidelines. After the dance was finished, they flopped into the big easy chairs exhausted. Everyone joined in the laughter.

It was time for a change of pace. Joe's little daughter, snuggled up on his knee, was watching the party. This little one was the unexpected later child, doted on by all the family. What a little blessing she was! Her big blue eyes won over everyone. And besides all this, the kid had talent. From the time she was three, she could pick out several tunes on the piano by ear, with no help from anybody.

Her mother said, "While you're resting up, we'll get Joanne to play a tune for us on the piano. Come along, dear, and play a tune for the people." Joanne crawled slowly from her dad's lap, but instead of going to her mother, she walked over to her Aunt Mary who was her "nanny" during the busy summer months. Aunt Mary whispered in her ear. Then her mum said again, "Hurry, Joanne. Play Buttons and Bows. That's a good one."

After a little more conversation with Aunt Mary, Joanne went to the piano. She climbed up on the big bench of the old Steinway, and without a second's hesitation, rattled through Buttons and Bows, verse and chorus. Everybody clapped. She got down from the bench and walked toward her dad who was bursting with pride at this little wonder.

The guests all pleaded, "Play us another one, please!"

She scrambled from her dad's knee and went back to Aunt Mary. They had a little chat. Then she went to the bench again and rattled off a few more tunes. They all marvelled at her music ability.

Soon a sumptuous lunch arrived. The homemade bread was made into salmon sandwiches – a favourite, and a meal in itself. There was scads of food, all you could eat and drink. The orchestra played a few more parting songs, ending as they always did with Now Is The Hour and Amazing Grace. It was another music night to remember.

After it was all over, Jean and Joe were tucking in the little one. "You played very well, tonight. But you mustn't have to be coaxed to play. When I tell you, I expect you to jump up on the seat and play."

"I don't like to play right away."

"Why not?" said her dad.

"Because if I don't go right away, Aunt Mary will give me a quarter to play. Look," she said. She opened her tiny fist to reveal two hot quarters.

"You little monkey! Don't let me catch you asking for money to play the piano! You just go and do it," said her Mum.

Her dad grinned. "Give me the money, dear, and I'll put it in your piggy bank." He gave her a wink. "Do what old mum says now, and go to sleep."

She gave him a big smile, and snuggled under the covers. "Pretty smart kid you got there," he whispered to Jean. "Got her Mum's knack for business!" They smiled at each other and turned out the light.

CHAPTER 30

Leaving her key to a stranger worried Sheila all day at work. What if this Brian was not the kind of person Mae thought he was? Surely she could trust Mae's testimonial to Brian's honesty, and the window certainly did need to be fixed, but the whole idea bothered her. She wished she had obeyed her first impulse and just said 'no'. Next time she would not be influenced by other people.

As soon as her shift ended, she was out the door. She knew she needed a few groceries, but instead of stopping at the corner store as she usually did, she drove straight home. She parked the car and walked directly to the frog. There was the key, exactly as she'd left it. She breathed a sigh of relief. City nerves in a safe country space. She had to learn to trust people more.

She let herself in and hung up her coat. Then she went straight to her porch. No sign of anyone having been here. Just as she'd thought. The town's favourite carpenter hadn't bothered to come. She'd given him a chance. Now she would find someone else. She flipped on the stereo and went to the kitchen. A coffee before dinner would calm her down. She had been so on edge all day, and needed to relax. As she reached for the jar of instant, she saw the note by the sink. It was like an intrusion into her private life. He had been here, and there was no trace of his being here except for this note. She read it. Nervy. He didn't say what he had to do. There was no mention of cost. She'd had enough of men making all the decisions without even consulting her. Whose house was this, anyway? And what all was he going to fix? The wall? The window? If that phone were in she'd call this minute and give him a piece of her mind. Did he expect her to leave the key available to the whole world while he took his time deciding what he was going to do and when?

She stabbed the kettle plug into the socket and spooned out the coffee, spilling some on the counter. Before the water had a chance to boil, she poured it into her cup. The very thought of this man threw her off. Or was it all men? She could almost feel Jim's presence, hear his voice undermining her confidence again, just when she'd thought she was over all that. She swallowed a lukewarm gulp of coffee. It was awful. She threw the rest down the sink.

113

Why hadn't they connected her phone, anyway? She would go back to that office and insist on some action. They had said 'soon' and that had been weeks ago. When was 'soon' on this Island? "We'll get your phone connected 'soon.'" "I'll drop down as soon as I can."

She would calm down and decide what to do. Maybe she was making a mountain out of a mole-hill. After all, the place was the same as she'd left it. Nothing had changed. The counselor had told her she wouldn't get over the emotional trauma of her marriage in a minute. There would be times when she might get emotional without apparent reason. That's what she'd said. Maybe this was one of the times.

She walked into the living room, pausing at the fireplace. The sun was shimmering through the west window, dancing on the little animals on her table. She was drawn to them immediately. In the sunlight, a dust speck crash landed on the elephant. She picked him up, rubbing him gently on her shirt. She suddenly felt calmer. Her animals still had their magical effect.

She glanced at the clock. There was time to get to the telephone office before it closed. And she needed milk. Maybe a simple TV dinner for supper. She would drop into Mae's and show her the note Brian had left. Maybe she was overreacting. She would get Mae's reaction. All these thoughts flew through her head as she grabbed her coat and purse and rushed out the door.

First stop. Telephone office. A girl sat behind the desk, working at a computer. She looked up as Sheila entered the door. "Can I help you?" she said.

"My name is Sheila Peters. I live on the subdivision by the lake. I've been waiting to have my phone connected. Can you tell me what the holdup is?"

"There's been some trouble on the line down there. But I'm surprised our service man hasn't been down to see you. I thought he had contacted all our customers."

"I work all week. Maybe he missed me. Tell him to come tomorrow after four."

"I won't be able to do that. He's booked off for deer season."

"But I didn't think that started until Monday."

"That's right. But everybody around here goes to camp early. The men do more getting ready than anything else. My husband has his hunting gear all over the kitchen. He's off in the morning."

"Does everybody on this Island close down for hunting season?"

"Pretty well. Some of the stores close. Most of the men own their own businesses and depend on their wives to look after things until they get back." She smiled.

"What is this fixation with hunting, anyway? Surely the world doesn't stop for hunting."

"It pretty well does. I'm just glad when it's all over and everybody's home safe."

"And how long does this last?"

"All next week. Until Sunday. Then, of course, there's the camp to clean up. Any excuse to stay in the bush another day." She smiled at Sheila. "I'll write your name here on the top of the list for Al. I'll see you get connected as soon as he gets back."

"Thanks. Thanks a lot." Sheila went out into the empty street. Where else in the world would you have to wait to get a phone connected? She dropped into the store, picked up a few groceries, and drove to Mae's. The door opened before she got there.

"Sheila! I'm so glad you dropped in. I've been thinking about you."

"I can only stay a minute, Mae."

"Sit down dear. I'm getting supper. Surely you'll stay. I always make too much for just Gary and me."

"Oh no, Mae. I must get home. I just wanted to show you something. Your friend, Brian, came to my house today. This is the note he left me."

Mae took the note and read it. "That's great! He'll fix it up for you as good as new."

"But Mae, I have no idea what he is going to do. Or how much it will cost. It is my house. I think I should make the decisions."

"He'd never overcharge you. He fixed my roof this spring and never charged a cent."

"But he's your friend Mae. I'm a stranger. I don't think he likes strangers."

"Now don't you worry. I'll call him. I know you haven't got your phone hooked up yet."

"And that's another thing. What is it with this place that everyone takes off for hunting, goes two or three days early, and stays later."

"Lots of people depend on venison in their freezers for winter. I don't mind people going hunting as long as they don't waste the meat. The men work hard in tourist season, and this is their time to relax."

"I guess I'll just have to get used to it. In the city, you can depend on services if you have the money. Here, money doesn't seem to matter."

"It matters more than you think to a lot of people. But this is an Island tradition. The dads even take their boys out of school for a day or two during season. Everything will be back to normal in a week."

115

"You always take things in your stride, Mae. I wish I could be more like you."

At this moment, steps sounded on the stairs, and Westicott appeared. "Hello, Sheila."

"I've just invited Sheila to stay for supper, Gary."

"That's great. Mae, I should have told you, I can't stay for supper tonight. I'm sorry. But if Sheila stays I won't feel so bad. Maxie sent word to me that he has a great auction coming up and asked me to meet him at West Bay for supper. I was just on my way."

Mae hid her disappointment. She would never get these two together. "You'll have to stay now, Sheila. I have a big dish of scalloped potatoes. And ham in the oven."

"I apologize again, Mae. Supper smells so good. This lady's a great cook, Sheila."

"I know. I'm tempted. I'll be happy to stay, Mae."

"I'll play my old victrola for you. I tried it the other day, and it works as good as new. Remember the records you looked at that afternoon?"

"I'd love to hear them. Let me help you set the table."

Gary was putting on his jacket. "You two have a great time. I'll be back about nine. If you're still here, Sheila, maybe we could have a coffee and sample one of Mae's biscuits. That is, if you both don't eat them all for supper."

"I'll keep some for you. And I'll keep Sheila, too. When you come back, we'll have a great visit."

"Seems as if everyone around here makes up my mind. All right. But I have to plan to be home by ten. My shift starts at seven, and I have to get my sleep. I can't slack off, even in hunting season." She smiled at her own joke.

"Then it's a date, ladies." Gary let himself out and closed the door. He felt for the shiny new key in his pocket. A perfect opportunity had presented itself. He would have lots of time to try out his new key in the door. He would find that knife and no one would be the wiser. He had seen the box she had got at the auction in the basement when he and Jamie had taken the chairs downstairs the night of the party. The traps were clearly visible. The knife would be in there with them. Number seven. His head began to pound with the excitement.

CHAPTER 31

As Gary drove towards Sheila's, he thanked his lucky stars for old houses. As he listened to the voices coming up through the grate, he was able to formulate his plan, and enter the conversation at just the right time. The date with Maxie had been an inspiration. They swallowed it without question. And asking Sheila to stay for coffee was another. She had committed herself until ten. Still, he would come back earlier than that. He was on a roll, and he wasn't going to mess anything up now that he was getting so close. He prided himself in his remarkable ability to control his emotions. That's where other people went wrong. They got careless and out of control. He could take time to reason things out carefully, leaving no trail.

Sheila would be at Mae's until at least nine, even if she didn't wait for him to come back. He would park his truck in some visible place and walk to Sheila's. He would simply let himself in, hunt for the knife, and return by nine. He would make an organized search, starting in the basement. If anybody should come by, or if Sheila should return for some unknown reason, he could leave unnoticed by the basement door. He could hide in the tall elder bushes that grew in profusion below her house, and make his way to the road with no problem. He would leave his truck at the bridge where the town had built a little parking spot to draw water. He had often parked there before, looking at the wildlife that frequented the river. If anyone saw him there, it would be fine. He was often there. Oh, it was almost too easy!

He began to execute his plan. He parked by the river, reaching across to get his binoculars from the glove compartment. He got out and leaned over the railing. A car passed, and he made himself visible, peering down into the water with his glasses. A second car passed. Again, he concentrated on the river bottom, leaning down over the railing.

It was almost five-thirty, still quite bright for a fall late afternoon. He molded the leather of his jacket around him, zipped up the front, and carelessly slouched his hands into his pockets. He was the picture of a nature nut, he thought, his glasses hanging by their long leather thongs around his neck. He walked down the side of the road. He was close to the golf course when he heard the voices. Likely a pair of walk-

117

ers. Everybody walked this trail and that was precisely what he was doing, walking the trail. Nothing suspect there.

As he turned the corner he saw them, two women, brightly dressed, both of whom he recognized from the town. They stopped chatting and one called out, "A great day for a walk, Mr. Westicott."

"It truly is. There was a wonderful family of ducks at the bridge. I got a great look at them up the river with my glasses and then they swam right to me. If you hurry, they may still be there."

"Oh. I thought the ducks were long gone."

"Not these. Better tell them winter's coming," he replied. Were the ducks gone now? He didn't think so. Even small lies were dangerous. Well, it was too late now. And it wasn't all that significant, anyway. All the same, he'd better keep a close watch over his tongue.

The women smiled in passing. Gary walked on, sometimes close to the water, just to make sure that anyone who might see him would think he was looking for birds, or whatever else people look for. He passed the cottages and turned left up the little hill towards Sheila's place. There were no cars at the closest neighbours, and no people evident. But somebody might be behind one of those curtained windows, and he was not going to take any chances. He walked right by Sheila's house, and stopped at the far end of the lot beyond Sheila's. He took the binoculars and scanned the sky. Then he focused on the government dock, presumably checking out the seagulls. At least, they were still around. He walked down the vacant lot to the edge of the hill, still looking through his glasses. Once over the hill, he darted into the elder bushes and disappeared.

Shortly after, anyone looking out a front window would see a lone woman walking along the road by the water. She turned up the hill, her short steps carrying her quickly to the top. When she approached Sheila's, she turned in, and walked straight to the door. In a moment she turned the key and walked in.

Gary smiled. He hadn't worn this skirt since the last time at the Soo. It was a soft, filmy thing, easily carried inside his jacket. All he had to do was turn his jacket inside out, revealing a lovely blue lining, slip on the skirt, roll up his pant legs, pull up his socks, and presto, he was a lady! The finishing touch was a French beret. He wore it saucily, almost covering one eye. Before he opened the door to the basement, he carefully folded his skirt, and stashed it into the beret. Then he turned his jacket. If he had to retreat quickly, he didn't need the added encumbrance of a long skirt.

It was still quite light in the basement. This house had scads of windows. He could work well and not use a flashlight. He saw the trap box, exactly where he remembered it. He carried it to the window. He rattled through the contents. Rusty old traps, some wrapped with bits of cloth, a few pieces of rusty iron scrap pieces, but nothing else. He lifted each trap out, looking closely at each one. Nothing caught or hidden anywhere. Where was that knife? He recognized his own beginning signs of panic. Calm down, he said to himself. Put the traps away. Just as they were. Pick another box.

He glanced around the room. When he and Jamie were here before, in late summer, there had been a lot of boxes. Now there were only a few. Most were full of books. He reached inside one, rubbing his fingers along the bottom of the heap of books. Dust and grit. He wiped his hands on his pants. Nothing there. Just an old jar of buttons.

Think. What would she do with the knife? She had moved it somewhere. He could imagine her looking at it. A little shoe. Likely she didn't even know it was a knife. Where would she put it? He went upstairs. Lots of time, he thought. There were windows all around the house. From his position at the top of the stairs he could see all around. Not a soul. He walked into the kitchen. He pulled out several drawers, checking each carefully. Some utensils. Tea towels. Garbage bags. Silverware. Nothing that even resembled what he was looking for.

Now the dining room. Little glass cupboards lined the wall. A few glasses and a pitcher in one. Nothing in the other. He turned to the fireplace. A perfect place for nickknacks on the mantle. There was a clock, a vase of artificial flowers, a small round tin. He opened it. Matches.

He glanced around the living room – a chair, a chesterfield, two easy chairs, an end table, a desk and chair, a glass-topped coffee table with ornaments. The desk first. He whipped open a drawer – paper, pens, paperclips. Nothing else. The book shelf above. A few old books, musty and smelly, in a pile. The coffee table. Only ornaments. Only ornaments? His eyes fixed on the glass zebra. A beautiful specimen. He picked it up and stared into its eyes. Number six! He carefully put him in his shirt pocket. His heart thumping loudly, echoed in his ears. Settle down, he told himself. One thousand, two thousand...

It was getting too dark to search thoroughly. No worry. He had a key. There would be lots of opportunities. There were still rooms he hadn't looked in. And he had the zebra. That was an unexpected bonus.

He would go back now, down the cellar and out the basement door, through the elder bushes, back to the road. If anyone saw him, it was just Gary, returning from his walk, having checked out the birds and the beaver – and the ducks who missed the last flight out. Now he would go back and spend a delightful evening with the girls, pigging out on Mae's biscuits.

It was on the way home that he saw the smoke, huge billows of blackness silhouetted in orange flames. The whole village was there.

He parked his truck at the end of the line and got out. Two fire trucks had drawn up close to the house. Men were manning the hoses, pouring water into the blackened windows while flames licked ravenously in and out the crevices of the walls. A circle of people had gathered around a family, clinging together in disbelief. Two children watched, wide-eyed and frightened. Westicott recognized the man, Fred. He'd met him at a Lion's Club meeting. He watched him now, ghost- white and staring at the fire.

Westicott joined a group of bystanders. "I just pulled in. What happened?"

"Nobody knows for sure. Just started all of a sudden. Likely a chimney fire."

"Anybody inside?"

"No. They all got out. They wouldn't have though, if it hadn't been for the neighbours. They saw the smoke along the eaves. The family didn't know a thing about it."

"Lucky to have neighbours."

"Yep. Not much happens around here that people don't notice."

"Take a long time for the fire trucks to get here?"

"Not too long. Somehow they couldn't get hooked up to the new water system and had to get water from the river. Some guy had parked his truck at the bridge. Made it tough to get the water. Kept them late."

Westicott didn't respond. Of course, the fact that it was his truck would be all around town.

"Hey, Gary. Give us a hand here." One of the firemen passed him an axe. "We've got to hack through here to get water between the floors. All the other guys are working at the back."

Gary took the axe. It would be good to be seen helping in such a visible way. "Sure," he said, and started chopping away at the wall. In a matter of minutes they were through and a cloud of trapped smoke belched through the hole covering Westicott with black soot. He fell to the ground. The fireman grabbed him, dragging him to an open space.

"Everybody back!" he shouted. "Make room, here."

Westicott gasped for breath.

"You gotta chop and run man, not stand around and fill your lungs with smoke. You'll be all right in a minute. Hey, Brian, look after this guy, will you?"

It was Brian Peterson. He put his big arms around Gary and practically lifted him to a cool place away from the house. "Just sit here quiet for a few minutes. Take some deep breaths and get some fresh air into your lungs. If it gets worse, I'll run you down to the hospital."

Westicott was struggling to get his breath. A small crowd soon gathered around him. "That's what you get for trying to be a hero," one man joked.

"Yeah. I'm okay. I just need a few minutes to catch my breath," Gary responded.

It took a long time for the fire to die down. Coffee and sandwiches appeared everywhere. There was enough for the whole town and it was still coming. Finally, clumps of people were beginning to disappear. Westicott was feeling better. He got up a bit shakily and headed for the truck.

"Sure you don't need a hand?" called someone from the sidelines.

"I'm fine. Thanks. Just need to get home." He waved to indicate he was going to manage to make it on his own. He got in his truck and drove to Mae's.

Chapter 32

Mae and Sheila were just finishing supper when a puff of rancid smoke curled into the partly open window. "Whatever is that?" Mae said, and rushed to the door. "Sheila, there's a fire!" Some people were rushing down the street. Mae called out, "What's on fire?"

"We think it's Fred's house. The family is okay as far as we know. It's just the house, but they say it's a goner."

Mae rushed in to tell Sheila. "There hasn't been a fire in town for years. At least now we have lots of water. I wonder what happened."

"What house is it?"

"Fred Whitely's house. They live down by the hospital. They just built it a few years ago. Fred works down at the garage. You may have seen him there." Mae immediately began to bustle about the kitchen. "I'll be no help down there. I'll just throw up some biscuits." She had flour in the bowl before Sheila had a chance to clear the table.

"Where will you take the biscuits?"

"To the church. That's likely where everyone will gather. Or maybe the hall. You'll be surprised how soon help will pour in. Folks become family when disaster strikes."

"Where I came from, no one would think of getting involved like this."

"Well, this isn't the city."

"Mae, I'm going home now. I'll go the other way in case the road's blocked. Will you have a way to get your biscuits up to the church?"

"Oh yes. I'll call Allie."

Sheila drove around the five mile block, avoiding the fire scene. At least there were no victims. She'd hear all about it in the morning at work. The drama of a small town.

She unlocked the door, thankful for her retreat. Yes, that was the way she had come to think of it – her retreat. A place of calm in the storm. It wasn't really a large house, but all the windows gave it such an air of spaciousness. She could be snug and warm within its walls and still explore with her mind the wide expanse of nature's backyard outside her windows. It was too dark to enjoy right now, but she had memorized every inch of it. This place was her small miracle – if one believed in miracles.

She gathered some kindling and started a fire. She was getting very good at this, she thought. The crackle of the kindling and the little licks of flame responded to her careful arrangement of cedar and paper. Jamie would be proud of her.

As she bustled about with her ordinary get-ready-for-morning tasks, she suddenly remembered she hadn't finalized anything with Mae about Brian. The excitement of the fire had erased her own problems temporarily. Well, she'd made up her mind about that. No more Mr. Brian fix-it. In the morning she'd talk to some of her friends at coffee break. They'd help her find a carpenter – somebody's brother or somebody's husband would be needing a job.

She thought about the people she worked with. Most of them were local, or at least from a neighbouring town. They were all bugging her to sign up for curling. Maybe she would try it. It would be a good way to meet people. But she'd certainly need lessons. Somebody had told her the rocks weighed forty pounds. Some idea of fun, throwing forty pound rocks down the ice.

She walked over to her animals. "Well, my little ones, if I'm going to be an Islander, I have to start somewhere. It's either hunting or curling." She picked the baby elephant and rubbed him against her sweater. "There you are, shiny and clean as a whip." She'd heard that expression at the hospital. Whatever it meant. Even the Island lingo was settling in.

Her eyes took in the whole family of animals. Something was missing. One, two, three...eleven. Which one? The zebra! She couldn't believe it. Where was he? Not on the floor. Not anywhere. A cold chill came over her. She hadn't moved it – or left it on the mantle. Where had it gone? No one had been...Brian! Brian had been here. The note. The missing zebra. What kind of game was this? A cold fury seized her. She grabbed her keys and made for the door. She passed the burning ruins, not even casting a glance towards the groups of people still gathered at the site. Five minutes and she was turning down Brian's lane.

She screeched her brakes to a sharp stop. She slammed her car door shut. Her sharp heels clicked over the wooden floored porch. She knocked loudly on the door. No answer. She pounded again.

"Hey," he said, "Sorry," opening the door as he spoke. "I was just getting some of the smoke off me, and didn't realize anyone was here."

"How could you? How could you have the unmitigated effrontery to come into my house when I trusted you, and take my zebra?" She marched into his kitchen.

"Just a minute. I didn't know you had a zebra in..."

She stepped towards him. "Don't play games with me. I trusted you with the keys to my house. You leave a rude note on my counter, giving me no information at all. You take over everything as if it were yours. And you stole my zebra. My grandmother gave me that zebra. Give it back!"

"Look, Miss Peters, I don't have your zebra." He grinned. "Check my barn. Just Daisy, my milk cow, and Peanut and Tulip, my horses. No zebras."

"Could you stop making those silly jokes which, by the way, are not funny. I suppose being a haweater gives you the right to make fun of newcomers. I do not intend to be made fun of. Hand over my zebra or I'll call the police."

"Miss Peters, I can see you are upset. And I'm sorry about that. But I do not have your zebra."

"Then how do you account for the fact that I had twelve animals on my coffee table and now there are only eleven? Answer me that."

"I didn't even see your coffee table."

"Then how did you manage to check out my window without walking around my coffee table?"

"Would you please sit down and try to calm yourself. I'll make some coffee and try to make some sense out of what you're saying. Actually, I'm a bit exhausted after the fire, and I could use some coffee."

"Mr. Peterson. I will not have a coffee. I will not sit down. I will not have you touch that window in my house. I am leaving right now, and I will stop at the police station on the way."

"You'd better call them on the phone. There is no one at the police station."

"You are fully aware that I do not have a phone. Everybody on this Island is out murdering deer. There is no one to connect my phone."

"Use mine."

Sheila was furious. She had no idea how to get the police. She didn't know if he was lying about the police station. She seldom let her anger get the best of her, but she certainly felt out of control this moment. She tossed her head like a defiant child and shot her last bullet. "This is not the end of this. You will pay for this." She turned on her heel, slammed the door, gunned the chevy, and sped down the driveway. She stopped at the police station and marched to the door. Nobody there. Tears of frustration welled up and spilled down her cheeks. She would not cry. She got into her car and started for home. A crowd of cars loitered in the church parking lot, waiting for their drivers.

People were carrying in boxes. One man was lugging in a chair, two others were carrying a dresser. She wanted to call out, "This town is a big sham. Everybody pretending to be so damn caring and underneath they'll steal you blind."

Sheila had to slow down for turning cars. Several people waved but she did not respond. In the morning she would call the police from the hospital. The receptionist would help her.

When she entered her own house, the fire was burning brightly. Thank heavens she had put the screen up when she lit the fire. The place could have burned down when she was away. It could have burned down right to the ground, and no one would have helped her. She wrapped herself in a blanket on the chesterfield and cried herself to sleep.

Brian poured cold water in the coffee pot and measured out three spoonfuls of coffee into the filter. He pushed the button, waiting for the responding gurgle in the coffee maker. What had the woman been talking about? She had certainly taken him by surprise. Was she furious! He grinned. It had been a long time since a woman had stomped around in his kitchen. Actually, she was kind of attractive, dancing about on those little sharp heels, tossing her head like an unruly colt. Too bad she was a bit daft. He'd never made a point of collecting zebras.

Well, he could scratch the window job off his list. He'd call the lumber yard and cancel the order. He had thought he was doing the neighbourly thing. There was no understanding women. He'd already found that out the hard way.

Meanwhile, Gary arrived at Mae's. He was still breathing carefully, his lungs crying out for oxygen yet hurting unbearably when he breathed. He opened the door. Mae was at the kitchen table. "Gary, did you hear about the fire? My lands Gary, are you all right?"

"Yes. Just got some smoke in my lungs. I was helping the firemen. I'll be okay, but I'm very tired."

"There's some clean clothes at the foot of the stairs. Just leave your soiled clothes in the bathroom and I'll put them in the washer when I get back. Allie and I are going to the church. They are starting a collection of clothing and furniture for the family. We're going to help sort. Get some rest now."

Westicott undid his shirt and threw it on the washer. Every piece of clothing smelled of smoke and burned his throat. He stepped into the shower, glad to be alive. He heard voices in the kitchen, then the slam of the door as the two old biddies left for their good deeds at the church.

It was in the middle of the night when he thought of the zebra. In the excitement of the fire, he had forgotten about it. Was it in his shirt pocket? Had Mae tossed it in the wash? Had she found it? Would it have fallen on the ground at the fire? His whole body trembled. He wanted to rush downstairs, hunt his shirt, race to the scene of the fire. He broke into a cold sweat. Get control. Get control. One thousand, two thousand...

Finally, his breathing regulated. He could plan. Get up early and check his shirt pocket. If the zebra was not there, then go to the fire scene. He could be interested and concerned. That would be a natural thing. Then check out the ground where he was sitting, catching his breath. That was the plan. Logically, everything could wait for morning.

Chapter 33

Mae was dead tired when she got home from the church. There were lots of people younger than she who could have handled the work, but she had taken over the organization like a retired general charging into battle one more time. There was no question about it, she knew how to handle the crowd: put the clothing there, separate the blankets and bedding and put them in the corner on the table, the furniture goes there, Ardith, you take over the dishes. There was a place for everything. The stricken family felt warm and safe in the hands of so many friends. The Everetts had invited them home for the night. Ned Perkins had offered them a vacant apartment, rent-free, until they were able to rebuild. An organized battalion of men was ready to deliver the sorted donations to the apartment the next morning. By the next night, the family would be safe and secure in their own place. They would need some time to make their plans. If Fred decided to rebuild, there would be lots of free help. A new home before Christmas was not a far-fetched dream.

Mae hung up her coat and put on the kettle. It was almost midnight, but she would unwind with a cup of tea before she went to bed. Gary must be sound asleep. She was glad he had gotten involved, helping with the fire. She thought about him. What a fine person, fitting right into the village – joining the Lions, fund raising for the hospital. She thought of the money he had made for her, selling the dresser. She hadn't touched that money yet. She might buy something for those two kids who'd just lost all their toys. That's what she'd do in the morning.

Yes, Gary was a jewel, so fond of his mother. A really caring person. She wondered what he'd seen to-night with Maxie. She hadn't heard of a sale, but then she'd scarcely had time to read the papers. She poured out her tea, and flipped through the unopened mail. Not much of interest – the telephone bill, a letter from the Handicapped Society, a bill from Sears, canceled cheques from the bank. She picked up the Expositor. As was her habit, she turned to the community news. She read the Mindemoya column. Not much this week. She checked out Tehkummah. Then Evansville. She knew quite a few people in that community and was always interested in what was happening there.

She enjoyed the chatty style: "We've just heard from Maxie who has arrived safely in Florida. He's back out on the golf course and in his spare time he visits all the flea markets, probably buying up stuff cheap to make a killing at the hometown auctions." Mae smiled. Maxie would not be offended at this good natured teasing. Then her eyes froze to the page. She reread the paragraph: "Maxie has arrived safely in Florida." But Maxie had met Gary tonight. That's strange. Surely Gary wouldn't make that up to get out of having supper with Sheila. That was nonsense. It was a small thing, but she didn't like that. Small lies, even in jest, could become big ones.

It was getting very late. Mae went into the bathroom. The acrid smell of smoke from Gary's clothes filled the room. She turned on the washer, and dumped in all the clothes he had left in the basket. She'd close her door and never hear it washing away. She finished getting ready for bed and reached for the light switch. Suddenly something sparkled on the carpet and caught her attention. She bent to pick it up. A little glass animal – a zebra – with little black stripes under the glass. What a pretty little thing. She had no idea where it came from. Some kids had been in earlier, selling candy for a school trip. One little girl had asked to go to the bathroom. That would be it. She must have had it with her and dropped it on the carpet. Lucky Gary hadn't stepped on it. Mae put the little animal in her housecoat pocket. Tomorrow maybe she could remember who that little girl was, and call her. Right now she was too tired to remember. She fell into bed and was asleep in a minute.

Gary was up at the crack of dawn. He had slept fretfully, twisting and turning as he thought about the zebra. Where was it? He must be careful and not draw any attention to himself. He crept into the bathroom, closing the door softly behind him. The clothes were gone. He lifted the lid of the washer. There they were, hugging the edge of the tub, partially dry. He found his shirt, pulling it out carefully, and checked the pocket. No zebra. He searched madly through the clothes. No sign of broken glass, no sign of the ornament anywhere. He must be careful. Mae would not expect him to put the clothes in the dryer. He must pack the clothes around the tub again, just as they were. Then he looked through the clothes basket. Nothing there. He checked the tub again. The clothes were falling down. Would Mae notice? Not likely. But he must be very careful. He poured a little water from a glass on the clothes, patting them in tightly to the side. There. That looked good.

He would go down now to the scene of the fire. If anyone were there, he could play the role of a concerned bystander. He knew exactly where the zebra would be – in the grass where he was coughing his lungs out.

The fire was still smouldering. Nothing remained of the house except the stone fireplace standing firm in what must have been the living room. No one was at the scene now, the danger having passed. He stopped the truck and walked in. If anyone were passing by, they would see a curious man studying the disaster. Then he walked around, looking for the exact spot where he had sat. There was nothing shiny in the grass. He moved closer to the house. That bear of a Brian had practically lifted him off his feet. That was where the zebra could have fallen from his pocket. He searched frantically. Nothing there. He broke out in a cold sweat. He had to find it. He called on all of his inner resources – one thousand, two thousand...he must keep control. He regulated his breathing and walked calmly to the truck. He would go back to the house. It shouldn't be hard to find out if Mae had seen the zebra.

When he returned, he noticed that the bathroom door was closed. Mae was up. He walked softly up the stairs. She would never know he left the house. Once in his room, he walked about, letting his footsteps be heard. He came downstairs at the usual time.

Mae had the coffee perking, and the water boiling on the stove for porridge. She was stirring in the oatmeal when Gary walked into the kitchen.

"Good morning, Mae."

"Good morning. I hope you didn't get too much smoke in your lungs from the fire."

"No, I'm fine. I was helping to chop in a wall when the burst of smoke hit me. I hadn't expected it. Got some in my lungs before I had a chance to get away."

"Your clothes were very smoky. I put them in the washer last night. I'll have to check to see if they should go through another cycle."

"Thanks, Mae. You're too good to me."

She filled his bowl with porridge and poured him a cup of coffee. Then she gave herself a smaller helping, and sat down opposite him at the kitchen table. They busied themselves with milk and brown sugar. There was no mention made of either Maxie or the glass zebra.

Allie broke into this happy little breakfast scene with a cheery tap tap tap at the door. "Morning, Mae. Hi, Gary. I wondered if you were ready to go to the church, Mae. A lot of extra things have come in, and we're going to have to decide what to do with them."

"People are so generous. There was almost enough to furnish a house last night."

"Right. And you should see what's there now. Have you got something in the oven, or can you come now?"

"I can come now, I've just finished breakfast. Will you be home for lunch, Gary?"

"No, you'll be busy all morning, and you won't need to be getting lunch for me. Could I be of help?"

"Are you going to be home? We could call if we need you."

"Actually, I have things to attend to. One more coat and I'll have the furniture mother wanted completely finished. But I could put that off if you need me."

"No, there's lots to help. You go ahead and finish your project. Allie, I'm going to get on my old comfort shoes and I'll be ready in a minute. Pour yourself a coffee."

"Thanks." Allie made conversation with Gary. "I don't know what this town would do without Mae. She's a born organizer."

"She's quite a lady, all right."

"Your being here has given her a new lease on life. There's nothing like young people to rejuvenate us old folks. I don't know whatever she'll do when you leave. Do you plan to be here for Christmas?"

(So, it's interrogation time.) "I plan to spend Christmas with mother. There's just the two of us now. She'd be pretty upset if I didn't come home."

"Your mother must be feeling better. Mae says she's able to run the store."

(If there's anything I can't stand, it's questions.) "Yes. She's doing pretty well. I have to go now, Allie, if I'm going to finish my project."

"I'd love to see the finished product. Mae says you've been working very hard. It must be lovely. Is it a dining room table?"

(Play the game. Play the game.) "It's a whole dining room suite. A table with eight leaves, a china cupboard, a sideboard, and twelve chairs." (Might as well throw in the works.)

"Eight leaves! We had a table with six leaves and it was too big for the dining room. Wherever did you get it?"

(One more question, lady, and I'll break your face.) Gary stood up and walked towards the door. "One of Maxie's sales. Got it last year. Have to go now. Things to do."

Mae walked into the kitchen, comfortably dressed. "Did Gary go?"

"Yes. Said he was going to work. Did he tell you he had a table with eight leaves?"

"No. Never heard of one that big. He doesn't talk much about his things. Allie, there's something that's bothering me about Gary."

"What is it, Mae?"

"Last night he said Maxie had phoned and asked him to meet him at West Bay. But I read in the paper that Maxie was in Florida."

"That is strange. Did he say he met him?"

"No. With the fire and all, we didn't talk about it."

"Maybe you misunderstood. Likely if you mention it, he'll tell you about it." Suddenly Allie's expression changed.

"Was it last night, Mae?"

"Yes. They were to meet for supper."

"I heard it was Gary's truck that was parked at the bridge and held up the firemen when they went for more water."

"Didn't they use the new system?"

"They tried, but there was a slip up somewhere. They had to pump from the lake, and Gary's truck was parked right in their spot."

"When was that?"

"Must have been about supper time. That's when the fire was reported."

"How strange. He and Maxie were meeting for supper. That's what he said. I'm sure."

"Well, I heard it was his truck. I could be wrong. You know how stories get going."

"That's very strange."

While they were talking, Gary's truck pulled into the driveway. Gary came in. "I thought you ladies would be long gone by now. I forgot one of my brushes. Had to come back. There's quite a few cars parked at the church."

"We're going soon." Mae looked knowingly at Allie. "I have a couple of things to do before. I forgot to ask you if you enjoyed your supper with Maxie?"

"We didn't have much time. Just grabbed some fish and chips and took them with us."

"Did he have anything of interest?"

"Not much. Just a few small things. Some dishes that were pretty old." He walked past them and up the stairs. They packed up their things and went outside. Mae was shaking. A deliberate lie. Her steps were slower, and suddenly her knees began to hurt.

CHAPTER 34

It was two o'clock when the donations got tidied up at the church. The restaurant had delivered sandwiches and pie to the volunteers, and the UCW had kept the coffee pot full. The mood was festive. Mae hid completely the black cloud that Gary had hung over her heart. She worked cheerfully and untiringly. Allie and two helpers were still sorting clothing and packing it in boxes.

"You have quite a bit left to do," Mae said. "I could help."

"No, Mae. You sit and rest. Take a break. You haven't stopped since you came."

"Actually, if you don't need me, I think I'll walk home. It's a beautiful afternoon, and the fresh air will be good for me."

"I could stop for a while and drive you."

"No. I'd like to walk. Really. Clear my head." She looked at Allie knowingly. "And I have my comfortable shoes on."

"All right. Go home and crawl into bed. I'll drop by after supper."

"Come for supper, Allie, please. I've got lots of leftovers."

"Okay." Allie recognized the hidden urgency in Mae's voice. She needed her. "Sounds great. I'll get a little rest myself, and I'll be there by five."

"Fine." Mae put on her coat. She wore a knitted tam, and pushed it down over her ears. She pulled the hand knit gloves from her pocket.

The sun shone brightly, but the air remained crisp. When had she walked? Not for a long time. She guessed she'd stopped gradually when her knees started to stiffen up. She took a deep breath, then another one. The fresh air was like a tonic. She decided she must walk more often. Allie had spoiled her, driving her everywhere. She blanked out the worries from her mind and feasted her eyes on the ordinary wonders of the great outdoors. Crisp, curled leaves took flight in front of her, propelled by little gusts of wind. She noticed that the Wallaces hadn't bothered to pullout their annuals. They stood grey and gloomy in their front flower bed. Some people did leave their annuals. She never did. It was nice to find a clean and uncluttered flower bed in the spring. Besides, there had to be lots of room for her early blooming tulips and narcissus. There were four cars at the restaurant – a favourite meeting place to talk over the affairs of the town. The stone fence in front of the Andersons' needed repair. She remembered when Doug Campbell had set the stones. Everyone in the town had admired the stone wall and the hollyhocks that stood like a row of chorus girls behind it. That was so long ago. The bank had customers, as usual. Today there were seven cars. Mae hated banking. Probably that was why she still had the money Gary had given her in her dresser drawer. It was folded into a plastic nylon package behind her stockings. Everybody was using bank cards to get money, but she had no idea how to do that. This way, she had control over what little she had. Once it went into a machine, who knew where it went.

She missed the old bank. They'd torn it down to build the new telephone office. It really wasn't the bank she missed as much as the huge old tree that used to stand in front of it. Well, it was gone now. No use crying over spilled milk.

The corner store was still here. It had been a focal point for the town since she could remember. She had heard rumours that it was going to close. She hoped not. It was a great store. You could buy dress material, clothes, hardware, groceries, even fishing tackle there. She knew every nook and cranny of it. One time it had boasted an ice cream parlour. As a youngster, she had sat upon a curved ice cream chair, tucked up close to a matching table. She remembered the chocolate milk and the orange drink they served there. She could almost taste it. And up the skinny stairs to the upper story she and her mother had gone to buy new shoes. The place had such a musty smell. But the shoes had been beautiful. Where did time go?

Finally, she reached her own place. Everything was tidy and ready for winter. Next spring, though, she'd have to paint the door. It was chipped at the bottom. It would have to be sanded first. That was the hard part. She turned the familiar knob and walked in. There was a note on the table. She sat down and read it before she took off her coat. "I won't be home for supper, Mae. Some unexpected things have come up that I have to attend to. Gary."

The note cut into her daydreaming. She had almost forgotten about Gary. It was great the way the mind worked. Some things could be put right out of the picture if you tried hard enough. Reality came back now in full force. She hung up her coat and hat in the bedroom, and stuffed the gloves in the pocket. Fine. Gary would not be home for supper.

She had some things to settle in her mind. For one thing, she had never been upstairs since Gary had come. He had specifically asked her not to – because of her knees, he'd said. He brought down his laundry everyday, and his bedding once a week. He dusted his own furniture with her Pride, and borrowed her dust mop on Saturdays. She had no need to go upstairs. Until now.

Today she felt compelled. She needed to know more about this man who was her boarder. She opened the door to the upstairs and closed it behind her. Her knees had not minded the walk. Climbing the stairs was another thing. She took each step carefully, her hand running along the wall, balancing her. She stopped for a few seconds on the landing, then hustled on up the next short flight of stairs. She opened his door.

The sun was shining through the partly open window, making the polished furniture gleam. There was nothing to suggest that anyone lived here. The dressers were completely cleaned off. There was nothing on the trunk except a clock, a roll of tape, a glass and a stack of books. A square cardboard box was beside the trunk, the top secured with tape. She looked in the closet. All his shirts were hanging neatly in a row, the colours blending. His pants were as neatly arranged as if they were for sale in a clothing store. Three pairs of shoes were lined up in twos, like soldiers. She turned and looked at his dresser. Not nearly as fancy as hers was. It was black walnut with lots of drawers. She tried one. Locked. She tried another. Locked, too. Everyone of them. What could be inside? Stuff he'd bought at auctions, she supposed.

She turned her attention to the bed. It was carefully made, the comforter folded neatly at the foot, the spread smooth and even at the sides. It was almost four inches from the floor, straight as a die. Her mind went back to the few times her husband had made the bed – the covers were more askew that when he started. She smiled at the memory.

Suddenly she heard the kitchen door open and shut. Who was here? Not Allie. Not yet. Surely not Gary! Should she call down? Something held her back. Whoever it was would come again. They would think she was still at the church. Lands. The stair door was opening! Gary. She couldn't let him find her here. There was no place to hide, except under the bed. She didn't believe her knees would bend, but somehow they did. Good job she was small. She lay on her stomach and slid herself along with her hands to the top of the bed. There was room to lie sideways and be hidden by the trunk on one side and the wall on the other. She lay there, cramped and motionless, but completely out of sight. Surely he would never look under the bed! She forced herself to be perfectly quiet, taking short breaths. Lord, keep me from coughing, she prayed.

She heard him close the door. She watched his feet walk past the foot of the bed and disappear. He dropped something on the bed, or maybe he was sitting on it. Her vision was limited to the four inches under the spread. He put a box on the floor by the bed. It was the one she had seen before. She listened as he ripped the tape from the top. He took out some cloth and put it on the floor. It was pretty fabric, and looked like a skirt. Then he placed two lady's shoes side by side, close

134

to the box. One of his feet disappeared, and she heard the flick of laces. A bare foot appeared on the mat beside the bed. The bed moved and creaked, and soon another bare foot planted itself beside the first one. He picked up the fabric and dropped it in the box. It had a silky sound. Now he was putting on stockings, his hand inside the foot, spreading it out to make room for all his toes at once. Then, one clothed, he dropped the sock which seemed to be connected with the other foot. My lands! Pantyhose! He stood up. Then one hand reached for a shoe. He squeezed his foot inside. Then the other. The feet left the bedside and walked around the room. She heard the heels tapping. He was taking short steps, walking up and down, up and down.

Mae's whole body trembled. Her legs were so cramped. Her elbows must be raw. She held her head so stiffly that her shoulders ached. There was nothing to do but wait. How long, oh Lord, how long.

She would force her mind to think of other things to keep herself calm. The tree at the bank. When had they cut it down? What was the name of the orange drink they had in the ice cream parlour so long ago? Green Spot, that was it, and the name was in large letters at the side. Where had she read that annuals might be better for the soil if they were left in the ground all winter? O God our help in ages past, our hope in years to come, our shelter from the stormy blast, and our eternal home. Did she remember the next verse? The beat of the song in her mind coincided nicely with the click of his heels on the wood floor. What kind of man was this?

Finally the short clicks stopped. He was sitting on the edge of the bed again, in his high heels. Finally, he took them off. He put them in the box, and then stood up. Then she saw his fingers, carefully removing the pantyhose. They fell for a moment on the mat, then were lifted and placed in the box. She heard him packing the box, securing it with new tape. He pulled the tape all around the box, patting it gently as he went. The box disappeared. Once more the bed creaked with body weight. She saw fingers reach for the socks and shoes – his own, this time.

Dear Lord, will I ever move again? The thought was a prayer. She watched his feet move to the dresser. She could see his shoes, standing there. She heard the click of a lock and the pull of a drawer. Shortly after, she heard it close. The lock clicked again.

He approached the bed, his two feet coming toward her. She cringed in her corner, a little fetal ball of skin and bones. Her heart stopped. He was patting the bed, smoothing the covers, she thought. Pulling the spread smooth after sitting on it. Finally, he finished and walked toward the window.

How long to wait? Another hymn – a prayer – Dear Lord and father of mankind, forgive our foolish ways, reclothe us in... Talk about reclothing – she'd had enough of that. She saw the feet turn and watched them pass the bed. She heard the door open and close. Her ears strained. Thank heavens for the grate in the floor. The sound filtered up clearly. What was that? Water in the bathroom. The flush of the toilet. An interminable silence. She quietly turned on her back and tried to stretch. How thankful she was for the small freedom of space to stretch, even a little. Quietly, quietly. She strained to hear. Sounds carried so well up the grate. Finally, the opening and closing of the kitchen door. Maybe it was a trick. Maybe he knew she was here all along and was just waiting for her. She lay still. The sound of a truck door closing. The sound of an engine. The sound of a truck leaving the driveway.

Could she crawl out? Her legs had been cramped for so long, would they still move? She had got in here, she would get out. She wriggled carefully. She grabbed the bed frame to steady herself. Finally, she got to her knees, then, leaning her hurting arms on the edge of the bed, pushed herself up. She made it to her feet, and her legs worked! Thank you, God. She opened the door softly, and closed it. She almost ran down the stairs, half sliding against the wall. She opened the stairs door and looked around. Not a soul. Her mind was spinning crazily with what she had seen. Hurry, Allie, hurry! If she ever needed someone to talk to, it was now.

Chapter 35

Allie responded quickly to the phone call. Mae sounded desperate. She usually didn't get rattled, but she was babbling nonsense on the phone. In no time, Allie was at Mae's door. Mae met her as she entered, and hugged her, a child needing to be consoled.

"Allie, I'm so glad you're here." she said, half sobbing.

"There, there, Mae. What is it? Sit down and tell me all about it."

"Oh, Allie, it's dreadful. Come into the living room so I can keep an eye on the door."

She took her chair close to the window. "I don't know where to start." She took a deep breath. "I had a really nice walk home from the church. I almost forgot the lie Gary had told me about having supper with Maxie, and meeting him at West Bay. When I came into the kitchen I found a note from him saying he would not be home for supper. And I suddenly had the feeling that I should go up to his room. I've never been up there, you know, since he came. Anyway, I went. I took my old knees up there, made the stairs just fine. I opened the door, and Allie, it looks just like an empty room. Everything is spotless. There is nothing on either dresser, and just a clock, a glass and some tape on the trunk. I opened the closet, and his clothes are all hung up in order, his shoes in perfect pairs on the floor. It surprised me to see a man's room so neat. I tried some of the drawers in his dresser, but they were all locked. I don't know what I thought I was going to find, but there was nothing there. Then I heard the door, and it was Gary. I had to hide. I squeezed in under the bed."

"Mae, why didn't you just let him know you were there? Make up an excuse or something? It's your house, you know."

"I know. I almost did call out. But for some reason, I was afraid to. So I hid. Allie, my old bones are so sore! I don't know whether I'll ever be the same again."

"How long did you hide?"

"I don't know. It seemed like hours. Well, I got home at two-thirty. It's four now. But wait till I tell you what happened. He opened up a box and took out a pair of lady's high-heeled shoes. And he put on pantyhose and walked around."

"What?"

"That's right."

"How could you tell?"

"There was a little space for me to see between the spread and the floor."

"I can't believe my ears!"

"Allie, I was never so scared. I just couldn't believe my eyes! I was so afraid I'd cough or make a noise. Every time he came and sat on the bed, I thought I'd die. I could have just reached out and touched his foot, it was so close."

"You should have reached out and given it a good grab. Then he'd have died of a heart attack!"

"It may seem funny now, but I tell you, I was scared to death. Allie, do you suppose he's one of those men who wants to be a woman? What do you call that?"

"Trans...something. I don't remember. We watched a talk show about that, remember? Transvestio. Something like that."

"Anyway, what will I do? I've never been in such a predicament before!"

"First of all, Mae, we have to pretend we don't know. That will give us time to think. We'll just carry on as before. Are you afraid of him?"

"No, I don't think so. I was never afraid before. I think I'm more shocked that anything else. And hurt. I've told everyone how wonderful he is. I almost thought of him as a son. He was always so caring."

"If we don't let on, he still will be. Look, we'll find some project we can do together. I can be over here lots. And we'll get a special gadget so you can call for help if you ever needed to. I can get one at the phone office this afternoon. Darlene took hers back when she went to live with the kids, and I know for a fact it's there."

"That would be great. I would never have thought of that."

"I'll pretend you're afraid of getting a stroke or something, and want to have it as a safety guard if you need help. Jim will believe that, and I know he will give it to me right away."

"But I think Sheila said he was deer hunting. She has to wait for him to come back to hook up her phone."

"He's back. Saw him at the locker at noon. Got himself a twelve pointer. He was bragging about it to everyone who'd listen."

"Thanks, I don't know what I'd do without you."

"Never mind. Now, why don't you bake to settle your nerves? If Gary comes back unexpectedly, you are doing a perfectly normal thing,

138

baking for...the church bazaar. That's it! The bazaar! You and I could piece a quilt for the church bazaar. We'd have to work fast because that event's coming up soon. That would give me a grand excuse to be here. I'll come after breakfast and work all day if he's around. When he's not, we can relax and watch TV. We haven't even had time to watch Unsolved Mysteries for weeks."

"Right. Instead we're in the middle of one. Never even heard the follow up to the last one – the murder at the Soo and Thunder Bay. Remember? The dead bodies and the little angels or whatever?"

"Yes. I'd forgotten about that. Anyway, we can have ourselves a good time and see what our lady-gent upstairs is all about."

"I feel so much better since you've been here. Look, I'm not even shaking. Before, I couldn't even make tea, my hands were trembling so. I'm fine now. I'll stir up some cookies. Something I can freeze for the sale."

"You sure you're okay?"

"I'm fine. When I get over the shock, I'll be as fit as a fiddle. I would feel better, though, if I had that little panic gadget."

"I'm on my way. I shouldn't be long. Have those cookies ready for me to try when I get back." She left Mae getting out the flour and butter, and reaching for the vanilla and spices in the cupboard.

Gary got home about eight. The two ladies were sitting in the living room, almost buried in fabric. What a pair! Gary almost liked them. Actually, Mae was fine. There were times when he felt smothered by her fussing, but she was a perfect testament to his good character. Once he'd done the deed, Mae would stand by him to the end if ever there was a question about him. The other old girl he could do without. Questions all the time. He couldn't stand that. He supposed they'd be clacking on into the night. Well, the place smelled good. He could put up with the conversation to have a hot drink and some of those cookies he saw in the kitchen.

"Hi, Gary. Glad you're home. Just in time for a snack."

"Hello, there. What are you two ladies up to?"

Allie responded. "We're piecing a quilt for the church bazaar. It's a lot of work, but if we work steady, we can have it done. Quilts bring a lot of money."

"How much will it sell for?"

"We won't sell it. We'll sell tickets on it. In summer you can get good money for handmade quilts, but in the winter you'd be hard pressed to find a buyer locally. Everybody around here makes their own quilts."

"You mean everybody around here can make a quilt?"

"If they can't, they have a grandmother or an aunt who can."

Mae went to the kitchen. "Do you want coffee, Allie?"

"I guess I can join you. I told you I wanted to sample the cookies!"

"You two chat while I get it ready."

Gary made himself comfortable, and picked up the new Macleans. He started to leaf through the pages, stretching his feet out leisurely in front of him.

As Allie sorted the fabric, she studied the feet out of the corner of her eye. Not very big. Maybe a size eight or a nine. She glanced up to his hands. Pretty hairy for a woman. If he were going to make the change, he would have to shave that off. Transvestite. That was the word. It just catapulted into her mind. She must tell Mae, later.

They all sat around enjoying Mae's cookies and tea. About ten o'clock, Gary announced he was off to bed. Mae and Allie tidied up and made arrangements to meet in the morning to work on the quilt. At the door they said their good nights, and Mae patted the pocket in her dress, beneath her apron.

CHAPTER 36

Westicott awoke to the sharp cracks of hail hitting his upstairs window. He looked out. A strong wind was blowing the freezing pellets and he could see them bouncing against the glass. He looked down the street. The hail was hitting and dancing on the little patches of pavement still visible on the street. It was a combination of hail and freezing rain. He decided to stay in today, and take stock of the situation. Perfecting his plan was essential. Things had been moving pretty fast. It was now time to assess his situation and formulate his plans to exit Mindemoya. Plan carefully, leave no stones unturned, leave no trail.

He took the keys from his pocket and unlocked each drawer in the dresser. He loved this part. He would empty each drawer, sort everything on the bed, and then replace everything carefully. Or maybe he shouldn't replace everything. Perhaps it would be wise to pack some things now so he could leave in a hurry if he had to.

He looked in each drawer. His beautiful collection. He could hardly keep from rubbing his hands in glee as they did in those cheap movies. What a wonderful scheme he had! The master formula for the perfect, undetectable, untraceable crime. He could hardly wait to begin to sort. But first things first. He must not arouse any suspicions in Mae's mind. He must have a reason for staying in his room. He would go downstairs, be polite and concerned for Mae. Little everyday things were important. He would see if she needed milk or anything for her precious baking. Say he felt a cold coming on and would just take a coffee upstairs and try to ward off the flu that was going around, with a sleep. She would probably pester him with a dozen homemade cold remedies. He would listen attentively, admire her repertoire of cures, take the least offensive one and flush it down the toilet, then retreat to the serenity of his room.

As it turned out, the remedy she prescribed was hot ginger tea, a vile, burning concoction that made his eyes water at the first sip. "It has to be good, Mae, it's so horrible," he said. Then, promising to drink the rest of it, he took it to his room. He set it on the trunk. It would be easy to get rid of it later.

He started the sort, beginning with the bottom drawer. Smiling up at him were the grinning marionettes, their strings neatly tied at the top. They were different colours and different shapes, but they all filled the qualification 'Floppy and old.' One, two, three, four, five. And the one Mae had downstairs was six. He could collect that one whenever he felt like it. What chance did he have of finding number seven? Actually, pretty good.

He had met the principal of the elementary school at the Lion's. They got talking, and when the topic of the school play came up, Gary said he had some experience making drama sets. He offered to help. The principal jumped at the offer. That was just what Gary needed – a chance to look around a school in old storage rooms. Who knew what he could find there?

So far, he had met the drama teacher and had a short time to case the drama room. She had left him there to check out the paint and bits of lumber he could use for the set. He had just enough time to collect that lovely pair of high heels and pantyhose. There they were, ready for the taking, tucked in behind a gallon of white enamel on a storage shelf. These shoes looked a lot more comfortable than the ones he had. It had taken quite a while for his feet to feel normal after his last trek to Sheila's. These did look larger, but what a messy place to store shoes. He hated untidiness, but in this case it would be to his advantage. Obviously, things had been stashed here carelessly over the years and no one would remember what was here. Nobody would miss the shoes, that was for sure. He stashed his loot under some old stiff paint brushes in an old box. When the teacher returned he told her he'd take the old brushes home to see if he could clean them back to life. She was pleased. It would help the drama budget if she didn't have to buy a whole lot of new brushes. Gary had put the box under his arm, and walked home. Next time he would have a really good search. There was a good chance that he might find an old floppy marionette in a public school drama cupboard. He would not pack the marionettes. He would move them to a drawer higher up. The almost completed collections would go in the top drawers. That was the plan.

He lifted each marionette carefully, and put it on the bed. In the same drawer were two kiwi birds. These were hard to find, and he had not collected them on the Island. These he could pack away. He put them in a separate place on the bed. He closed the bottom drawer. Then he pulled open the one above it. What a lovely collection of treasures. Three china rabbits and a set of three mottled yellow rabbits with the orange eyes and pure white whiskers. These were the ones he'd lifted from the box Sheila had bought at an auction about a year ago. It was such a simple deception. He had seen her eying the box. The only thing he wanted was the rabbits. It had been so easy to remove them and put them in another box. He didn't think she'd notice, but she had raised a major stink about it. Even stopped the auction while Maxie dressed down the crowd. Who would ever switch things in auction boxes? How low would some people stoop? He smiled to himself.

In the same drawer were three blue fish. And, in three little soft bags, were little pieces of gold nuggets. These had been easy to get when he was in Thunder Bay. He could easily have finished his collection of seven, but had been 'called away' before he could get them all. Also, lying beside the bags, were three beautiful quills. The poem hadn't been specific about the quills, but he had added his own qualifications. They should be quills used at weddings. White and beautifully shaped. The quills, the nuggets, the fish, the rabbits, could all be packed. He put them on the bed and moved to the next drawer. This was a deep, box shaped drawer in the centre of the dresser. Because of its size, he stored his bigger things here. He had three xylophones, four yule logs and two tea urns. These things didn't seem to show up at auctions on the Island. There was little hope of getting seven in a hurry. These he would pack. They were a little awkward because of their size, but he had a little carry-on bag in the shed for these. He would put these back in the drawer until he had a chance to get the bag.

On each side of the box drawer were two smaller ones. He opened the one on the bottom right. Here were his five little glass zebras, twinkling in the reflected light. There should be six, he thought. He had to find that missing zebra. Behind them were violin strings. It was easy to get individual strings, but finding sets of four was difficult. He had only one complete set. He would keep the zebras out and pack the strings. The top drawer on the right housed two gypsy moths and three old ink wells. Tucked in behind were two lorgnettes. All these could be packed. He placed them on the bed.

The bottom small drawer on the left held three owls, four glass cows, one bundle of beeswax, and four small pairs of duck salt and pepper shakers. Folded in front in a straight line were five handkerchiefs with tatted edgings. He smiled. Mae just hadn't looked in the right place for her handkerchief. He would pack everything in here except the handkerchiefs.

Finally, the last drawer. The top left – the backbone of the master plan. There were the spoons, nine face down, one turned up revealing the word Manitoulin, and three wrapped in velvet. Behind the spoons was his collection of knives, all shaped in the perfect image of a lady's boot. He loved these. He had great luck at the Soo. There had been an auction at the home of a knife collector. He had been able to buy a perfect collection of six. Ha. Guess who had the seventh one. And he had the key to her house. He had been down several times to continue his search, but so far he had come up cold. What would she have done with it? That was a puzzle.

Now for the final arrangements. He spread out the tatted handkerchiefs in the shape of a fan, one fold missing, in the top right drawer. He placed the zebras carefully behind them. In the drawer just below, he arranged the marionettes. These two drawers held his potential winners. One more of each – checkmate. The rest of the articles he carefully wrapped in some soft cloth he had brought home from the school. He stored all the wrapped articles in the two bottom drawers. Now, if he had to, he could pack in a minute.

He had been concentrating so hard on his work that he had been unaware of any sounds or activities around him. The wind was howling at his window, and the noise of the two old biddies clacking away downstairs beamed directly up through the grate in the floor. He listened to them now. "Do you have more pink patches?" "Yes, I have lots." "I need two for this corner." He was going to have to put up with all this babbling until that quilt was finished for the bazaar.

Having completed his sorting, he now checked his wardrobe. His skirt was neatly folded into the lining of his jacket, along with his pantyhose and beret. His high heels fit snugly into his binocular case. The slender coil of copper wire was tucked inside one shoe. His hands were sweaty. The more he touched these things, the more excited he became. It was the moment before the race began. He was aware of his heart jumping inside his chest. Hold back, hold back. One thousand... Meanwhile, in the room below, the ladies chatted and listened. Gary was walking about, from the dresser to the bed, back and forth, back and forth. They monitored his steps – to the dresser, to the bed, to the closet, to the window. For a sick man, trying to sleep off the flu, there was a lot of walking about. What was he doing? Putting things in the dresser? Taking them out? They could only imagine. Maybe his drawers were full of lady's clothes and he was trying them all on. For all their curiosity, they maintained complete disinterest when he finally came downstairs.

"Feeling better, Gary? I hope we didn't disturb you when you were trying to sleep."

"No, no, not at all. I feel a lot better. Slept like a log."

"That's good. Next to my ginger tea, sleep's the best thing."

The evening passed uneventfully. The same old routine, the same mindless chatter. Westicott excused himself as soon as possible and retreated to his room.

In the middle of the night, he woke up in a cold sweat. He had been dreaming, and his plan hadn't worked. It brought him to a stark realization. Sometimes you can take care of the little details and let the big ones slip by. That's what had happened in his dream. He had left the object on the body, and they had traced it to him. Mae would certainly recognize the tatted handkerchief and draw conclusions about

144

the marionette, even if it weren't hers. He could use one from the school, if he found one, or one from his drawer. But in order to have his seven, he would somehow have to get Mae's. It was hard to say how smart she was. Once in a while she seemed to have a glimmer of intelligence. She just might get the connection. And if he left the knife, Sheila would be sure to make a case out of it. He hadn't really worked out yet how he was going to leave an object on the body that was untraceable. But it was still all right. He had time, and the challenge was stimulating. He would put his mind to it and devise the perfect plan. He must keep foremost in his mind that this was not the Soo – this was Manitoulin. He tossed and turned for a little while, then fell into a dead sleep.

CHAPTER 37

Sheila felt much more secure when Al finally came to hook up her phone. Now she had a connection with the outside world. She had heard no more from Brian. She did report the loss of the glass zebra to the police, but a lot of time had passed, and still no word from them. She had a feeling that her story about Brian and the key had made no impression on them. What was this Brian, a sacred cow? She wouldn't think about that anymore. It always upset her. Right now she was getting ready for her foray into curling. She knew she didn't have the proper clothing, but first of all she was going to see if she liked the game before she invested her hard earned money. Amy had invited her to come early.

When she arrived at the rink Amy was waiting for her. "Hi," she said. "Ben is going to give you a few quick lessons before the gang arrives. He's out there on the ice now, waiting for you."

"Thanks a lot, Amy."

Ben saw her through the window and came in. "Come on, Sheila. Let's give these rocks a whirl before everybody gets here. You may have a little trouble with those shoes you're wearing. But you'll get the idea, anyway."

"I really didn't know what shoes to get. I thought I'd get good advice here."

"Yeah. We're full of it," he laughed. The two of them walked to the ice surface. Amy watched her friend through the window. Ben would be a good coach. Sheila was taking off her coat, getting right into it. Other curlers were coming in. This was the first game of the season, and everyone was anxious to see whose team they were on. They all hoped they had a good skip. Winning didn't really matter all that much, but if you had a good skip you certainly had a better chance.

Gary Westicott walked in. Everyone greeted him warmly. He was really getting involved with the community. Most of the men knew him from his association with the Lion's Club. He had helped with a few fund raising events, and the local people appreciated the involvement of a newcomer, especially when that person wasn't always bragging about how much better they did it at some place he'd been before. The regulars welcomed him now.

"You curl before, Gary?"

"No, can't say that I have. But I'm game to learn."

"Good. Ben's out with another newcomer giving her some pointers. Go out and try a few rocks."

Gary went out to the ice. There was Sheila. He watched her strain as she lifted the rock, bringing it back, then forward, letting go too late and sliding part way down the ice with it.

"That's the way, Sheila, but let go sooner. When you get your shoes you'll have a slider on your right foot. That will help you make a smooth delivery. You'll soon get the idea. Try another one, and I'll give Gary a hand on the other sheet. Gary, grab one of these rocks. Watch me. I'll show you what to do." Ben picked up a rock, swung back easily, leaned forward and slid smoothly, following his rock almost to the red line.

"It may be a while before I look that good," Gary said. He picked up a rock and tried to copy the delivery. It was harder than he thought. They both threw a few more rocks until Charlie called them into the clubhouse. "Okay, guys. We've got the teams drawn up. Give a listen. We'll have this all typed up and on the wall for tomorrow, but for now I'll read off the names. These teams play at seven."

Sheila was on Henry Smith's team, playing lead. She tried hard, aimed at his broom, but didn't come near it. That didn't bother Henry. He told her that her biggest problem was her shoes. Not to worry. At least she was getting her rocks over the hog line and that was better than a lot of beginners.

It seemed like a long game to Sheila. She couldn't understand the sweeping part, couldn't even keep up with the rock. She was really glad when it was over. There seemed to be a lot of protocol in the game, people were courteous, and shaking hands all round seemed an accepted part of the game's end. They all went into the clubhouse and the vice skip bought drinks for everyone. There was no booze on the regular nights, just coffee and hot chocolate. Sheila tried the chocolate. She hadn't had this drink since forever, she thought. It was a treat. They all sat around chatting, and everyone made Sheila feel welcome. She was glad she had come. Suddenly she felt as if she were being watched. She turned, and Gary was staring at her. The necklace. With all the exercise, the little knife had slipped outside her shirt. It was there, in full view.

"You've caught me staring at your necklace, Sheila. That's a beautiful little shoe."

Instinctively she placed her hand over it. "Thank you. I like it very much."

"Did you buy it at an auction, by any chance?"

"Yes, I did."

"I remember. I wondered who got it. It was something that really caught my eye. I must admit, I did a perfectly inexcusable thing. I found it in a box and slipped it in another box with less in it. I don't know why I did that, except I wanted the shoe without all the other things. When I looked in the box, the shoe was not there."

"That's because I watched you hide it and so I moved it into another box. I thought I'd teach you a lesson."

They all laughed. "It looks better on you than it would on me," said Gary. "I'm glad you got it."

"Why did you want it?" she asked.

"I thought it would be a nice little item for my mother's store."

"Would you like it now?" She was testing him.

"No. You bought it fair and square. Besides, I've learned my lesson. I hadn't realized at the time that it was a no-no to change things from one box to another."

Suddenly Sheila felt relaxed with Gary. He was all right after all. Quite gracious, really. And all this time she had been a little bit afraid of him.

The nine o'clock curlers were arriving and the women from the seven o'clock draw were washing up the cups. Sheila said her good nights and walked out. This was going to be fun. She was glad she'd come. She jumped into her car and turned on the ignition. There were a lot of cars now. She hoped she could get her car out. She accelerated slowly, and her back tires started to spin. She tried again. This time she slid sideways, coming dangerously close to the next parked vehicle. She opened the door to assess the situation.

"Having trouble?" It was Gary's voice. "Looks as if your rear tire's on ice, Sheila. I'm not sure if you can get out."

"When I parked, these cars weren't here. I'm kind of boxed in."

"Likely they all belong to the players on the ice now. Look, take your keys and leave your car. I'll drive you home."

This man was surprising. "Are you sure you don't mind?"

"Not at all. Jump in." They chatted all the way. Sheila invited him in for coffee.

"I had forgotten how lovely your place is. You have really made it look homey."

"Thanks. I'm making some progress. I have lots to do yet. I'll put on a fire. That's something I'm quite good at." She knelt on the hearth, building her little house of cedar filled with paper.

"I didn't think a city girl could build a fire like that," he said.

"You'd be surprised what a city girl can do," she said. "It was Jamie who taught me."

They drew two big chairs close to the fireplace and watched the flames twist and curl and catch on the log she had placed on top. She got the coffee and they sat there, two friends enjoying one another's company. He had to steel himself from grabbing that little knife that dangled so temptingly as she leaned forward to adjust a log with the fire tongs.

In no time, it got too hot by the fire and they had to push their chairs back. Gary's brushed the coffee table. He adjusted his chair to keep it from hitting. "What a lovely glass collection," he said, apparently noticing it for the first time.

"Thank you. It's very special to me."

He picked each one up, one at a time. "They are so perfectly made. Such smooth little bodies. I wonder how they got the paint inside."

"I don't know. I think it's blown in. I've had them a long time. There's one missing."

"There is? What one?"

"A little zebra."

"Did it break?"

"No. Someone took it."

"Surely not since you came here."

"Yes."

"Do you know who?"

"I lent my key to a carpenter to fix my window. I came home and my zebra was gone."

"You were talking about that window one time at Mae's. Surely not that Brian chap."

"Who else?"

"I don't know. Everybody speaks so well of him. Kind of a local hero."

"I reported it. I haven't had any follow up. Maybe this place isn't what it seems to be. Maybe it's run by the mafia." She laughed. "Gary, look at the time. It's eleven-thirty."

"Time goes fast when you're enjoying yourself."

"Yes. We've bumped into one another lots of times but this is the first time we've really had a chance to chat. I've enjoyed it very much. But I'd better get my car. I have to work in the morning. I think the fire will be all right. I'll just put the screen up."

Together they made the fire safe, and Gary took her to the rink to get her car. He could tell that she could be very easily won over, if he applied the charm. He was very pleased with his own performance. He thought it was at least worth an Oscar. He would use Sheila in his plan. She was convinced Brian had her zebra. All he had to do now was find one more zebra. He could make his kill, leave the zebra on the body, stay at Mae's while all fingers pointed at Brian, after they heard Sheila's accusation. Then he could just make a leisurely exit and let justice take its course. The only trouble was he had to find Sheila's zebra, and another one. He would intensify the search. He had a fixed course now. Gentlemen, start your engines.

CHAPTER 38

Sheila had invited the ladies for supper. They were her first guests. At first she had been worried that things wouldn't turn out right. It had been such a long time since she'd entertained. Sometime, maybe, she'd tell them that she'd cooked the same supper the night before for a practice run.

"That was a wonderful meal, Sheila. You are a great cook."

"I'd have to go a long way to top you, Mae."

"I just cook ordinary things. I'd never tasted carrots with cinnamon before. They were really tasty."

"Thanks. Now you two ladies pull up a chair by the fire and toast your toes while I clear the table."

"Can't we help?" asked Allie.

"No, you are my first dinner guests. I want you to make yourselves perfectly at home. I've been so long returning all the kind things you've done for me since I came to Mindemoya."

"It seems as if we've known you forever, Sheila. You seem like one of the family."

"Thanks. I appreciate that more than you can know. While you two are getting cosy at the fire, would you like to look at some old books that were left here when I came? I know you both knew the previous owner."

"Love to," Mae said.

"I'll get them. Here's the last bunch I was trying to sort, and then I fell asleep in front of the fire." She placed a box of books between them on the floor.

Each of the ladies picked up a book. "Look at this one, Allie. Remember how Jean loved anything about the royal family? Here's one on the Queen Mother."

"Yes, she never wanted to hear anything bad about the Queen or her family. She was upset when there was trouble between Diana and the Queen. She thought they should just try harder to get along. I wonder what she would think if she were living now."

"Dear knows." Allie reached for another book. "Here's a pattern book. I remember this one. It has those slippers in it that we used to knit. I bet you couldn't count how many you did, Mae."

Mae laughed. "Yes, I sure knit a lot of those. But I don't remember now how I did them. Are the directions there? I wouldn't mind making a pair."

"Take the book home, Mae," Sheila said. "If ever I want to knit a pair of slippers, I'll know where the book is."

"Better still, Sheila, ask Mae to whip you up a pair."

"Sure," said Mae. "I'd love to. I've got scads of wool at home wanting to be knit up. Any special colour?"

"You ladies are something else! Any colour would be great."

Mae reached into the box, pleased that she could do something nice for Sheila. She pulled up a child's book. It had beautiful illustrations. It was an ABC book. She flipped through, looking at the pictures. She stopped at one of the pages. 'H is for handkerchiefs, tatted in white.' "This picture reminds me Allie. I had forgotten to look for that handkerchief with the tatting that you wanted. It went right out of my mind."

"Did you put it away?"

"No. It just disappeared. Gary was going to look behind the dryer for me. I washed it along with the other doilies, but when I ironed them up, the handkerchief wasn't with them. I'll remind Gary to look for me." She flipped to the first of the book. 'A is for angels with feathery wings.' Where had she heard that before? It sounded familiar. 'B is for beeswax you rub on a string. C is for..." Suddenly it hit her like a bolt. That was the line pinned on that dead woman in Thunder Bay! They had found that on her, along with an angel with feather wings. It was on Unsolved Mysteries. A clammy, nauseous feeling crept into Mae's throat. She thought for a minute she was going to be sick. She closed the book. Almost mechanically, she bent and picked up another book. She slipped the ABC book inside it. "There's another book here, Sheila," she said when she had control of herself. "It's on gardening. I want to know whether I should clean my annuals out of the flower beds in the fall. I think this would tell me. Could I borrow it?"

"Sure. Find everything out, then tell me." The phone rang. Sheila excused herself and chatted away for a few minutes on the phone. The ladies kept leafing through the books. Mae didn't dare say anything to Allie about her discovery.

"I'd love to go, Gary."

Mae picked up her ears. Sheila was on the phone to Gary!

"It doesn't matter to me. You pick the place. Yes, I'll be ready. Bye now." She hung up the phone.

"Guess what, ladies. I have a date."

"A date? How nice. We'd like to pretend we were not listening."

"Mae, you've been trying to set me up with Gary ever since I came. I didn't really like him much at first, but we've had a few opportunities to chat at the curling rink, and I'm beginning to think you have very good taste in men."

"Sometimes I'm wrong," said Mae.

"Not likely this time. You have a perfect chance to know him when you see him every day."

"May we pry and ask you where you are going?" asked Allie.

"To dinner. At Tehkummah. It's his birthday. Funny, at first I was a little afraid of Gary, but I realize now I had nothing to be afraid of."

"Why were you afraid?"

"It was something that happened at an auction. I thought he had taken something from a box I had bought at an auction in the fall. So I kept my eye on him. One day I watched him take something out of a box and stash it in another one. So, when he wasn't looking, I felt around in the box and sneaked out a small object. I put it in another box. He bought the one he thought it was in, and I bought the one I knew it was in! Actually, this is what it was," and she showed them the necklace. "It was afterwards I put this chain on it. Here, have a look at it." She took off the necklace and passed it to Allie.

"Looks like a little boot to me. Oh, I see. It's a jackknife. Mae, look."

"That's very unusual. In all my born days I've never seen anything like it. Must have been a lady's knife. Likely wore it for protection."

"Maybe. It certainly isn't very big. Anyway, I didn't want Gary to see it. I always wore it under my shirt. But it slipped out one night at the curling rink. We were all sitting around the table after the game, drinking hot chocolate, and he saw it. He asked me about it. In front of everybody, he said it was wrong of him to have slipped it into another box, and that I'd taught him a lesson. We both had a good laugh about it."

"When is your date, Sheila?"

"Next Wednesday. That's his birthday."

"After dinner, come back to my place. I'll make a birthday cake."

"He thought we should do something afterwards. Maybe just go for a drive."

"I think you should come in afterwards. I'll make something good."

"I'll let him decide, Mae. I don't want to be bossy on our first date."

"The side roads will be slippery. I'll be worried about you."

"Mae, you sound like my grandmother. She used to worry about me when I was a teenager. When I think back, I maybe should have listened. Mae, I'm a big girl now. I'm thirty-five." She gave Mae a hug.

Allie chipped in. "It's getting late and I should be getting home. I don't like driving in the dark anymore. Are you ready, Mae?"

"Yes, it is getting on. Thanks so much for letting me borrow these books. Sure you don't care what colour I knit those slippers?" asked Mae.

"Surprise me." Sheila sounded excited and happy. Was it the slippers or the phone call, Mae wondered.

"It was a wonderful evening, dear. So thoughtful of you to invite us."

"I'll never get even for everything you've done for me." Sheila helped them into their coats. "Now you ladies go straight home," she teased.

"What else would a couple of old codgers like us do?" laughed Allie.

"Think about coming in after your date, Sheila. I'll work on Gary."

"Mae, it's good you didn't have kids. You would have worn yourself out worrying about them." The two of them smiled and helped each other to the car.

As soon as they were in and had the door shut, Mae burst out, "Allie, I'm so worried. I don't think she should be going out with Gary."

"I don't like the idea, either. But just because he's a – I've got the word now – a transvestite – doesn't mean he's dangerous. Maybe we should tell her what we know."

"I think there's a lot more to it than that. I found an old book in that bunch we were looking at. I sneaked it out in the gardener's book. There's something I have to show you."

"Does it have to do with Gary?"

"I'm afraid so. It just about made me sick. Come in and have a look at it as soon as we get home. No, we can't do that. Gary may be home. Stop right here and turn on the inside light."

"Someone will come along and think we're in trouble. We'll go to my place."

"Hurry. You have to see this."

Allie put her foot on the gas and was at home in no time. She and Mae hurried out, and they were in the living room, Allie pulling the drapes while Mae was getting out her concealed rhyme book. "Look," she said. She already had it opened to the A. She read the verse, "A is for angels with feathery wings. Does that ring a bell, Allie?"

"It is familiar. Let me think."

"I'll tell you. Remember that murder in Thunder Bay – the one on Unsolved Mysteries? There was an angel on the dead body, and part of the verse pinned on her shirt."

"Heavens! That's right. Whatever does this mean?"

"Do you remember the message on the dead body at the Soo?"

"I can't think!"

Mae was flipping through the pages. "And look here. H is for handkerchiefs tatted in white!" Her eyes opened wide. "My handkerchief is missing. Allie!" They stared at each other in horror. When she first saw the picture down at Sheila's the full impact hadn't hit her. Her whole body trembled. She almost fell and Allie reached out to steady her. They clung together, two old bodies frozen in a momentary ecstasy of fear. A murderer was living at Mae's house. They could be in danger. Mae was the first to get hold of herself. "Now, we mustn't jump to conclusions. We could look like a couple of old fools if we raise a big commotion and we're wrong. Let's be calm, and read through this whole book."

They sat on the couch together. Mae read aloud, "A is for angels with feathery wings, B is for beeswax you rub on a string. C is for cows chewing barley and malt..."

"That's it, Mae! They found a glass cow on that body."

"Oh, you're right." Mae started to shiver.

"Allie, I've just taken a cold chill."

"Get hold of yourself. Read on."

"D is for ducks filled with pepper and salt. E is for eagle's nest high in the trees, F is for blue fish that swim in the seas. G is for ghosts that go bump in the night, H is for handkerchiefs tatted in white. I is for ink in an indigo blue, J is a jackknife in the shape of a shoe..." Mae caught a scream in her throat. Sheila's jackknife. "Allie, he wanted Sheila's jackknife!"

"Keep reading Mae, keep reading."

"K is for kiwi a bird that can't fly, L is a lorgnette you hold to your eye. M is a marionette... Allie, he asked me all kinds of questions about my marionette."

"Keep reading Mae, keep reading."

"M is a marionette, tattered and old, N is for nugget, a rough lump of gold. O is for owl with orange blinking eyes, P is a pilot who flies in the sky. Q is for quill what you use when you write, R is for rabbits with whiskers of white. S is for spoons with the name of a place, T is for thimbles for Mae and for Grace..." Mae shuddered at the word Mae. "U is for urn that is used to hold tea, V is violin strings E, A,

D and G. W is a winkle that tickles your palate, X is a xylophone you play with a mallet. Y is a yule log you can burn Christmas night, Z is a zebra with stripes black and white." Mae shrieked. A zebra! She had forgotten about the little glass zebra. "Allie! I found a little glass zebra in the bathroom the other night."

"You did?"

"Yes. I forgot all about it. I put it in my apron pocket. It was there the night of the fire. I had just put Gary's clothes in the washer and when I turned to go out the door, I saw a shiny thing on the floor. I bent over and picked it up and it was a little glass zebra. Some kids had been in the house in the afternoon selling tickets, and a little girl had asked to use the bathroom. I thought it must be hers, and that night I was too tired to think of her name. Now I know who she is...Marty Wilson. I never called."

"Call her tomorrow, Mae. Then we'd know for sure if it was hers or not.

"What if Gary had dropped it there? He didn't mention it at all? Never a word. There's something very strange going on."

"I should stay with you tonight, Mae."

"No. He must never suspect that we know anything. I'll just catch my breathe and I'll be all right. He's planning this date with Sheila. You don't suspect he is going to do something to her?"

"We must see that never happens. We'll think about this and make our plans tomorrow. Are you really sure you will be okay?"

"YES. My mind is made up. You keep the book here. He must never know we've seen it. I've got my magic button on my new phone, thanks to you, and I'll keep it beside me all the time. I'll take it to bed with me and keep my hand on it all night. I'm fine." She smiled bravely at Allie.

"All right. I'll take you home now. I'll go in for a few minutes in case he's up." But when they got there, the truck was parked in the driveway, the light was still on in the kitchen, but Gary had gone to bed.

Chapter 39

The tantalizing aroma of coffee drifted through the grate into Gary's room. He had slept in. Now that he had worked out his plan, he was more relaxed. He had made up a new birthday date for himself, and was going to wine and dine Sheila on Wednesday, maybe even get a little bit romantic in a gentlemanly way. It was time to pour on the charm, endear himself to everyone. Sheila had to be firmly on his side. If he could find an unobtrusive way to shed suspicion on Brian's character, he would. But that would have to be carefully done. He could throw hints, and Sheila could draw the inferences. That would be the way to do it. That he would have to play by ear.

He was humming a little tune under his breath as he went down the stairs. "Morning, Mae. You and Allie have a good time last night?"

"We certainly did. Just stuffed ourselves with good food, then toasted ourselves by the fire. We had a wonderful time. How about you?"

"Oh, nothing out of the way. Well, maybe something did happen. You probably heard. I'm taking Sheila out Wednesday night."

"Yes, we heard about your birthday, too. You should have told me."

"I know you've been trying to get Sheila and me together, but I've been so focused on my projects that I thought I didn't have time. But I got talking to her at the curling rink, and found we have a lot in common. I took her home, and we really had a good time together."

"She didn't tell us."

"I'm glad she's discreet. Anyway, you were right all along. She is a very nice person."

"Since it's your birthday, I'll make a cake. You and Sheila can come back here after you have your dinner, and we'll all celebrate!"

"I hadn't decided what we would do after dinner. Maybe take a drive. We could zip over to Sudbury and catch a movie."

"I'm always so worried about people on the roads in the winter. That highway to Sudbury is noted for accidents."

"Now don't fuss, Mae. We'll talk about it...that bacon sure smells good. I didn't know I was so hungry. It's just what I need for a little extra stamina today. I'm going to start to work on the set for the school play."

"That's a wonderful thing to do. Then you'll be home for lunch."

"Actually, the principal is treating. He and the drama teacher and I are going out for lunch. We have to come up with some decisions about the set."

"Then I won't look for you until after school. Allie and I are working on the quilt all day."

"Will it be done in time?"

"We're almost finished." She took down her calendar. "Today's the tenth. And the church concert, I'm counting on you to go, is on Sunday the thirteenth. The bazaar is on Tuesday, the fifteenth. And your birthday is on Wednesday." She was laboriously writing all this down as she spoke. "Quite a busy week."

"You're right. And the school play is on the eighteenth. Just gives me eight days to build the set." He wiped his mouth carefully with the serviette. "I'd better get going if I'm to get finished. See you around supper."

As soon as he left, Mae was on the phone to Allie. "He's gone."

"I've been sitting here waiting. I'll be right over."

She was there in a matter of minutes. Mae poured them each a coffee and they sat down at the kitchen table. "They are going out on Wednesday. We have five days, that's all."

"I've been thinking about it all night. Whatever happens, he can't take her out. It's too dangerous."

"We could tell Sheila. But it would be better to catch him red-handed. We'll have to keep track of him every single minute."

"He has a lot to do on the school set. That will keep him busy during the day, and Sheila works. We just have the evenings to worry about."

"Not Sunday. Sheila doesn't work on Sunday."

"Then we'll have to account for Sunday."

"Let's do it one day at a time. This is Friday."

"There's a special curling draw tonight. She told me that, because she was a little upset about being on Brian's team. Of course, she didn't let on to anyone else. They just draw the names out of a hat, and they go with the luck of the draw."

"Then there's tomorrow."

"Sheila's working. We could invite her for supper. We can pretend we're cupids and try to get them involved in something...maybe we could play the old victrola."

"I'm sure they'd love that! Really, Mae, we're in the twentieth century! What about a game of rook? We can tell them they can't be true Islanders if they can't play rook!"

"Good thinking. But Sheila really did want to hear more songs on my old victrola."

"Now let's get on with Sunday. We're both helping with the food for the pageant. Maybe we can get them both to go. Or one of them."

"I think we can handle that. What happens Monday night?"

"There's curling again. That should be all right. Usually Gary comes right home after curling."

"Tuesday is the bazaar and the supper for the hospital. Gary has been involved with the fund raising, and I'm sure he wouldn't miss that."

"And then there's Wednesday."

"Gary told me about his date with Sheila. Told me it was his birthday, and I said I'd make him a cake. I think he was pleased."

"We could tell Sheila we're going to have a surprise birthday for him, and we're inviting some of his friends. That way we'd be sure she would get him here. If he knew we were waiting for him, he wouldn't dare do anything to Sheila."

"Now let's go over that again. We must be sure of what we're doing. Tonight, curling. You have Gary's schedule on the wall. Let's see. She plays at nine on Brian's team. If Gary is not home by eleven thirty, call me. I'll be up. Saturday, Sheila's coming for supper. And the evening. Sunday, the Christmas pageant. Monday, curling. I see they both play at nine. Tuesday, the bazaar and supper. We should be able to keep one of them to help clean up."

"So what are we going to do to catch him?"

"We need some pretty solid proof before the police get in on it. They will just muck it up, ask a lot of questions, tip off Gary, and he'll outsmart us all."

"I've got an idea. We'll phone and see if that little girl lost a glass zebra. If she did, then we have to change our thinking. But if she didn't, we can make it easy for Gary to get the zebra. If he takes it, we know for sure he is the killer."

"But he already has the handkerchief. He mightn't need the ze-bra."

"He's had that for a long time. He must need something more. Maybe he needs one of everything on the list. Or maybe he needs a certain number of each. Did the poem mention numbers?"

"I can't remember. But I have it right here in my bag." She reread the poem. "Not a number. There's twenty-six letters. He'd have a pretty hard time collecting twenty-six zebras. Let's see. There are four violin strings. Maybe he needs four of each."

"I think he is short of marionettes too, because he hasn't got mine." She rushed into the living room. "Here it is, safe and sound."

"You gave me a scare for a minute."

"Do you think we're really onto something?"

"Let's think some more about this. We know he is collecting zebras, tatted handkerchiefs, marionettes and jackknives. Do you think it is the jackknife he wants? He let Sheila think he didn't want it. Would that be a way to throw her off guard? Or does he want marionettes and knows exactly how to get mine when he needs it? Who knows, he may have a whole collection of things locked away up there."

"We can test our theory. Leave the zebra out in full view. If he shows an interest, tell him it belongs to Marty."

"That won't work. He knows who it belongs to."

"Right. Tell him you found it and that a little girl was in the house and you think it belongs to her."

"That would work."

"And I could say I didn't remember her name."

"What happens if he does take it?"

"Then we call the police."

"I wonder if we should tell anybody about this as a safety precaution. He might come in here and kill us both and then he would never get caught."

"I was wondering about that. What about Brian? We could tell lots of people, but you know how news travels around here. Brian is about the only one I know who can keep his mouth shut."

"Somebody really should know. I wish the police lived in Mindemoya like they used to. Now that they're all stationed somewhere else, I don't feel as safe. And I wouldn't know who to tell without a big fuss and alert Gary."

"Mae, I'll go and see Brian now. I'll be right back. If Gary comes unexpectedly, you can easily find an excuse for me not being here. Let's say I had to go to the store to get more thread."

"I thought I might have to write all this down to remember it, but my mind's as clear as a bell."

"Maybe all we old folks need is a bit of excitement to keep our heads clear." They smiled at each other.

"I think you're right. Allie, I haven't felt so well in a long time. I can even crawl under beds and not suffer any after-effects. My knees aren't even hurting." Watson and Sherlock gave each other a hug.

"When I'm gone, you phone Marty's mother. Incidentally, where is the zebra?"

"Just a minute. I'll get it out of my apron pocket." She rustled into the bedroom. "Here it is. Isn't it a beautiful little thing?"

Allie picked it up. "Indeed it is. Expensive. Not a toy. Marty's mom would certainly know if it was hers. You call. I'll be back soon."

CHAPTER 40

At Christmas time, loneliness walked into Brian's kitchen, pulled up a chair and stayed for the week. Every year he struggled to ward off this Christmas visitor with a frantic schedule of extra work. Every year that old human heart took over at the first Silent Night on CBC. He struggled against it, but it was heart over mind every time. He had many friends in the village. He knew that. And he would be included in many activities during the holiday season. But he would not be invited anywhere for Christmas day. He understood that. He was really too proud to accept an invitation at first. Now, nobody asked. They felt it would be an intrusion on his privacy. And he had given them every reason to think so.

He pondered one more time that age old question: what is it that keeps people from being absolutely honest with each other? Why, for example, could he not go to the Watson's with all the kids who met him every day with the milk, and just say, "Could I be included in your Christmas this year? I'd love to watch the kids open their gifts. I could bring some extra presents." Why couldn't he say that? He knew they would welcome him – probably appreciate the opportunity to pay for the milk with kindness, share their kids and commotion. What kept him from asking?

Pride. That old deadly sin built a little tougher wall around him every year. It was pride that brought him back to this Island. He would take that rundown farm and make it into the best dagnab farm on the Island. He would prove to everybody that he didn't have to have a big city job to be a success. He had gone about this task methodically. He fixed the barn first, then the yard, then the house. And all the time he worked the farm. Planned the crops, ploughed the furrows straight, built the hay loads right, arranged the bales in the loft with precision. He fed the stock at regular hours, groomed the horses, coddled his cows. He grew almost all his own food, wasted nothing, was generous to a fault with extra milk and vegetables.

Then he set about the house. He did all the things he knew his mother had wanted when they were scraping money together to send him to university. He could hear her now – a new counter top can wait, we'll get new flooring when you finish school, it would be nice to replaster the wall, but we can do that later. He'd done it all. He wondered what she'd say if she could see it now.

And now it was almost finished. The only thing this house needed was a little noise, a little untidiness, things on the floor to pick up. Again he heard his mother's voice: "Brian, if you don't pick those cars up off the floor, I'm going to package them up and send them away." But she never did. And when he was at university, he'd bring home all his papers – essays to write and books to read. "Brian, I declare, when you come home you scatter your papers all over the living room. There's hardly a trail through." But there was a kind of pride in her voice. His dad recognized this and smiled at the two of them. They were both happy. Their son was going away to university. He would become some-body. It was worth the scrimping and saving.

And he did what they wanted him to – studied hard, got good grades, and that coveted piece of paper that said he was a success. But he hated it. He hated the fancy job and the stylish shirt that went with it, the big desk, the constant deadlines, the 'yes sir, no sir' of the office staff. The only positive thing about it was that he could send his mother money every month. And what had she done with it? Hadn't bought a counter top or fixed the wall. No. She put it all in savings bonds ear-marked for him. And that's where it still was. He hadn't touched a cent of it. Did all the fixings by the sweat of his brow.

Strange. They had given him the gift of an education, he had given them the gift of money. Neither had used it. One could deduce it was the giving that made one happy. And where did that fancy educa-tion put him now? Happiness is merely a state of mind. He could make himself happy. If giving helped, fine. He could take bags of potatoes and carrots and onions and freshly churned butter down to that scrawny Christmas tree at the corner and put up a big sign: HELP YOURSELF.

The sound of a car coming up his lane interrupted his musings. He went to the door and opened it. There was Allie, looking as if she had a mission. "Allie, come in. Can I help you?"

"Can I sit down a minute? Something very strange is happening and I have to talk to someone who can keep a secret."

"Is Mae all right?"

"Yes. So far. Everybody is all right." Allie looked around. "You sure have fixed this place up. If your mother could see it now."

"I was just thinking the same thing. Glad you like it."

"I've wanted to come. I knew you were working on the house, but I was afraid you would think I was just being nosy. Someday, will you show me through the whole house?"

"Sure. I'll show you now."

"Brian, I haven't time now. I don't know where to start."

"Maybe you should start at the beginning."

"All right." She took a deep breath. "You know that man that's staying at Mae's. Gary Westicott. It's about him. Mae has been so good to him. Cooks for him, does his laundry, waits on him like a king. And he's been good to her, but it's all been a complete lie. A week or so ago, he told her he was going to meet Maxie at West Bay for supper and Mae was reading the paper and found out that Maxie was already in Florida. She couldn't believe Gary would deliberately lie, so she asked him about the dinner and he told her all about it. Said Maxie showed him some things that he was going to auction off. It was the night of the fire."

"It was his truck parked at the bridge and we couldn't use our regular place to get water. Held us up a bit. Some of the guys were pretty mad, but he has done a lot for this town and we decided not to say anything about it."

"That's just it. He volunteers for this and that and people like him. But he deliberately lied to Mae."

"I wonder what reason he would have to do that?"

"That's just it. And what's stranger is this." Allie leaned towards him. "Mae had never been in his room ever since he came. And she determined to go up there. And no sooner than she got up there, he came back, and went straight to his room."

"What happened?"

"She crawled under his bed and hid."

"Mae did?"

"Yes. Now here's the weird part. She could peek out the space between the floor and the spread, and she saw him put on pantyhose and women's shoes. Then he walked up and down, up and down the room. Finally, he put his own shoes back on and went downstairs."

"He never found out she was there?"

"He doesn't know to this day! But there's more." Allie's voice became conspiratorial. "He collects things and keeps them hidden in locked drawers. We were quilting downstairs and listening with all our ears but pretending, of course, not to. We kept chatting, but listening to the noises coming down the grate. He was walking from the dresser to the bed, from the bed to the dresser. Then he would go to the clothes closet and back. Walking constantly. He must have been sorting things. One thing we know for sure, he has Mae's tatted handkerchief."

"Whatever would he want with a handkerchief?"

Allie went over the whole story. About the murders, the ABC rhyme, the marionette, the jackknife. She told him about the date he had with Sheila, and their plan to keep them apart.

"Allie, this is a job for the police."

"No. Not yet. We are so close, and we must have proof or he'll get away. And I forgot to tell you about the zebra. Mae found a little glass zebra on the bathroom floor the night of the fire. She thought a little girl who had been to her house had dropped it accidentally. But that is in the poem, too. We think Gary dropped it. He was pretty shaken with smoke inhalation when he came in. If Mae puts the little zebra in full sight, and if it goes missing, we will know for sure and catch him red handed."

"I know who the zebra belongs to."

"Who?"

"Sheila."

"You don't mean to tell me. How do you know?"

"She came here one day all fired up and accused me of stealing her zebra. I had gone down to check out her window, and she thought I had taken it when I was there."

"How did Gary get it?"

"Must have gotten in somehow. She said it was in full view on her coffee table, but I hadn't noticed it."

"Isn't that a caution. Wait till Mae hears about this."

"If he's been in once, Allie, he can get in again. It's too dangerous not to phone the police."

"No. Not yet. Promise me. We've got it all worked out. We just wanted you to know in case we needed extra help. Somebody we could trust." She looked at him hard. "Now, I must go. Mae is waiting for me."

Brian was taken aback by this sudden explosion of information. Now he was an accomplice to a very dangerous plan. These two pistol packin' mommas had fixed him on a path he didn't want to travel. Here he was, thinking how alone he was and, might as well face it, feeling sorry for himself because he had no real family, and suddenly, out of nowhere, a major murder case is handed to him to sit by and watch. He shuddered at the responsibility. What course of action did he have? This would take some thinking, and tonight he had to curl. He checked his schedule. He hadn't even taken it out of the envelope yet. He unfolded the paper. Who was on his rink – Sandra Brown, John Vickers, and Sheila Peters. He thought she wouldn't be too happy about that. Well, at least he could keep an eye on her tonight.

CHAPTER 41

Allie was in her car and down the lane before she even thought about fastening her seatbelt. She screeched her brakes at the entrance to the highway and looked both ways, hoping no one had heard. She drove with one hand, trying to fasten the seatbelt with the other. Fortunately, there were no cars on the road as she careened down the centre like a kid taking a crash course in obstacle driving. She landed a full stop at Mae's door. She saw the kitchen curtain shiver and knew Mae was waiting there. She opened the door and almost ran her down.

Before Allie had a chance to speak, Mae said, "Little Marty never had a glass zebra. Now we know for sure it must be Gary's."

"Wait till I tell you, Mae. That zebra belongs to Sheila. She thought Brian took it when he went down that time to check her window. She went right up there and gave him what for!"

"Brian wouldn't steal a drink of water if he was dying of thirst. What a thing to accuse him of. My lands, Allie, it's Sheila Gary's after. How on earth did he get into her house? Do you think he broke in?"

"Probably easy enough. She likely never locks her house. I never do."

"She locks it alright. Made a big fuss about leaving a key for Brian to go in and fix the window."

"Maybe he crawled in a window. She might have left one open."

"We will just have to keep track of Gary's whereabouts every living minute. If he's after her, she's in real danger. Tonight, when he comes home, we'll have the zebra in the window sill by the table. We'll make some kind of conversation about it and watch close and see how he reacts." Mae was holding her hands tightly to her chest. "My whole skeleton is shivering, but my hands are still warm. How can that be?"

"It's nerves, Mae. That's all. Do you feel up to this?"

"Yes, I do. I hate to be made a fool of and that is precisely what Gary is doing to me. I'd be the laughing stock of town. Here I am, bragging about my boarder, and all the time he's a murderer. I want to have a hand in putting him in a place where the landlord won't be baking him biscuits."

"That's the spirit. Tonight is going to be very important. All we have to do is have proof before we call the police. If we have the sense that he is dying to get his hands on this zebra, we have it."

Allie nodded approvingly. "And as long as we know where he is every minute, Sheila is safe." She took a deep breath. "Mae, I'd like to take a look at his room. Would that be alright?"

"Yes, but hurry. I'll be scared all the time you're up there. I'll keep an eye out the window and watch, just in case he comes back."

Allie was up the stairs in a minute. The room was neat as a pin, just like Mae said. She tried the drawers. All locked. She opened the closet. The clothes were all hung neatly. There were the shoes, all men's. She closed the closet door. The bedspread was smooth, tucked in evenly under the pillows. Only the glass, and some books, and the clock on the trunk. An empty carry-all bag was folded on the dresser. Absolutely nothing else. He certainly left no tracks. She hurried down the stairs.

Mae was still by the window. "Did you see anything?"

"Not a thing. I would say it is uncommonly neat for a man. If he is a man," she added. "Gives you an eerie feeling, doesn't it? As if there was a ghost up there. Maybe the ghosts of all the people he's killed."

"Let's not scare ourselves silly. We should be quilting to settle our nerves."

"Good idea. I'll put the zebra on the window sill right now. It'll be right in his line of vision. At supper, we'll mention it."

They quilted and practised what they would say. Just like getting ready for a play, they thought. Their needles flew in and out, in and out, then pulled the thread taut. "My stitches are not very even. Hope nobody looks at them closely."

"Most detectives can't even quilt, Mae, so don't worry about them." They both chuckled.

"I'll make him his favourite dish – chicken and dumplings. He'll love that. And we'll have carrots and a salad. And I have a berry pie ready to go in the oven. I always like to thaw them out a little after I take them out of the freezer."

"Some people plunk them right in, frozen solid, but I don't think the bottom crust gets a chance to cook that way. I'll make the salad, Mae, when it's time."

"I'll stop and put the pie in now, and get the vegetables ready. We can practice our speeches while I'm peeling the carrots."

"Okay, I start." She cleared her throat. "That is a very interesting little animal on your window, Mae."

"Yes, it is. It is a zebra."

"Where did you get it?"

"I found it on the floor. It is a glass zebra. A little girl was in my house and she must have dropped it."

"It is very pretty."

"Yes, it is. I must call her mother and tell her it is here." (Now I take the zebra in my hands.) "Look how the stripes are painted inside the glass. See, Gary?"

"I think we have it down pat, Allie." Together they set the table, and Allie fixed the salad. They did what they knew best – making a good, hearty meal. They froze in their tracks the minute they heard Gary's truck in the driveway. Then they each took a breath and swallowed their nervousness. Gary opened the door.

"Smells great in here. I sure am hungry."

"Hi! How's the set coming along?"

"Just fine. But I feel all grubby. That old junk has been in storage for so long and never cleaned or taken care of. I'll wash up before supper." He disappeared into the bathroom. Then they heard him go upstairs and close the door.

Gary opened up his closet and took a shirt off a hanger. That chicken smelled so good. He sniffed appreciatively. Actually, he had worked hard all day. He was very hungry. In the act of buttoning up the third button on his shirt, he stopped. What was the other smell? A faint perfume of some kind. Just a trace. He tried to recognize the smell, but it was gone. He buttoned his shirt, smoothed down his hair and went downstairs.

Mae put the casserole on the table. "Your favourite dish, Gary."

"I do appreciate that. Carrots, too. What's sprinkled on them?"

"Cinnamon. We tasted that for the first time at Sheila's. Really good."

"Are you saying grace, Mae?" asked Allie.

Mae bowed her head. "Bless this food to our use, and us to Thy service. Amen."

They all ate heartily. Gary was more talkative than usual. "I have to make a fireplace for Santa, a door that really opens, and a window. I have to build a wall first to put the window in. That may be hard."

"I'm sure you can do it. How many kids are in the play?"

"I haven't seen it yet, but I think there are eight."

"I can remember the old school concerts. It was so frightening, standing there in front of all those people. Then you'd look back into that sea of faces and try to pick out your own family – your dad smiling proudly, and your mother with tears in her eyes. But they were happy tears."

Allie said, "That is a very interesting animal in your window, Mae."

"Yes, it is. It is a zebra."

"Where did you get it?"

"A little girl was in the house and she must have dropped it."

"It is very pretty."

"Yes, it is. I must call her mother and tell her it is here. Look how the stripes are painted inside the glass, Gary."

The speeches went like clockwork. Gary contained his original reaction of shock and disbelief. He calmly took the zebra from Mae and put it on the window. "Very nice," he said. Then he went back to devouring his dumplings. Mae and Allie were quiet. Gary sensed danger, like a fox who gets a whiff of human scent before he touches the bait. He kept rigid control, not a flicker of hand or heartbeat changed his expression. Then they all talked at once, of the bazaar, the church pageant, the weather, any little tidbit of local news.

"Mae, you sit while I get the dessert." Allie took her plate and Mae's and came back for Gary's. As her arm brushed in front of him, that same whiff of perfume he had smelled upstairs froze him to his chair. She'd been up there, the meddling old witch. He maintained total outward composure while his inner emotions came to a full rolling boil. Control, Gary, control. "Delicious, Mae," he said as he took his first bite of berry pie.

"Thank you. I always keep a few frozen berry pies. It's a little taste of summer on a winter's day."

"That was a wonderful meal, Mae. I must excuse myself. I have a few things to do at the school, and I curl at nine. I'll go straight to curling from there."

"I may be asleep when you come home. I'll leave the light on in the kitchen."

"Or we may still be quilting," Allie said.

Westicott went up to his room. He sat on the edge of his bed and held himself in his own arms, rocking back and forth, back and forth, trying desperately to control the seething anger within. His body jerked in spasms. His arms, crossed tightly in front, squeezed his shoulders. One thousand, two thousand... The old trick was working. Slowly. The rocking was becoming less violent. He gradually loosened his grip. That snarky old she-devil had been up here. It was her perfume he smelled. And when they talked about the zebra, it was a trick. So rehearsed. "That is a very interesting animal in your window. Where did you find it?" It sounded like a kid's play. Every syllable so distinct. Those old dames were onto something. As if they could ever outsmart him. Well, there was nothing to find in his bedroom. Everything was in place, according to plan. His mind was playing tricks on him. He was imagin-

169

ing things. Two old broads like that didn't have brains enough to fill a teaspoon. So what if they thought he had something to do with the zebra? He had acted perfectly calm. He had fooled them completely. Even so, he had to be sure whether Allie had been in his room. He would have to be certain of that if he was to be secure. He was in perfect control now. He went down the stairs two at a time and left for the school.

As soon as he closed the door, both women started talking at once. They had bottled up their reactions all the time Gary was upstairs. Now all these emotions fizzed out like spilled pop, Allie got control. "Mae, he didn't react at all."

"Very nice," he said. "That was it. He didn't show any sign of recognition or even interest." Mae was deflated. "Our hope of proof is gone. What can we do now?"

"I didn't see one flicker of recognition. But we've got to remember, we're dealing with an expert here. He's never been caught. He wouldn't dare show any interest."

"When you think of it, not showing any interest at all is a good sign that he is very interested."

"I hope we're not in over our heads, Mae."

"We'll be okay if we watch our step. Nothing to do but wait. We may find our zebra gone after all."

Gary struggled to keep his mind on curling. After the game, he didn't stay to socialize. When Sheila came to talk to him, he almost forgot the romance thing. He excused himself abruptly, saying he was very tired.

The old girls were just packing up when he got there. The faint scent was still in the air. His eyes caught the glass zebra, shining reflected light on the pane. He would not touch that zebra, yet. He hadn't found another, but he would have a good chance to look around the church at the pageant. A thought had hit him that every church should have a Noah's ark. And any good Noah's ark should have a zebra. There had been so much activity around the church, he didn't dare go before the pageant. He could wait.

He said good night and went upstairs. He listened at the grate while they said good-bye. Nothing unusual there. No whisperings. He took an envelope out of his pocket, unsealed it gently, and examined the contents. He got down on his knees and poured a little on the floor. Perfect colour. In the morning he would sprinkle this dust ever so carefully, just where a person coming into his room might put her foot. Let that old snark poke her nose in his door, and he'd know, once and for all.

Chapter 42

Before noon on Saturday, Gary called Sheila from the school. He apologized for bothering her at work, but wondered if she'd meet him at the restaurant for lunch. He told her that he realized how rude he had been at the curling rink the night before, and wanted to make amends. She said she would be glad to meet him, but only had a half an hour for lunch. She said she would get there as close to twelve as possible.

Gary went into the restaurant at ten to twelve. It was crowded for lunch, and he remembered there was a work crew in town, working on a leak in the water line. Gary spotted an empty table, and sat down. He busied himself squaring a placemat in front of him, and arranging the silverware so it would line up exactly with the pattern. Having finished this ritual, he lifted his head. The waitress was standing there. "Please bring two specials as soon as the lady comes," he said.

"Would you like a coffee now?"

"Please."

She poured his coffee. He stirred in the cream and looked around the dining room. Just his luck. There, in full side view, was that lummox Brian, who'd almost broken his ribs the night of the fire. He was sitting there, his elbows on the table, cap on backwards, gibbering away with some of the local yokels. For that matter, they were all wearing caps, the peaks staring backwards down their dirty necks. He'd often seen this bunch in the fall, playing with the fire hose at some of the town celebrations. One of them spotted him. "Hi, Gary old chap, how ya doin'?"

"Fine. Or as they say around here, just dandy."

Brian had seen Gary come in, but only now acknowledged his presence. "Hi, Gary. You're looking better today. Thought you were pretty tuckered out the last time I saw you. Hope you got over the smoke attack. Say, I could give you a hand with that drama set I hear you're building at the school."

"Thanks. I'm sure..." Just then Sheila walked in, easily seeing Gary, and sat down opposite him, her back to Brian. Gary ignored Brian's comments and turned his attention to Sheila. They began to talk earnestly across the table. "I really want to apologize for my behaviour last night. I feel badly about it. I was so tired. I'm afraid I wasn't even civil."

"Don't apologize. I know what it's like to be overtired. I used to get that way sometimes, before I came here."

"I guess it's just that I'm not used to carpentry work. There's quite a bit of building on this set."

"Those jobs always turn out to be bigger than what they start out to be. I used to do some stage work when I was in high school."

He smiled. "You are looking particularly beautiful today."

"Thank you."

She felt the colour rising to her cheeks. "It's been quite a while since I had a compliment like that from a man."

Just then the waitress appeared. Gary said, "I've taken the liberty of ordering two specials. I knew you didn't have much time."

"Thanks."

"Hello," the waitress said. "Are you ready for your meals?"

"Yes, please. We are in a hurry." The waitress hustled off.

Gary said, "Have you decided where you want to go after dinner Wednesday?"

"That's up to you, Gary."

"Mae's trying to get me to take you back to her house. She wants to make me a cake. I didn't know what you would think about that. We've not had much opportunity to be alone."

"That's true. But we have all winter, unless you are planning to leave?"

"That's up in the air right now. Mother says she's having trouble with the books and needs me to straighten them out." He smiled at her. "I find I'm beginning to like this place better and better."

"I'd like to meet your mother. She must be something special."

"She is."

The waitress delivered the food. "I don't have a mother anymore," Sheila said. "She died a long time ago. I think I'm beginning to find a surrogate mother in Mae."

"She is a dear thing. But I've been wanting to ask you...do you have any personal attachments away from here?"

"I was married, Gary. We were...incompatible. I'm divorced now. Does that make a difference?"

"No, not at all." He smiled. "Don't look now, but our friend Brian is coming to our table."

Brian was casually buttoning up his jacket as he stopped beside Gary. "Hello, Miss Peters. I hope you enjoyed the game last night. You threw some good rocks." Then he turned to Gary. "I'll give you a hand this afternoon with that set. I'm not very experienced with that kind of

172

thing, but if you tell me where to put the nails, I'll drive them in. Do you have enough lumber? I have some spare boards at my place."

"Really, I can..."

"I hear that Mr. Peterson is a fine carpenter." There was something in the way she said 'carpenter' that made Brian cringe. She was implying that this was the only fine thing about him. "Why don't you take him up on his offer? After all, this is a community responsibility. Let him help, Gary."

"I could use another hand. You'll have to bring an extra hammer."

"See you in about an hour," Brian said and walked up to the cash desk.

Sheila spoke softly. "Make him work hard. And keep a close eye on him. If you can get friendly with him, he may brag about stealing my zebra. You can be my detective agent. Everybody else thinks he's as pure as the driven snow."

Gary smiled. "I'll do that." Panic! He'd have to move that zebra from sight on Mae's window!

Sheila checked her watch. "I have to go now. I'm almost late. Will I see you again before Wednesday?"

"Tomorrow for sure at the pageant. I promised Mae."

She smiled, touched by his concern for Mae. "We'll get a chance to talk about Wednesday night. Thanks for lunch." She hurried out the door.

As Gary waited to pay for lunch, he assessed the situation. Everything was fine, now, with Sheila. She could be counted on. He would have to move that zebra. And, in spite of the fact that he couldn't abide Brian, he would have to gain his confidence. Better to act surprised when Brian was accused of the murder. He paid the bill, quite satisfied with himself. Now, off to the school.

He hadn't had any luck finding anything on his list in the drama room. There was every other thing but what he needed. There were a few cupboards he hadn't checked out yet, but on first look they seemed to be full of paint. He was pinning his hopes now on the church. He wondered why he had been so long thinking about that. A much better place to find a zebra. Maybe a pair of them.

Brian's arrival cut into his musings. "Okay, chief, what do you want done?"

Gary took out the drama teacher's sketch. "Here's what we need. We have to have a door that opens. There's a door here, but somehow we have to frame it. And in the wall, here, we have a window that opens. Maybe you will have some ideas about that. I am working on the fireplace."

173

"If we have to have a window that opens, then I guess we have to build a wall."

"Right. I'm glad you came. I'm better with a paint brush than a hammer. Anyway, where do we start?"

"I'll look around and see what we have to work with. Same old place. I went to school here when I was knee high to a grasshopper. That varnish smell never left the place. And I don't think they've changed that fountain since the day they put it in."

They were walking towards the drama storage room. Gary had the key. "I don't think this room's ever been cleaned. Layers of dust everywhere. Help yourself to whatever you can find." Gary hauled out the fireplace. He had been stapling paper that looked like bricks around the frame. Brian searched around and found some two by fours. He checked the dimensions on the sketch and set about to build a wall. In no time at all he had a frame, ready to nail the boards to. "How big's that window?"

"I'll measure it." Gary found a tape. "It's three by five."

"Gotcha. Three by five." Brian set about making a frame to fit. The two of them worked away all afternoon. It was evident to Brian that Gary hadn't done this kind of work before. He wondered why he had volunteered to help. But he was working away, and at least, he wasn't getting into any kind of trouble. He really didn't seem like a bad sort of guy. About five they decided to quit. "I can give you a hand on Monday. Meet you about ten? I'll have my chores done by then."

"I really appreciate your help, Brian. I hate to admit it, but I don't think I could have done it without you."

"I was born with a hammer in my hand. See you at ten on Monday. Are you going to the church pageant? It's a major tradition around here. Good food, too."

Gary was putting his stapler away in a cupboard. Something caught his eye behind the paint cans. He reached in. There was a broken recorder, a harmonica, and packages of strings...six of them!...clearly labeled, EADG. Violin strings! Never opened. What a find! He was elated. Good citizenship was paying off. He almost lost the thread of the conversation with Brian.

"What'd you find, good buddy?"

"Just some old broken instruments. I hate to see things broken like this." He showed Brian the recorder.

"That's been here a long time. They used to teach music here. I was in the band way back then. Had a C sax. We were pretty careless with the instruments, I guess. Anyway, as I was saying, everybody goes to the pageant."

"Yes, I'm going. Promised Mae."

"The place will be packed. It's the one night when everybody's house is empty. Can't understand why robbers don't steal us blind."

"You're very fortunate. You wouldn't think of leaving a street open where I come from. Well, I'll see you at the church tomorrow night. Thanks again for your help."

They both left together. Gary's hands trembled in his pocket, clutching the strings. The line from the poem filled his mind: V IS FOR VIOLIN STRINGS, E, A, D and G. He had them all. Seven sets. He had been searching out doilies and zebras and marionettes and never even thought he had a chance of finding violin strings. A sudden sense of his own divine power made him momentarily giddy. Nothing could stop him. Things were presenting themselves to him without his even looking for them. He could probably turn stones into bread if he wanted to. He had the Power.

This was the best time. His plan was perfect. But he must not get too confident. He went over everything again. He had the seven sets of strings. From this very moment, the third woman he encountered would be his next victim. Once identified, he could take all the time he needed to execute the murder. He would not actively seek out the third woman. He would let her present herself to him, just as the strings had presented themselves. He relished the electric flow of adrenaline surging through his body.

Gary got in his truck and started to drive. He was too excited to be composed at supper with Mae. He had told her he might work late, so she wouldn't be looking for him. He had some cheese, chips and doughnuts in the truck. He devoured them ravenously. His mind was so filled with excitement that he didn't really know where he was. It was starting to get dark. He began to pay attention to road signs. Highway 6, Sheguiandah. He turned left, towards Mindemoya.

He was approaching Mae's house. The lights were still on in the kitchen. He collected himself, acquiring a tired demeanour before opening the door. Mae was sitting in the living room, reading the paper. He casually flicked the curtain in front of the zebra, hiding him nicely with one quick, undetected motion. "Hello. I was hoping you had the teapot on. I could sure use a good cup of your tea."

"You came at just the right time. The kettle's just starting to boil." She came to the kitchen. "You have been working so hard, you must be tired."

"Actually, I am. But your friend, Brian, was a great help. He helped a lot with the walls and the window."

"He should be pretty good at that. Will you get it all done in time?" Mae reached for the mugs.

"No problem. We got a lot more done today than I thought. The kids will have their set in lots of time."

They sat opposite each other, drinking their tea. Mae could hardly believe that this man, whom she had trusted so completely, was a cold blooded murderer. She had to keep up a conversation to settle her nerves. "Since you're so close to being finished, you won't have to work tomorrow, then. Tomorrow night's the pageant, you know. I'm so hoping you will go. I'm so proud of my boarder, and I guess I want to show you off to my friends. Of course, you know most of them already."

"I know how much you want me to go, Mae." He reached over and patted her hand. "I will be there. You can count on that." He smiled at her. "Brian says everybody goes to the pageant. Is that really so?"

"It would be hard to find anyone at home in this town when the pageant's on. Whenever their kids are involved, you can be sure their parents will be there, even if they never set foot in the church at any other time."

"How long does the pageant last?"

"That depends on how long you want to visit after the pageant's over. The main part will be finished about nine or nine thirty."

Gary got up and took his mug to the sink. "I wish my mother could be here. She would be pretty proud to see her son in church."

"I'm sure she would be. And I'm so proud, too. You are like a son to me, Gary." Might as well lay it in thick, she thought.

"Mae, you flatter me," he said. He turned and placed his hand on her shoulder. "In my book," he said, "You're number one."

She didn't flinch as she felt the warm pressure of the murderer's hand. She wanted to yell, to run, to push the help button on the gadget in her pocket, but she did none of these things. Instead, she raised her eyes to his and smiled. "I think your mother's number one. But I'm your guardian angel while you're here." Angel, she thought. Why on earth did she say angel? The line from the poem rang in her ears.

"I think you are, Mae." He took his hand from her shoulder, trembling a little, he thought, by his closeness. "I really am pretty tired. Thanks for the tea. I'm off to bed to get myself in good shape for tomorrow. Good night."

"See you in the morning, Gary. I'm going to finish reading the paper, and turn in myself." Relief had swept over her like balm of Gilead. She pretended to read, but the words blurred in front of her. She heard Gary's steps retreat. He opened the bathroom door and closed it. She heard the toilet flush, the water run in the sink, the door open, his feet cross to the upstairs door, heard it open and close. One more night. She was safe.

CHAPTER 43

Gary woke to freezing rain pellets on his windows. A persistent wind rattled a loosened shingle on the dormer, determined to carry it away with the rest of the loosened landscape it had managed to hurl down the street. He crawled out of bed and looked out the window. A perfect day for a perfect deed, he thought.

How quickly things change. Yesterday he had pinned all his hopes on finding the zebra. He had made all his plans with the zebra in mind. After he made his kill, he would place the zebra on the victim's body, and what a commotion that would create. Sheila had lost her zebra, Mae had seen it and Allie had seen it. Sheila was sure Brian had stolen it from her. The only problem was that the one on Mae's window would have to be removed to add to his collection, and that might have been tricky. He hadn't quite figured that out yet but he could certainly have pointed the finger at Brian. Even though that would have been enjoyable, there was an element of danger involved. Yes, finding the strings was better.

He thought about the strings. They were certainly way down on his list. Suddenly all six sets had presented themselves in front of him. It was an omen, clear and simple. No one would ever connect him with violin strings. It made his work much easier. Even so, he must pay particular care to the job at hand.

This was the exciting part. Who would the next victim be? The third woman after the finding of the strings. Not Mae. She was number one. He'd even told her that. Silly old woman. If he had his druthers it would be Allie. There had been no tracks in the dust he had left upstairs, but she had been snooping around, he was sure of that. Well, he had certainly not left any clues, so she could snoop around whenever she wanted to. Still, it would be gratifying to get a confession out of her. And that wouldn't be hard as the wire tightened around her throat. He smiled at the picture that was focusing in his mind. He forced himself back to reality. It was never safe to let his imagination wander. It was much too easy to get over excited. Especially now, he had to keep rigid control over his emotions. The big moment was approaching.

Was he completely ready? Yes. The clothes. The wire. The violin strings. The spoons, ready and waiting. First, coil the wire neatly, and put it in his top right jacket pocket. Then place the packet of strings in the left pocket, and the line from the poem, and a pin to fasten it to the body. Make sure the skirt is folded neatly and fastened to the jacket lining. Tuck the beret beneath the skirt. Never mind the high heels. Such a nice effect, but it was just too icy out for safety. Besides, he would do the deed at night, and everyone would be at the pageant, so no one would see him anyway. It would all be so easy when no one was around. Thanks to Brian, he had the perfect time and occasion for the murder. He smiled to himself at the thought. Brian, the town do-gooder, an unwitting accomplice to a murder.

He checked everything once more. Everything was in order. He looked at the clock. Almost noon. He would put on the helpful boarder attitude and go downstairs. He took the steps two at a time. Mae was in the kitchen. "Can I do anything to help, Mae? Sorry I slept so late when I might have been helping you."

"No, I don't think there's anything I need at the moment. I have the loaves almost ready for tonight. I would appreciate a hand to get everything to the church, though. It is pretty slippery out."

"Sure. Allie coming over?"

"No, she's involved in the decorations. She'll be there all day."

This little bit of information disappointed him a little. So Allie wouldn't be dropping in. Too bad. "Anybody coming to help you?"

"No. Everybody has a specific job for the pageant. Some are making costumes, some are rehearsing the kids, there's tables to get ready, and music to arrange. It's a major effort. Every year it gets a little more elaborate."

"What exactly happens?"

"The church basement is set up like the Bethlehem Inn. The townspeople arrive and are served by the innkeeper and his servants. Suddenly a knock comes to the door. It's one of the bigger kids playing the part of Joseph. And the whole story is acted out just as if everything was happening now."

"I am amazed at the involvement of this community. Don't tell me everybody attends." (Might as well double check.)

"Yes, everybody goes. And I must say, you got pretty involved yourself, spending all your spare time making that set for the play at the school. That's the kind of thing that makes strangers well-liked by folks in a small town. And it makes you feel a part of us too, don't you think?"

"Yes, you're right. I do feel a part of this town. It's a good feeling to belong. And you've made me so welcome, Mae. I can't begin to thank you for that."

"You are like a son to me, Gary. Now you get along and leave me to my baking, or I'll forget what I'm doing." She smiled up at him. Mae was so glad he was here. As long as he was here, Sheila was safe. She was surprised at how calm she could be as she smiled into his eyes.

Gary went into the living room and settled himself comfortably on the couch. He thought about that old woman in the kitchen. She was devoted to him. She might have had some suspicions over that zebra, but he had played it so cool that she had never doubted him. She hadn't said one more word about it. It was still in the window, completely hidden now by some Christmas cards, as well as the curtain.

He picked up the paper and glanced at the headlines. Nothing of interest there. He went through a pile of magazines on the coffee table. Only the Macleans was fairly recent. He forced himself to read, determined to be patient and in control of his emotions. He read it from cover to cover. What a lot of violence in the world. Mae brought him a sandwich. She hoped he didn't mind if he didn't have a full course meal. She wanted him to be hungry for the sumptuous feast they would partake of later.

Mae continued to bustle about the kitchen. Finally, she announced that she had six loaves ready and she was going to catch a little rest before they went. "Are you going to be here, Gary? I just need a half hour or so."

"Sure, I'll be here. I'll take any calls if the phone rings. Are you expecting anyone?"

"No, everyone will be up to their ears in work. Don't let me sleep past four thirty."

"Have a good nap. I'll look after things." He went to the kitchen and poured himself a coffee. Then he sat down at the kitchen table. An old Chatelaine was opened to a recipe. He leafed through the magazine. Surely there was something better to read. He went into the living room and started sorting through the old books in the bookcase. He could use a good classic, something to make you think and take your mind off the present. What was in here, anyway? Dickens. Hardy. Some Shakespearean plays. All pretty ancient copies. He took out Macbeth. This was one of his favourites. The thing about Shakespeare, you could read his plays again and again. Every time you found something you hadn't completely understood before. He opened the book, noting that this was probably a very collectable edition. He'd settle himself comfortably and have a good read. Macbeth was such a loser. Falling to pieces like that in front of everyone when he could have pulled off the perfect murder. You could learn a lot though, from his mistakes. He opened to the first page. "When shall we three meet again, in thunder, lightning or in rain." He heard the chant of the witches in his ears. The

179

wonderful control of words that compelled you to see the whole scene in your mind.

He became completely absorbed in the story. He must have been engrossed for an hour when a tap on the door startled him. It came very appropriately, just as he had reached the porter scene. "Who's there?" he said, then went to open the door.

"Hello, Mr. Westicott. Is Mae home?" It was a little girl he had seen at the school.

"She's having a nap right now. Do you want something?"

"My mother sent me down to see if she had some candle holders for the tables."

"She probably has. Can she call you at the church?"

"Yes. There's a phone there."

"I'll make sure she calls."

"I see you everyday making the sets for our play. My mom says you are a good person to do that."

"Thank you." He smiled as she turned and walked away. He had never considered that his next victim might be a child. No, that would be too easy. However, he would count this little girl as number two. But he decided that number three had to be over sixteen. Anyway, he wouldn't worry. Children came very seldom.

He made himself comfortable again. The next female adult would be number three. He went back to his reading. Where was he? He read on. Lady Macbeth was washing her hands. "Who'd have thought the old man would have had so much blood in him?" That was another careless thing. He should have killed Duncan some other way. Then, Macbeth made it worse by killing the guards. Blood everywhere. Stupid. He settled into the story.

The clock struck four. He heard Mae walking around in her room. She came out. "I was dead to the world. Guess I was tired."

"A little girl was here looking for candle holders for the tables. You are to call the church."

"I have lots. Now, what's the number? Oh, here it is. I'll call right now."

"Hello. It's Mae."

"I have at least four sets. They're not fancy. Suitable for the inn."

"That'll be fine. Everything going all right there?"

"I'm dying to see it. See you at five thirty. Bye."

Mae began searching for the candle holders, talking to herself as she rooted through the cupboards. "Every year these things get harder to find. And my old knees get harder to bend. Here they are... finally."

She hauled out four pair. Gary could hear her washing them in the sink. He was engrossed again in his book. He was used to the noises in the kitchen. Suddenly a different noise shocked him to attention. Someone was opening the door...

CHAPTER 44

Sheila couldn't remember when she had been this excited. She stepped out of the shower and wiped the steam from the mirror. When she caught a glimpse of herself, she seemed to see a younger Sheila, cheeks highly coloured, eyes bright and smiling. She caught herself studying her reflection. Do I really look like this? Yes, that's the way I feel, definitely younger and prettier. Gary told me I was beautiful. She smiled, remembering.

She sorted through her closet. What to wear? Something lovely, but not fussy. This was a new situation. She wanted to blend in, not stand out from the crowd. Finally, she picked a deep purple wool skirt and matching turtleneck. This would do. It was comfortable and classy, and someone long ago had told her that purple did something for her eyes. Deepened the blue. She smiled. What should she choose to wear for jewelry? A necklace of some sort. Not pearls, not the chunky purple beads, the little knife on the chain, maybe? Yes, that was it. She tried it. Perfect. Simple, yet charming. And a conversation piece. Besides, it was a kind of bond between herself and Gary.

She was ready. She checked her image in the long hall mirror. Everything was right. She looked good. Her face was positively glowing. Whatever had come over her? She smiled. All for a simple country pageant. Or was it in anticipation of a growing relationship with Gary? Giddy as a girl on her first date, she hurried out the door. She thought she might stop at Mae's to see if she needed any help getting her things to the church.

Allie was hustling about the church, trying to keep her mind on the decorations. She was worried about Mae, alone in her house with that murderer. But she knew she had her phone in her pocket if she needed help. Would they ever get over this night?

She climbed up on a two step ladder, balancing cedar branches in one hand and tinsel in the other. Somehow she managed to fasten the branches to last year's hooks concealed behind the fasteners that held the furnace pipes. On any other occasion, this was a job she loved. But not today.

Then she set about placing the wreaths on the window ledges. Where were the little crystal angels stored? The mere thought of glass angels made her heart pound. Her hands trembled as she opened the storage cupboard and reached for the box marked 'angels'. She opened the box carefully, trying to control the fear clutching at her heart.

Finally all the wreaths were perfect. She found the miniature lights and set them twinkling. The reflected light seemed to give the angels life. So beautiful, but so terrifying. She didn't dare tell anyone why she was so worried. Let this secret out and the whole plan would be shattered. She had to make up some excuse.

"I'm afraid Mae will forget those candle holders in all the excitement," she announced to one and all. "I'll just take a minute and run down and get them myself."

"I can go, Allie. I'm almost finished and it will save you going out in all that ice. Just take me a minute."

"No," Allie replied firmly. "Mae might need me for something else." She grabbed her coat and sped out the door.

CHAPTER 45

Sheila and Allie pulled into Mae's driveway at the same time. Sheila got out and walked carefully on the icy pavement towards Allie who was just getting out of her car. "Careful, Allie. It's slippery. I thought I might be of help to Mae. I know she's baking up a storm."

"No need to bother," Allie replied. "I'll help her. You go along to the church."

"I'd like to help, Allie."

"I know, dear. But I'll take her things. You can be of help after it's all over." Allie certainly didn't want Sheila going into Mae's house. That would give Gary a perfect chance to offer to take her to the pageant, and who knows what would happen then. It would be delivering the innocent fly right to the spider himself.

"Then I'll just pop in and say 'Hi' and let her know I at least offered." Sheila walked to the door. Allie pushed past her, almost blocking her way.

"Allie, is something wrong?"

"No, no, dear. It's just that these things get me all on edge. Sorry." There was certainly no way she was going to be able to keep Sheila from going inside. Allie opened the door, making frantic facial motions to Mae. Just behind her, Sheila said, "I just wanted to know if I could help, Mae. Allie thinks you don't need me, but I wanted to check."

Allie was talking at the same time. "Mae, I told Sheila to go on to the church and I'll help you."

After this burst of conversation, silence hung suspended in the kitchen. Mae was momentarily tongue-tied. Gary came out from the living room. "A lot of excitement out here. Sheila, hello. Both you and Allie are here to help Mae, and that's my job. Everybody wants to help my favourite lady." He put his arm around Mae. "See how much people care about you. Now, let me help decide. Who got here first?" For the life of him, he really couldn't tell with both of them talking at once.

Sheila laughed. "Well, I got to the door first."

"And I got in first," Allie said. "Then that decides it. The person who got in first is it. The one who helps."

184

Mae took her cue. "Allie's first – and she knows how I like to pack things. But Sheila, dear, I do appreciate you coming. I'll tell you what. You can help by taking the candle holders on ahead. They'll want them to finish decorating the tables. Here they are, all ready. Hurry along now, and we'll see you soon."

Gary smiled at Sheila. "I think it's times like this we foreigners do what we're told," he said. "I hope you'll save me a spot at the table."

Sheila gave him a knowing look. "I'll do that," she said, and went out and closed the door.

"Now, Mae, let me help you wrap that baking." She had to busy herself to keep sane.

"I'd better get ready. How dressed up are you supposed to be at this party?" Gary asked.

"You don't need to really dress up. That blue sweater of yours would be nice. It looks very good on you."

"Okay. Now if you'll excuse me, ladies, I'll go and get dressed for the occasion." They heard his feet climb the stairs.

Allie and Mae hugged each other. They were both trembling. "Close call," Mae whispered.

"I was scared to death," Allie said in a quiet voice. "We must carry on talking as we usually would in case Gary's listening." In a louder voice she said, "I've got a splitting headache. I'm certainly not staying late after the pageant. Someone else can help with the dishes."

"That's too bad. You've been looking forward to this for so long."

"I think Sheila will help. Maybe we can convince Gary to help, too."

"I thought you said I was the matchmaker," Mae replied, laughing.

These words carried very nicely up through the floor grate. Gary could feel the excitement rising, and was struggling to control it. He must keep cool. This was the most important part – making sure he was completely ready for the task ahead. The ladies had just helped with the little piece of news that Allie was going home early. He planned it as he dressed. He would go to the pageant. He would talk to as many people as he could, making sure they would remember his being there. He would play up to Sheila. It wouldn't be hard to win her over. A few compliments, a hand on her shoulder with a slight message conveyed through his fingers that if they weren't in public he could do better than this. Then he would just relax and enjoy the show. It was all so easy. He didn't even have to look for a zebra!

Then, after the pageant and the feasting were over, he would whisper to Sheila that he had to put one more coat of paint on the window at the school so it would be ready for Brian to put in the next day. He would actually go to the school and do that. He would leave his truck parked in full view, and put on the lights in the storage room in the school. Then, in the darkness, he would put on his long skirt and beret, just on the off chance he should meet someone on the street. He would simply walk into Allie's house, since he knew she never locked it, and wait for her to come home. When the deed was done, he would change into his own clothes and go back to the church. Of course he would have to go back to the school to put out the lights.

He dressed carefully, choosing navy pants to wear with his sweater. He would take his leather jacket, all packed and ready. The shoes and the binocular case he locked in the bottom drawer. What a great dresser this was. How lucky to have one that locked. All ready now, he went downstairs to help Mae. By the sound of things, Allie was already gone. How nice of Mae to confirm for him that Allie was first in. Things were certainly working for him. He took the steps two at a time.

Chapter 46

Mae and Gary arrived at the church at five. Many people were there already. Mae hurried out to the kitchen with her breads. Gary soon found someone to talk to. One of the local husbands was quick to start a conversation. "I see Mae's talked you into coming to the pageant. I'm surprised she hasn't got you into preachin' the sermon on Sundays." He laughed at his own joke.

"Well, it isn't as if she hasn't tried to get me involved with the church. She's quite a lady."

"Yep. Sort of the town grandmother, though she never had any kids herself. Can't help but go straight when Mae's got you on her leash. A bit pushy, maybe, but we all take her with a grain of salt."

"She's sure been good to me." Gary spied Sheila. "Pardon me, there's a young lady over there who's keeping me a chair." He walked over to Sheila, anxious to rid himself of the town idiot.

"Glad you came. I thought I might have trouble saving you a spot."

"You can bet I would have found a space. You are looking particularly lovely in that deep purple. And there's that little knife with a history!"

"Yes. I wore it for you, actually. Kind of a symbol of our friendship. I can't believe, now, how I didn't trust you!"

He took it in his fingers, studying it closely. "It's strange how we make hasty decisions and then find out we were wrong. I'm glad you wore it. It makes me think you like me," he teased.

Sheila felt the colour rising to her cheeks. "It's probably not a good place to discuss this with all these people watching."

He put his hand on her shoulder and squeezed it gently. "Some other time soon. That's a promise."

As if by magic, food arrived on the table – turkey, potatoes, carrots, peas, salad, deep brown gravy.

"This is a feast fit for a king," he said.

"That's what it's all about," she said, smiling. "How long since you've read that..." Her sentence was interrupted with a loud knocking. It was Joseph, of course. The crowd hushed as the innkeeper explained that there was no room in the inn. They were led to the manger and then came more loud knocking. This time it was the wisemen. More knocking... The words echoed in Gary's head: "Wake Duncan with thy knocking, I wish thou could'st." That was the beginning of Macbeth's downfall. Scared all the way. Silly fool. Well, that's not me, he thought. Everyone participated in the pageant. They all sang, laughed at the donkey's head that kept slipping, were amazed at the costumes of the kings. And it was true, the inn was crowded to the rafters.

A beautiful little girl held a doll which actually cried when she put it in the manger. Joseph stooped to pick up the baby, while angels hovered behind him. The scene touched Sheila. She felt herself there, at the manger, kneeling with the shepherds. Gary touched her arm, bringing her back to reality. "I hate to interrupt, but I have to go to the school to put one more coat of paint on a window. Brian has to put it in the wall tomorrow, and the paint has to be dry. I don't want to make a big thing out of leaving early. I'll just duck out quietly. If I get finished in time, I'll be back."

"Did Brian mention my zebra?" she asked.

"No, not a word. He may, yet. He's a pretty impressive carpenter, though," and he smiled at their in joke.

"Please come back. I'll stay and help with the dishes. I'll be waiting."

"Count on me," he said, and left.

The weather had changed while they were in the church. The wind had quieted, but it was very cold. Ice hung from the trees. Gary got in his truck and drove to the school. He got out his brushes and carefully painted the window. This was good self discipline, keeping his emotions under control. He was using yellow paint and some had got on his fingers. That was certainly proof that he had been here. Then he put a few finishing touches on the fireplace. It didn't take long for an hour to pass. They'd be starting to tidy about now. Allie would soon be going home. It was time. He kept the light on in the room, and closed the door. In the dark hall, he turned his jacket inside out, and put on his skirt and the beret. He checked his pockets for the wire and the strings. And the line from the poem. All there. But had he remembered to clear these things of fingerprints? No. He went back in and found a soft cloth. He rubbed each item carefully. He put on his gloves and replaced the articles. Everything was immaculate. He was ready.

He opened the door. Nobody on the street. What a perfect night. He walked down to the corner. Not a soul. Not a light in a house. Actually, the moon provided the light. The trees were like chandeliers, hanging with prisms of ice. He walked unhurriedly to Allie's house. He opened the door and walked in. She was not home yet. How simple. He would wait for her to come, strangle her quickly and go back to the school. Of course, he would have to prepare the body with the strings and the poem, but that would take no time at all. He would wait by the window until he saw her coming. Then he would hide behind the door and grab her from behind. Pulling the wire tight. She wouldn't even have time to struggle. Then he would yank her body out on the carpet, and pin on the note and the strings. He would go to the school, turn out the lights and go to the church where Sheila was waiting. And he would still have the yellow paint on his fingers. His mind kept going over and over the details.

He waited. Patiently, at first. What time was it now? She said she was leaving early, he'd heard her tell Mae. He could wait longer. The minutes crawled by. He forced his mind to think of other things to pass the time. He thought of Sheila. He might as well carry on the romance thing, see how far she would go. He needed a good alibi, and she would provide it. And why not enjoy himself! He deserved it. Then he thought about the spoons. Where would they take him next? After he was safe in his room tonight, he'd turn one over. That was always exciting. He liked that part. He wondered then when Mae would be home. If she missed him, she might send someone to the school. Such a busybody, running everybody's life. Why wasn't Allie home? He started to pace. What if Mae did send someone to the school and found no one there? Lights were coming on in all the houses. How long he had been here! He couldn't risk staying any longer. Mae would expect him home and try to find out where he was. He had to make a reasonable lie about where he'd been. Where was that witch, Allie? Now he knew why he always called her a witch. If Macbeth had murdered all the witches he'd have been better off.

This could have been the perfect setup but Allie had ruined it all. Well, he didn't have to kill her tonight. Any night would do. He'd just have to revise his plan. The street was still quiet. It was dark, now. Any people he saw would just be unrecognizable shadows. And besides that, he had committed no crime. He had no worries, none at all. And it would be rather pleasant planning his next move. Nothing could stop him now.

He opened the door and stepped softly out. He checked the street. No sound. He took in a deep breathe of crisp air that filled him with exhilaration. No, indeed, he had not failed. He had simply been given a second chance. Another opportunity to challenge his superior mind. Killing in a small community was much more of a challenge than killing in a city. Although the people here were a simple minded lot, they had an uncanny sense of knowing what was going on in the community. He placed a confident foot on the top step of the porch, checked the darkening street once more, and started down the small paved walk to the road. Little patches of ice caught reflected light and he was glad he had decided against the high heels tonight! He smiled to himself. They were such a neat touch but a little impractical in winter. He inhaled deeply. He felt the Power welling up in him.

189

What he did not hear were the quiet steps of two dark figures creeping out from the shadows of the cedars by Allie's house. They moved quickly but carefully, trying to avoid making a sound. Brian held a yellow nylon rope in one hand. Fred was almost three feet from Gary when a twig snapped beneath his foot. Gary spun around. Fred lunged forward grabbing Gary's foot and throwing him to the ground. A rush of adrenaline filled Gary's body with momentary superhuman strength. He writhed wildly, jerking his foot loose. Brian grabbed an arm and it was all he could do to hang on as Gary lurched forward toward the street. A patch of ice betrayed him and he lost his footing. Brian seized the moment to pin him to the ground, but it took all of Brian's and Fred's strength to secure him with the rope. A loud animal howl rose from Gary's throat, piercing the darkness. Spasms took over his body. He rolled into a ball, writhing and foaming at the mouth. Brian spoke for the first time. "What a pitiful piece of humanity," he said. How thankful he was that they had prevented a tragedy tonight.

Fred spoke. "I'll go into Allie's and call the cops while you catch your breath. That's enough for me for one night."

CHAPTER 47

Sheila felt a little deserted when Gary left. He could have told her earlier that he was going to the school to finish the painting. But he was coming back. She turned to Amy who was sitting beside her and explained why he'd gone. Soon the two of them began to chat. Amy had helped to mastermind the pageant. All the angels were in her Sunday school class. She explained that they were making crafts to try to raise money for a tape cassette player and the big sale was on Tuesday. Sheila was interested. "I'll show you what we've made so far. Come with me."

They made their way through the crowd to a little classroom off the main hall. Crafts littered the table. There were angel ornaments made from glass beads, at least a dozen huge pine cones painted like trees, a papier-mache creche, and several reindeer and santas made from bread dough. Sheila was impressed. "You work long shifts and you've still been able to do all this!"

"I love it. Some of the mothers help and I find it a nice break from work. Here's a bunch of patterns I picked up, but I'm afraid we won't get time to make many of them."

Sheila leafed through the patterns. "Here's a cute one. A doll made out of buttons. I think this would sell. For sure, I'd buy one."

"Yes, it's a good one. But it takes a lot of buttons. I'm not sure I could find enough."

"I've got lots of buttons. I bought a whole big jar of them at an auction. I'll never do anything with them. I could leave them here at the church on my way to work tomorrow. But that's silly. I'll give them to you at work in the morning."

"That would be wonderful. Would you like to help us make them?"

"Yes, I would. I'd like that very much. I love doing crafts, and I haven't done any since I've come here." She picked up the pattern. "It looks as if the arms and legs are made of different sizes. The leg ones are bigger."

"And the feet are bigger still."

"If it's all right, I'll take the pattern with me and I'll sort the buttons beforehand. Everybody is so involved in the bazaar, and I'd like to be a part of the action."

191

"Would you do that? Thanks a lot. Here, put the pattern in your purse. And we could meet tomorrow night, if that's all right."

"Sure. Want to come to my house?"

"That would be lovely. I'll gather up what kids I can, and we'll be there. Say about seven?"

"I'll be waiting for you."

Sheila felt good about this. She hadn't got involved with anything and now she was beginning to know people, she wanted to be more sociable. After all, this was her town, too. The evening's events were winding down. People were starting to clean up. Sheila had intended to help with the dishes, but it was obvious that no more help was needed. There were at least ten women in the kitchen, and the men were wiping off the tables and getting ready to vacuum. Allie was collecting the decorations. The place would soon be back in order. And Gary hadn't come back. She said her good-byes and left for home.

The night was beautiful. The moon was shining through the icy trees, casting strange shadows in the snow. Sheila felt excited about the little craft, and warm and happy with the friendships she was making. She was impressed with the pageant, the newness of the old story brought to life by the children. She could still see their faces in her mind, radiant with their involvement in the Christmas story. And the fact that Gary didn't come back was simply that he didn't get finished. You could hardly be upset with someone so involved with helping out the kids.

As soon as she got home she went straight to the basement to hunt the buttons. They were exactly where she had put them. She brought them upstairs and spread them all on the kitchen table. This was the first time she had looked at them. There were some lovely ones. Odd shaped ones, not familiar to her. One that stood out was a ruby red bead with a little string and a piece of paper attached to it. There had been words on the paper, but they were too faded to read. She wondered what had been written there. She set this one aside. The rest she started to sort into sizes.

It took a long time. Finally, she had fifteen piles of buttons on the table. Each pile would make a doll. If they charged four dollars a doll, that would bring in sixty dollars. That would be a good start towards the cassette player. She carefully packed each little pile of beads into plastic bags. She put some antique buttons in a rose bowl, making a lovely display. She studied the little red bead, and tried again to make out the tag. Where would it have come from? She took it into her room and put it in her jewelry box. Someday she might do something special with this precious ruby bead.

Chapter 48

Crime in a small town doubles the coffee trade. The restaurants could hardly keep up on Monday morning. A steady flow of customers came in, anxious to add to what they already knew. Nothing of this magnitude had ever hit this little town before. People edged their bodies closer to the centre table where they could glean bits of information from the firefighters. They sat there, caps on backwards, leaning into their conversation. They had been planning their strategy at this very table two days before. The murderer had been sitting right beside them, fussily fixing away at his placemat. Now it was all over.

They went over the whole scheme again. Brian had got them together before the curling game on Friday. He had sworn them all to secrecy. He had it all planned out. They had to keep a watch on every woman in town. They mapped out the area. If a woman lived alone, there were special precautions. They went over all the families and divided up the watch. Actually, it was all quite easy. All firemen were equipped with walkie talkies, a perfect way to keep in touch in an emergency.

Pete lived across from Mae's and reported every time Gary came and went. Chris lived across from the school, and reported Gary's comings and goings from there. Brian worked with Gary during the day, and Lorne did a little extra sweeping at the school before Brian arrived, and after he left, keeping his eyes on Gary. Mae never knew that Charlie spent the night and part of the day sitting on the top step of her cellarway, head close to the door, listening to make sure she was all right. Sunday evening, the night of the pageant, every lady in town had a guardian fireman.

That night, Jason saw Gary leave, and casually went to the washroom. He summoned Chris on his walkie talkie, telling him to watch for him at the school. He alerted Peter, who was on the ready, waiting in his truck outside, to follow Gary wherever he went. Chris reported Gary's arrival at the school, and the departure of a woman an hour or so later. Lorne watched her turn left at the corner, go past Mae's and turn into Allie's. He watched her raise her skirt as she climbed the stairs, then pat it in place before she walked to the door. She opened it. As soon as she was inside, Lorne alerted Fred, who was behind Allie's house, hidden in the trees. Fred called Brian, who was across the street from Sheila's. He knew he would need extra help when the time came, and he wanted Brian to be on hand for the climax of the plan.

It was a surprisingly complicated network, but it worked like magic. Brian stopped his truck at the post office and walked through the shadows of the cedars to help Fred. They both waited, one on each side of the porch, behind the big cedars that shaded her house.

Allie, unsuspecting, had gone to Mae's. She was too hyper to sleep. They needed to talk, and as long as Gary was not at home, they were free to. It was getting fairly late, about ten thirty, when Brian showed up at Mae's door.

"You ladies still up, I see," he said, coming in and closing the door.

"We were too tired to sleep," Allie said. And in a lower voice, "Gary hasn't come home yet. We hope he is at the school."

"Could you spare a cup of that coffee, Mae?"

"Of course. And here's some bread left over from supper. Wasn't it a wonderful evening?"

"Indeed it was." Brian took the cup from her. "I've got something to tell you, Mae. And Allie. Everything is fine. Now, I don't want you to worry, but I want to call a good friend of yours up from the cellar. He's been watching out for you just in case Gary got any funny ideas."

Mae's eyes widened. Brian went to the cellar door. "Charlie, you can come up now. It's all over."

"My lands, Brian, what are you saying? Charlie, how long have you been in my cellar?"

"Just last night, and today until you went to the pageant. Then I slipped back in before you got back."

"The whole town doesn't know your secret ladies, but I had to tell the firemen to protect you and all the other ladies in town. I don't mean to frighten you, Allie, but Gary was after you."

Allie dropped her cup. Coffee splashed on the tablecloth. "Me? Why was he after me?" Her hands shook uncontrollably.

"That's the part I don't know. Nobody knows. But he went to your place disguised as a woman, went right into your house, and was waiting for you to come back from the pageant. Since you came to Mae's, he must have gotten tired of waiting for you to come back from the pageant. When he came out, Fred and I just happened to be there, and slipped the rope around his hands and feet to keep him secure. He's in police custody now. Nothing to worry about."

The two ladies reached across the table and took each other's hands. Now that it was all over, the starch seemed to come out of them. They were like two droopy houseplants starving for water.

"Now you both have done a very brave thing. Without you, no one would have suspected Gary, and there would have been a great tragedy

194

in our town. You are the heroines who saved the day, and it is because of you a very dangerous criminal is in the hands of the police. By the way, did he take your zebra?"

Mae looked in the window. "No, it is still here."

Allie said, "He must have been collecting something else." She started to search through her bag. "It will be in here, in the book. I've kept it here for safekeeping. Mae found it at Sheila's. Whatever he was collecting will be in this rhyme. It will be locked in the drawers of his cupboard."

"We'll have to wait until the police come to look in there. We'd better give this book to them when they come."

"Are they coming tonight?" Mae asked.

"Yes, any minute. They will be coming to seal off his room to keep all the evidence untouched."

Mae smoothed her hair and took off her apron. She got up and went to the cupboard. "I'll put on more coffee and cut up some bread. They'll all need coffee."

"You are the perfect hostess, Mae." Brian said. "Allie, you'd better stay the night here. It will be better for the both of you."

"I couldn't move from here, Brian. I don't think my legs would carry me."

A knock came to the door. Two constables from Gore Bay appeared when Mae opened the door. "Sorry for the intrusion. We hate to bother you so late at night. Did a Gary Westicott live here?"

"Yes. Where is he?"

"Safe in our care, ma'am. We'd like to see his room, please."

"It's right up those stairs."

"Thank you." They were not upstairs long. They simply fastened the door with a special lock and put tape across it. Then they came back down.

"Will you have some coffee? I made a fresh pot."

"No, thank you all the same. Some officers will be back tomorrow morning, about nine o'clock. Good night, now." And they left.

Mae was disappointed. She had expected more drama. "If the police still lived in this town, they'd stay for coffee. Now I've wasted a whole pot."

"We'll all have another cup, Mae. We likely won't be able to sleep, anyway. And how about some of that good bread? Got any more with the cherries in it?"

Mae smiled. Brian appreciated her cooking. All was right with the world.

Chapter 49

Sheila didn't hear the news until she went to work the next morning. The place was buzzing with the details. What were they talking about? She listened.

"He seemed like a decent guy."

"Yes. People liked him."

"He was doing all that work at the school for the kids' play."

Sheila stood still. Gary! What were they talking about? "Excuse me please. Can anybody tell me what has happened?"

Amy said, "You didn't hear? Of course. No one has told you – I'm sorry, Sheila." She took her by the arm to withdraw her from the conversation. "The firemen caught Gary Westicott in the act of committing some kind of ritualistic murder. He was disguised as a woman, and waiting for Allie to come home from the pageant. He was right in her house. She had stopped in at Mae's and I guess he couldn't wait for her any longer. He stepped outside and they nabbed him."

"Who nabbed him?"

"Brian and Fred. They were hiding there, waiting to protect Allie."

"How did they know to be there?"

"Somehow they suspected him. They were taking every precaution. They had men posted to watch the houses of any lady living alone. Rumour has it that he has already murdered three women. Allie would have been the fourth.

"Was somebody watching my house?"

"I'm sure there was."

"And Gary was dressed as a woman?"

"Yes. That's so weird. It must have been a disguise."

"Amy, he was at my house one evening last week. He was charming. He invited me for dinner this Wednesday. It is his birthday."

"Sheila," Amy said, "maybe you were on his list. Count your lucky stars that you're safe."

"Amy, can you take over for me for a few minutes? My stomach is churning. I think I'm going to be sick. I was just going to room nine. Routine blood pressure check."

"Sure, I'll fill in. Take your time."

Sheila hurried into the washroom. She was stunned by what she had heard. How wrong she had been again. How could she be such a poor judge of character? She grabbed the edge of the basin and caught a glimpse of herself in the mirror. She looked white. She sipped a drink of water, trying to keep from being sick. She sat on a stool, bending over, holding her head in her hands. Her face started to perspire. She sat there, rocking back and forth. Finally, her body quieted. She sat perfectly still, collecting her emotions. She washed her face with a cool face cloth. She had a job to do. She was a professional. She could get through this. She fixed her hair and put on some lipstick. If she kept busy, she could handle it. No one needed to know about her personal involvement with Gary. She stood up, squared her shoulders, and walked into the ward.

All through the day, little bits of information filtered in through the visitors to the hospital. Each had a slightly different version, but all were clear on one thing – Gary Westicott was a murderer. He had already killed a number of women – the numbers varied from three to seven. The firemen were all heroes. Brian was getting the credit for the master plan. He was denying it and giving the accolades to Mae and Allie. Sheila couldn't believe how those two ladies could be involved.

Sheila wrestled with her changing feelings – fear, anger, pride, thankfulness, guilt. Her emotions were in turmoil. One thing she knew, she owed Brian an apology. She had to do that right away. How wrong she had been.

Finally, her shift was over. She just wanted to go home and lock the door and crawl under the covers. But the kids were coming tonight. If she were going to get this apology over, it had to be now. She got in her car and drove up to Brian's. She was hoping he might not be home and she could just leave a note. She got out of her car, inhaled deeply, and walked up to the door. She knocked twice, and waited. He had probably seen her come and didn't want to talk to her.

Brian had not heard the car. He was studying the set design he had inherited from Gary. There was a lot more to do than he had thought. He had only seen page one. He heard the knock. He went to the door and opened it. Sheila was standing there.

"Miss Peters."

"Sheila. May I come in, please?"

"Yes. Of course."

"I'll just remove my boots. They're covered with snow." She did this, then proceeded to unbutton her coat. She handed it to him. "It may take a long time to say... what I have to say."

He was taken aback. Could this be the same person who had stormed in here before? "Please, have a chair."

"Do you have any more of that coffee you offered me last time?"

"Not the same pot." He smiled. "But I can make more."

"Please do," she said. She sat down at the kitchen table.

He hunted the filters. He'd just had them this morning. Where in the devil had they gone? Where were they this morning? And the coffee. Everything seemed to have disappeared. She watched him. "The coffee is beside the sugar canister."

"Right. Should have known that. By any chance, do you see the filters?"

"Beside the coffee."

"I knew that." Whatever had come over him. He poured the water, filled the filter with coffee, and plugged in the coffee maker. He reached for two mugs from the cupboard, and put them on the table. Then he brought out a pitcher of cream from the fridge. He hunted around for the sugar bowl and was relieved to see it in full view by the spoon drawer. The coffee started to gurgle and burp in the coffee maker.

"You have a beautiful kitchen. I'm afraid I didn't see it the last time."

"Thank you." He paced around the kitchen, looking for the Shriners' Christmas cake he'd bought. Where had he put it?

"Please come and sit down," she said.

"I'm searching for the Christmas cake. I seldom get a chance to entertain guests."

"I don't need cake. Just coffee. Please, sit down."

He was being asked to sit down, in his own house. He came over to the table and pulled out a chair opposite Sheila. He sat down.

"I have so many things to say. I have been wrong about so many things..."

He looked at her and smiled. "Some things don't need saying. You've come. That's enough."

It didn't seem important now to talk about Gary – enough had been said all day. "There's something I need to know."

The coffee maker indicated with a dying gurgle that it was finished. He got up quickly and poured the coffee.

"I heard that you were watching my house last night. Is that true?"

He looked at her and smiled. "I drove down your way for a while," he said, casually. Then, more seriously, "I was afraid that you might be in danger. I wasn't spying or anything. I hope you understand that."

"Thank you." She looked at him. "I appreciate that...more than I can say." She held her hands around the mug, feeling its warmth. He poured too much cream in his, stirred it too violently and slopped a little coffee on the cloth. She seemed not to notice.

She hunted for the words. "Jamie said you didn't always live here."

"Yes. No, I was born here. I went away. I chose to come back." He wanted to tell her the whole story, but nothing more would come out.

"You may think this strange. But I had the feeling that this place chose me. The Island, I mean. Someday, perhaps, I'll tell you about that."

"Islands have strange effects on people," he said. "I know this Island has a strange effect on me. The moment I cross that bridge, either way, I feel different." He smiled, proud of that long sentence he'd just uttered. "Come into the living room. The chairs are more comfortable." he led the way. "Bring your coffee."

Sheila walked into the living room. There was the faint, fragrant smell of new wood. "The peacock," she said. There he was, perched on a table, looking out the window. "It was you who bought the peacock. I had forgotten. He was so dusty." She reached her hand up to touch the shiny neck feathers. "You have made him beautiful."

He grinned. "I had to add a few feathers to his tail. I bought him for sentimental reasons. We used to have one on this farm when I was a kid. After I brought him home, a friend told me he belonged to a man who used to own that island you see out your window every day. Apparently, it used to be his pet when he was a kid. Seems that a cat killed it. You can see the scars on its neck. If that's the case, he's a pretty old bird."

"It's nice to have old things. Last night I found a ruby red button in a jar I bought at that same auction. It had a tag on it, but the writing had faded too much to read it. I've put it away. Things like that somehow connect you with the past. Somebody else besides me loved that button. Just like someone else besides you liked that peacock."

"Yes, I like him even better now I know who he belonged to. I have the feeling that I'm looking after him for Joe. Kind of a trust, I guess."

The room was full of old things. Likely things belonging to his family. Keeping them in trust. She felt very at home in this room. She sat down on the chesterfield and tucked her feet up under her, balancing her coffee on her knees.

"I don't have many old things. My family moved a lot, and things got lost." How was it she felt so comfortable saying these things to a stranger? She babbled on. "Actually, I was only allowed to take one thing with me when we moved – except my clothes. It was a collection of animals."

"Could one of those be a glass zebra?" He said. "If, by any chance it's missing, Mae has one on her window sill."

"She has?" She couldn't believe it. "I'm really sorry about that. I really lost…"

He interrupted her. "I'd be pretty upset if anyone took my peacock," he said, smiling.

Sheila returned the smile. His words were so…comfortable. He wasn't pushing an apology, or expecting one. "I love your home, Brian. It has wonderful vibrations. It makes me feel welcome."

"Thank you. I hope so." She looked so right there, sitting back against the cushion, holding her cup. Why didn't he just up and ask her what she was doing for Christmas. Could he dare ask her to come for Christmas dinner. He could cook it. He'd ask her. If he could just find the right words. If they didn't all blurt out and mess everything up. Things were perfect now. Should he risk spoiling…

"Brian, I have no family connections. I am alone for Christmas." There, she'd said it. "I wonder if you would come down for Christmas dinner." When he looked at her strangely, she felt embarrassed. She had assumed he was alone, and likely he had a lot of friends who invited to him for Christmas. She hurried on. "I was thinking of asking Mae, too. And Allie, if she's alone. I just thought I'd like to warm up my new home with a few friends, but if you're busy, that's…"

He finally found his tongue. "I'd love to come. I'll bring the tree. I know a Scotch pine that wants to be a Christmas tree. And in the attic there are scads of decorations. I haven't used them since Mom died." He was babbling now. "Mother loved Christmas. I'll bring them all. That is, if you'd like some extra ones."

"Yes," she said, relief flooding over her. "That would be great. I don't have any decorations. You can tell me about yours as we sort through. They likely all have their own story." The old gingerbread clock on the mantle sucked in its breath and struck six. They listened. "What a beautiful sound. But it reminds me that I have a bunch of little girls coming to make crafts at my house in one hour, and I'm not quite ready for them. I must go." He reached for her cup. "I'll take it to the kitchen," she said.

He found her coat and held it for her. "I've had a wonderful time, Brian." She reached out her hand. "Thank you, for everything."

He had nothing left to say. He couldn't spoil this moment with some crazy words. She was putting on her boots. The words came. "That window of yours…is it pretty cold? When would be a good time to fix it?"

"Anytime," she said, and smiled. "I'll leave the key under the frog."

Chapter 50

It was getting dark. Mae was still sitting by the window. She had not turned on the lights. The phone had rung incessantly all day, friends had called, the police had arrived, carting Gary's things down the stairs and out the door. The big dresser was the last to go, its drawers still locked. Nothing to remind her of Gary was left in the upstairs room – only the empty space where the dresser had stood. She didn't want to go up there. Not now. Later Allie and she would scrub that room from ceiling to floor with pine oil, but not today. She had no heart for it.

Actually, she had no heart for anything. She was strong as a prairie housewife when the storm was on. Now she had no energy to clear away the dust. She was lifeless, like that loose-limbed marionette grinning on the couch. What was there to smile about? The world was a cruel joke. She had pitted her wits against a killer and solved the mystery. And all she felt was emptiness. It was like a gnawing in her whole being – something she couldn't talk about to her friends – not even to Allie. She could hardly put it into words herself.

If Ernie were alive, she could have told him. If he were here, in this space beside her, what would she say? Maybe if she could put this feeling into words, she could put this sadness away, once and for all. She sat quietly, concentrating, calling up the words from the depth of her soul. She spoke the words aloud. "It was as if I had a son, Ernie, the son we both longed for. It was as if he were ours. I was so proud when people talked well of him. It seemed a reflection on me. I felt needed. I had a purpose. My whole body felt young again. I could even climb the stairs, without stopping for a breath on the landing." As the words came, she could almost feel Ernie beside her, feel his strong arms around her shoulders, drawing her close. In the circle of his arms she said the cruel words. "He lied to me. His whole life was a lie." A sob escaped her, shook her for a moment. "I lost my son."

Having said the words, some of the heaviness lifted. She sat perfectly still, absorbing the sensation. She no longer felt Ernie beside her. It was as if he had lifted the shawl of sadness from her shoulders and taken it with him as she sat here alone now in the kitchen. She had felt his presence once before, shortly after he had died. She had never told anybody about that. She would treasure these moments privately, for the rest of her life.

A soft tap at the door roused her from her reverie. "Mae, are you here? It's Sheila. Can I turn on the light?"

"Come in, dear. Yes, please do."

"I wanted to come earlier, but I had Amy's class at my house making dolls for the bazaar. Everyone around town is singing your praises, Mae. You are a heroine! And from what I understand, I owe my life to you."

"I was so worried about you! It was at your house that I found the book that solved the mystery. It was a child's rhyme, and it had in it all the things that Gary was collecting. I'm not sure of all the details, but I know he had to collect a certain number before he committed the next murder."

"It's so horrible, Mae. I was getting to like him. And I know you trusted him completely. You must be devastated. It's so hard when someone you love turns out just the opposite of what you would expect."

"Yes," Mae said. "I felt very...let down. But I have come to terms with that." She squared her shoulders and put on a bright smile. "I'm glad you understand how I felt. I didn't think I could talk to anyone about it."

"I know. There's a lot of personal things I haven't shared with anyone. When I get around to doing that, it will be with you, Mae. You're like a mother to me, you know."

Mae reached for her and hugged her tight. "You don't know how wonderful those words are to me, dear. Now, let's put on the kettle. We could both use a cup of tea." Mae's spirits lifted. A daughter. She felt very close to Sheila. Yes, she thought, I could be a help to her. She had seemed so excited about Gary, and now so disappointed. She must see if she could find a wonderful person for Sheila. Somebody completely trustworthy. Somebody with no surprises. Her mind did somersaults! Why hadn't she thought of it before? Brian! What a perfect match for her. She would see what she could do about that.

EPILOGUE

She was so light, so free, so young – so able to leap and twirl and pirouette to music sweeter than she had ever experienced. They were all there – the violins, the guitars, the autoharps, magical instruments so beautiful and somehow so familiar. Hundreds of thousands of spirits danced to the music, stretching, bending, flowing, falling back, frolicking like licks of candle flame. Filled with wonder and amazement, she watched the fireworks of heaven.

Suddenly a bright soul spirit shot towards her like a falling star. It totally encompassed her, pulled her up and led her in the rhythm of the Dance.

"You've been a long time coming, Jeannie."

"Joe."